THE COMPLETE PACKAGE

• ANN ROBERTS •

Bella
BOOKS

2014

Other Books by Ann Roberts

Furthest from the Gate
Brilliant
Beach Town
Root of Passion
Beacon of Love
Keeping Up Appearances
Petra's Canvas
Hidden Hearts

Ari Adams Mystery Series:
Paid in Full
White Offerings
Deadly Intersections
Point of Betrayal

Acknowledgments

Fans of western Colorado may recognize the Ouray area and see the similarities between the very real town of Ridgway and fictional Pinedale. A few summers ago our friend Barb Steele suggested we get out of the Phoenix heat and come to Ridgway for a visit. The setting was definitely inspirational, and I appreciate Barb's hospitality and retelling of interesting local color, which became the basis for a few key plot points.

Fortunately I don't experience everything I write about, and I relied on my sister-in-law Diane, a veteran of the airline industry, as well as her pilot friend Tim for their expertise about safety protocols and emergency landings.

My editor Medora MacDougall coached me through some of the trickier scenes and made sure my timeline worked. She asked probing questions and pushed for the best story possible. I appreciate her talent and collaborative approach.

I was going through old files recently and found my first rejection from a rival press dated 2004. How lucky for me. Instead I found a home at Bella and Spinsters Ink, and I am grateful for the continued support of Linda Hill and the production staff. I hope we have a few more decades together.

Finally, by the time this book is published my partner and I will be nearing our twentieth anniversary. While I have no recipe for our success, I feel incredibly fortunate to live in my own on-going romance novel. I love you, honey.

About the Author

Ann Roberts is the author of several romances, including *Beacon of Love*, a Lambda finalist, and the Ari Adams mystery series. A 2014 winner of the Alice B. Medal, Ann lives in Phoenix, Arizona, with her partner. Please visit her website at annroberts.net.

For my son, Alex
A kite needs to soar as high as possible

CHAPTER ONE

2007

When the call came Sunday afternoon, Lenny Barclay excused herself from parenting. Her son Seth provided a logical reason to sever their relationship and she didn't fight it. For Lenny, who always believed she was an inferior parent at her best moments, it was like someone showing her the exit door in a dark theater after a long movie. A *really* long movie.

She'd given up analyzing why she wasn't a good mother, willing to accept the easy explanations she'd heard endlessly throughout his childhood from countless sources. Her own mother faulted herself for Lenny's free spirit and inability to create proper boundaries. The counselor at Seth's school suggested Lenny and her son were growing up together since his conception was the surprise present she unknowingly received at her eighteenth birthday party. A friend-of-a-friend had got her drunk and convinced her—at least for fifteen minutes—that she wasn't a lesbian. At first she'd thought the counselor might be on to something...until the woman propositioned her during their second session.

It was the other parents, though, that she encountered during Seth's childhood who displayed open disdain for her, whispering behind her back, snickering at her ideas during PTA meetings and refusing to allow their children to attend his yearly birthday parties (even the pirate-themed one) that convinced her she was a terrible parent. She didn't fit the mold and never gained acceptance, no matter how hard she tried.

She and Seth had endured mainly because she found a partner who was a natural parent. She attributed Seth's fine qualities to Pru, a woman who was everything she was not. Then after high school graduation, he announced he was leaving, moving to South Carolina to be near his father, a man who'd actually been a *worse* parent than she had.

He'd made the statement blithely at the conclusion of Christmas dinner, and she doubted he'd noticed the dropped jaws around the table, particularly hers and Pru's. There was no foreshadowing, no emotional swell behind the words, no tears. Sometimes he could be *such a boy*, and at those moments during his life, she'd found herself wishing for a daughter, someone who was like her and possessed a greater level of empathy and foresight.

A *girl* would never have announced such a life-changing decision as the homemade pumpkin pie was being served. A *girl* would have realized guests and extended family were prepared only to discuss lighthearted anecdotes, the weather and the follies of past Christmases. Such an emotional hairpin turn was more than they bargained for when they agreed to attend a meal on Jesus's birthday, not that many of her friends or family were religious. A *girl* would be cognizant that once the words were spoken, the pie would cease to be the center of attention as everyone reflected on what Lenny had done to drive her child away. Girls got it. Boys did not. She had a boy.

So, the last week of January, she'd driven Seth to the airport and dropped him at the curb. He'd given her a hug and the perfunctory "I love you" as he got out of the car. He'd disappeared through the sliding doors, and she'd circled the terminal five more times searching to escape the numbness that enveloped her. She wanted to feel an emotion, *any* emotion.

Then a homeless person stepped in front of her Jeep and she slammed on her brakes to save him. After he'd flipped her off and she'd returned the gesture—totally pissed—she'd gone home. *Anger*. It was something.

That was over a year ago. They'd been reduced to phone calls on Sunday, and he continually kept her waiting, as he was doing now. *He is such a boy*.

She checked her watch and refilled her iced tea in the kitchen, carefully stepping over the three dogs that had parked themselves on the cool ceramic tile. Pru, the love of her life for the last seventeen years and her son's second mother, busied herself with work from the office. She casually tossed her long, graying ponytail behind her shoulders and studied the spreadsheets in front of her. She was fifty-four, but hardly looked a day over forty. She attributed her youthful face to her vegetarian lifestyle, something Lenny couldn't embrace but apparently didn't need to because at thirty-seven she was still getting carded.

Pru was a flurry of paper, shifting her attention between the multiple stacks covering the dining room table. When she worked, it was a whole body experience. She scanned the pages with her pencil, sometimes shaking her head in disagreement or murmuring an "uh-huh" when a projection was spot-on. She would often crosscheck figures, transferring documents over the table in the complicated ballet that had assured job security and thirty years of success at a company she'd helped establish. Her retirement was set, unlike that of Lenny, who'd spent her entire adult life avoiding a boss, too busy looking for the next cause to support or underdog to defend.

Lenny loved watching Pru work, and over the years Pru's industry often inspired her to be a better person or at least get a better job. She'd never graduated from college, unable to accumulate enough classes to complete a program of study and gain a diploma. Yet, she had one hundred and seventy-five credits and was rumored to be the only UNLV student to have taken courses in *every* discipline. She viewed it as a point of pride, but the slew of academic advisors who'd met with her over the years had shaken their heads and talked with her about focus and goals.

The focus part she understood. With Seth's arrival shortly after high school graduation, she'd balanced school, a job and parenting, relying heavily on her own parents for support. She'd started as a business major but took a philosophy class for fun and loved it. Then there was psychology and marketing and computer graphics. She loved learning but nothing seemed to click.

Equally intriguing were the university's student organizations. She'd always sought justice, and as a child she'd found herself in the principal's office more than a few times for protecting the weak or refusing to abide by an unfair school policy—such as the one that forbade her from asking a girl to the school dance. She'd always been on the outside until she got to college. There she met entire groups of people who wanted to save the earth, defend helpless lab animals and feed the starving children in third world countries.

She'd throw Seth on her back and go to sit-ins and protests. He'd learned quickly, and she had a great photo of him as a two-year-old, shaking his fist at a pro-choice rally. All the while, she worked jobs like "Customer Service Coordinator" or "Comptroller II." Work was something that happened after classes in the morning and before evenings of playing with Seth and studying.

When she turned twenty-one, she went to work on the Vegas strip as a blackjack dealer, making ridiculous money at night and taking courses during the day. It was the ideal life—until her mother had invoked some tough love and refused to care for Seth anymore. He was three by then. Lenny made plans to move to Reno, but fate stepped in the night Pru slid onto a stool at her blackjack table. They flirted for two hours until the end of her shift, and when Pru's accounting convention concluded at the end of the week, Lenny packed up Seth and went to Arizona with her. Just like that.

"Why don't you call *him*?" Pru suggested without looking up.

It amazed her how Pru could be so invested in her work and cognizant of her surroundings at the same time. "He's supposed to call me. It's his *turn*."

"He probably forgot."

She settled in the chair across from Pru, cell phone in hand. She checked to make sure it was on and had juice. It was fine. "He's probably too involved with his new girlfriend."

"Could be," Pru agreed.

"You know, he went to church with her last week. Did I mention that?"

Pru looked up. "You didn't. What religion?"

"I didn't ask."

"Chicken."

Lenny laughed. "I love you, you know?"

Pru returned to her numbers. "You'd better. As your accountant, I can tell you you're stuck." When Lenny continued to fret, Pru grabbed her own phone and hit speed dial. "This is bullshit."

Lenny heard it ringing and her anxiety grew. A part of her didn't want him to answer, but it was always that way. She hated phones and he wasn't any better, so their conversations were a series of short phrases and questions. Pru, on the other hand, was a master of dialogue and could engage anyone in long conversations, even their son.

When he answered, Pru said, "Talk to your mother. Shame on you for forgetting it was your week to call. You owe us another fifty bucks in the Lousy Son Jar." She handed Lenny the phone.

"Hey," she said.

"Hey."

"Are you busy?"

"No, not really."

"Did you forget it was your week?"

He paused and the anxiety returned. He knew it was his turn to call. He knew it, but he hadn't done it. He was avoiding her. Pru's eyes darted from a file to Lenny's face. Although she couldn't hear Seth's part of the conversation, they had decided Pru was the phone monitor, and it was her job to keep Lenny's tone in check so the call didn't devolve into a shouting match as it had in the past.

"Look, Mom, I've been thinking these weekly calls are a bit much."

There it was. "Oh. How often would you like to speak on the phone? Were you thinking every two weeks?"

"Um, well, I think I just need some space."

"You need space? You're in South Carolina and we're in Arizona. How much more space can you need?"

"No, not that kind of space. More like mental space."

"You need mental space?"

Pru dropped the file and rested her chin on her clasped hands. She was squeezing them tightly to control her anger.

"What's going on, honey?" Lenny asked evenly. She'd learned it was impossible to lecture him across the country. He either hung up or set down the phone and started doing something else while he said, "Uh-huh," when she paused at appropriate points.

"I'm having concerns about our relationship, or, well, actually your relationship with Pru."

"Excuse me? What *about* my relationship with Pru?"

"I've been going to church with Jennifer—"

"Is that your new girlfriend?"

"Mom, she's more than that. We're in love."

"You're nineteen and you've never had a girlfriend. You've fallen for the first girl you've met. Are you having sex?"

"Mom, that's none of your business! Anyway, Dad likes her. He even went to church."

"Your father is going to church with you? The man who said Nietzsche was right and God was dead?"

Pru started waving her hands, their signal for Lenny to back off.

She heard paper rustling in the background. He cleared his throat and said, "Mom, I know this is probably difficult for you to understand. I've been reassessing my relationship with my Lord and Savior, and as much as I love you, I can't approve of your lifestyle."

Lenny hung up the phone.

CHAPTER TWO

2012

A three-and-a-half million-dollar deal depended on the next twenty-six minutes. Racing through Midway Airport, Sloane McHenry was almost certain she would miss her connecting flight to Portland, which was scheduled to leave in twenty-six, no twenty-*four* minutes. Leslie, her travel agent, always allowed for at least an hour between connections so Sloane could work her routine. But even Leslie couldn't control the weather or the unpredicted snowstorm, the first of the winter season.

She'd have to do everything twice as fast. Thank god she was wearing her two-inch heels and not her stilettos. First stop was always the terminal restroom, since she refused to use airplane lavatories. While her niece constantly reminded her about the studies on bacteria from the toilet spray, Sloane found it abhorrent that men and small children couldn't hit the hole in such an enclosed space. Fortunately, there wasn't a line, and she was an expert at the fast pee. *Nineteen minutes.*

She barreled onto the moving sidewalk, muttering "Pardon me" repeatedly as she wiggled her carry-on past the passengers who didn't understand that the left side was reserved for people in a *hurry*. A few travelers gave her a sharp stare when her carry-on failed to navigate the human obstacle course and crashed into a hairy leg that should not have ever worn shorts and, worse, a large woman's derriere that clearly stretched beyond the halfway point of the walkway. When Sloane's bag rolled over a child's dropped teddy bear, she caught the glare of the appalled parents.

"What? It's not like it's real," she hissed as she ran past.

The sidewalk ended and she turned left, ignoring the father's threatening reply. *Whatever. Seventeen minutes.* She charged into a news shop and grabbed a *Wall Street Journal* and a Red Bull. There was only one person ahead of her, a middle-aged woman fumbling through an oversized bag covered in a gaudy floral print. On the counter were the woman's purchases: a bottle of water, a pack of spearmint gum and a *People* magazine.

"I know my wallet's in here somewhere," she said while her hand groped the depths of the purse.

Sloane glanced at the zoned-out salesclerk, who couldn't have cared less about the woman's scavenger hunt. Unlike most everyone else in the airport, he was going nowhere. The customer seemed to be moving in slow motion and recognition crossed her face each time she realized whichever object she was touching in the bag. It reminded Sloane of a similar game in school where each person had a chance to guess the identity of something placed in a sack based on how it felt. She thought the game was pointless (*Just take out the damn thing and look at it!*), and she didn't have time to wait now.

"Let me get that for you," Sloane said in her electric PR voice, the one that energized entire rooms of people to do exactly what she wanted. It was always accompanied by a dazzling smile and a stare that was slightly hypnotic.

"Oh, I couldn't," the woman said. "I have the money but somehow my little leather wallet manages to get buried in the cracks and crevices, like it's hibernating for winter," she added. Her roly-poly face brightened. "I think I found it." She pulled out a small red billfold and frowned. "Oops, these are my pictures." She dropped it back in the voluminous bag and swirled the contents some more.

Sloane dropped a twenty on the counter and held up the Red Bull and the newspaper. "This is for me, and in the event that anyone else walks up who has to catch a plane sometime *today*, I'll pay for them too but not *her*," she added, motioning to the woman.

Her jaw dropped and Sloane heard her say, "Well, I never!" but she didn't hear the rest. She'd already passed two gates down the concourse.

They announced last call for her flight. She scowled. She'd make it, but she'd have to read the newspaper on the plane rather than at the gate. She didn't like that. She needed to prep for her meeting while the plane was in the air.

She sailed down the gangplank and into the shiny silver tube. She found her first-class seat next to a young butch in an ill-fitting black suit and purple silk shirt. She looked as if she were playing dress up, and when she smiled, Sloane felt the corners of her mouth turn up automatically. Whatever she did and wherever she was going, Sloane imagined, the heavy hitters were going to eat her for lunch. *I'd like to eat her up as well.*

The butch returned to the SkyMall magazine she was reading, and Sloane dug her mint tin out of her briefcase. Although the container hadn't held any candy for a long time, the faint smell of peppermint lingered and disguised the true contents—her stash of Vicodin. She popped two in her mouth and washed it down with the Red Bull.

"Worried about your breath?" the butch asked. Her gaze remained on the magazine, but she wore a knowing grin.

"Very," Sloane replied. She leaned back in her seat and closed her eyes, waiting for the chemical combustion to occur. The energy drink kept her going at full speed and the vikes lessened the inevitable stress of work. It was her version of yoga without the sweating and stretching.

She ignored the requests of the flight attendants to read the pocket brochure on water landings, preferring to scan the *Journal* instead. She wasn't about to ruin her pleasant buzz by watching the ridiculous oxygen demonstration for the twelve hundredth and fifty-fourth time. She'd kept track and knew she'd accumulated millions of frequent flyer miles, which she occasionally used for vacation jaunts but, more often than not, transferred to friends or Regina, her "adopted" niece and vice president of new accounts. Regina was her pride and joy, a young woman whose drive and determination rivaled her own. *Maybe someday she'll take over—if she doesn't wander off down the trite route of mother and wife. Now that there's a man in the picture...*

The takeoff was uneventful, and she was amused at the sight of the butch gazing through the tiny window, studying the disappearing landscape below. Sloane remembered a time when she regularly claimed the window seat and spent the first five minutes enjoying a bird's-eye view of the world, but that was about a thousand flights ago. She'd realized that from the sky most every city in America was an unoriginal collection of rectangles and rhombuses topped by gray roofs.

The customary ding traveled through the cabin, and the pilot gave the okay for electronic devices to be turned on. She wistfully abandoned the newspaper, unwilling to squander too much time away from work. She reached for her iPad and noticed the butch doing the same. The flight from Chicago to Portland was four hours and nineteen minutes long, which meant she could get all of her weekly reports read and annotated without any increase to her blood pressure, thanks to the calming effect of the Vicodin, originally prescribed for a neck injury she'd sustained during a fall at an indoor climbing facility. She'd feigned pain long after it was gone, and the prescriptions from her understanding and ancient physician kept coming. It just felt too good. Once she discovered the Red Bull, everyone around her benefited.

No longer did she rip off castigating emails to employees for innocent mistakes or fire people at will for fumbling company protocols. When she was high on vikes and Red Bull, her empathy for the human condition soared and music played in her head like a soundtrack for her life.

Case in point: an employee named Curtis Bean could thank the Red Bull company, Van Morrison's "Bright Side of the Road" and the Pfizer drug company for his job, which he would *not* be losing upon Sloane's return to Boston despite the sloppy quarterly report he'd submitted on the Seattle store. She composed an email to him, and instead of creating a subject line titled "CLEAN OUT YOUR DESK," she merely wrote, "See me upon my return." No screaming, no capital letters or ultimatums that she and Curtis would regret.

When she looked at her watch again, an hour had passed. She'd finished her reports and was about to start answering her general email, when she felt the first bump. Sparkling water sloshed out of the plastic cup on her tray table, and she quickly moved her iPad and dabbed at the puddle with her tiny napkin.

She glanced at the butch, who was wiping gin and tonic off her pants. "Damn."

The captain announced there was some significant turbulence ahead, and he was turning on the Fasten Seat Belt sign, which would suspend further food and beverage service. While Sloane had flown often enough to experience rough turbulence, she knew it was bad if the flight attendants were ordered to the jump seats. Still, the captain's silky voice told the passengers he wasn't concerned. *Maybe he's taken* his *vikes.*

She attempted to work as the turbulence increased, but she couldn't concentrate, her mind focused on the next bump—when it would come and how hard it would be.

The butch had given up working completely. She'd put away her iPad and was gripping the armrests. When she realized Sloane was watching her, she said, "I'm not a good flyer."

"I can tell," Sloane replied. "What's your name?"

"I'm Chris. I'd shake your hand, but I'm worried that a hole is going to appear in the ceiling, and if I'm not clinging to my seat, I'll be sucked into the atmosphere." She tried to be witty and sophisticated, but her nervous expression belied her youth.

She can't be more than twenty-five. So young. So fresh. Just my type.

"I'm Sloane and I'll forgive your manners." She leaned toward her and linked their arms together, caressing her clenched fingers. "This way, if a hole appears, you won't go through it alone."

"That's mighty nice of you," she said, offering Sloane a huge whiff of her gin-laden breath. "Aren't you even a little worried?"

"I'm used to it. Are you going to be sick? I'm not going to be happy if your gin and tonics wind up all over my Armani suit."

Chris shook her head as the aircraft bounced twice. Both women joined the collective gasp that came from the passengers. Sloane's stomach had just recuperated when the plane hit another bump, one so hard it felt as if they'd landed on pavement. The little yellow masks toppled from above and a flurry of arms grabbed for them. Sloane calmly affixed her own mask over her head and then helped Chris with hers. She tried to breathe normally, remembering the one other time she'd used the oxygen mask—on a vacation with Sunshine, a woman who had not lived up to her name.

A few cries for help could be heard in economy, from passengers too panicked or too stupid to stick the cups over their mouths. A flight attendant's voice reinstructed the passengers about the masks and reminded them to put their seat and tray table in the upright position with their seat belt fastened.

A brave flight attendant hustled down the aisle, checking on the passengers. She was knocked to the floor when the next bump came and slid the plane into a sideways skid. She quickly scrambled back to her jump seat. The passengers would have to figure things out themselves.

Chris's face was a white sheet against the bright yellow mask, her terrified brown eyes staring into Sloane's. "How are you so calm?"

"Years of flying," Sloane replied easily. "You need something."

She quickly grabbed her purse and popped two vikes in Chris's hand before the next bump came, one that made her stomach leap into her throat. Across the aisle, a man retched into a barf bag, his entire front already covered in vomit.

Chris studied the pills in her hand, a questioning look on her face.

"It's candy."

She pulled off her mask long enough to swallow the pills. She nodded her thanks, and Sloane knew it would only be a few minutes for the drugs to kick in given the amount of alcohol she'd already consumed.

She closed her eyes and attempted to steady her breathing. She'd never experienced anything like this, and even though she was a veteran traveler, it was getting harder to keep calm. The cries and shouts from economy class were increasing and the plane didn't sound right. A high-pitched wheezing, like metal scraping against metal, resonated above the man-made din.

After fifteen hundred flights, the hum of an airplane engine was white noise, a pleasant mask against crying babies and drunk college students, the two groups most hated by business travelers. The engine noise kept her sane, but now, she knew, something was *mechanically* wrong. She could hear it.

She realized the turbulence had stopped. The shrieks of the passengers subsided, leaving only the strange sounding engine. A flight attendant answered the cockpit phone and stayed on the line for a long time. When the ironically soothing ding sounded, indicating the captain would address them, the plane finally went quiet, and she knew they were in trouble.

"Well, folks," he said, "I won't lie to you. That was some of the worst turbulence I've ever encountered in my twenty-six years of flying. We're through it now, but some caution lights have come on, and we're going to make an unscheduled landing in Jackson Hole, Wyoming, which is only thirty miles away. You absolutely must stay in your seats with your seat belt buckled as we make our descent, just in case there's more turbulence. We are flying below ten thousand feet, so you may remove your oxygen masks at this time. After we arrive in Jackson Hole, members of the airline staff will help you with a connecting flight."

Her throat was dry. Never had she heard a captain *order* the passengers to remain in their seats. The flight attendants breezed down the aisle, plastic smiles glued to their faces as they checked seat belts and offered words of encouragement.

"What's going on?" Chris slurred. "Are we gonna die?"

She shook her head, although she wasn't entirely convinced. Emergency landings meant something wasn't working or could stop working at any moment.

"You finally look scared," Chris observed.

"I am a little," she conceded.

Chris sat straighter in her chair, her courage fueled by Seagram's and Vicodin. She leaned very close to Sloane. "If I'm gonna die, then I wanna die kissing someone, and if I live, I'll have a great story."

If she weren't so cute, she'd be creepy. What the hell.

She expected a sloppy kiss from the young and inebriated butch, not a sizzling connection with just the right amount of tongue. A tingle crept down her back and settled between her legs.

The idiot covered in vomit across the aisle uttered a homophobic protest. With her free hand, she flashed him the bird, all the while enjoying Chris's tantalizing mouth and the swell of her left breast, which fit nicely in her hand.

Their distracting behavior lasted only a few seconds until the ding overhead broke the kiss. Sloane gazed at Chris, her eyes still closed and wearing a broad grin. *If we die, I will have fulfilled her last wish. I'm a fucking saint.*

"Okay, folks, we're nearing Jackson Hole, and we're going to ask that everyone lean forward in your seats, placing your head between your hands. We're expecting a difficult landing."

Chris began to cry. "Shit."

"Take my hand," Sloane whispered.

A chill gripped her, and she noticed her knees were visibly shaking. Chris's grip was vise-like, but she couldn't feel it. She was cold and numb. *Perhaps this is fear.*

She realized the last time she'd sat like this—bent over with head bowed—was in church as a child. Crash position and prayer. Maybe there was a reason they were identical. Maybe she should start praying now, but she didn't believe it would really matter. She doubted God, if she or he existed, would listen to such a late arrival.

She wasn't a religious person and couldn't stand all of the hypocrisy, greed and judgment she felt existed in most religions. She was a straight shooter, but since she might be moments from dying, she also should admit she wasn't a very nice person. She didn't even think she was a good person, although she'd done a few *good* things in her life, such as raising Regina.

Again, though, that hadn't started out as a good deed. Her best friend Mimi had inherited Regina after a tragic set of circumstances. For a while Sloane had resented her for intruding on the fun life she and Mimi had enjoyed. She'd laugh at Regina and call her Stickgirl because she was thin and awkward.

The resentment faded when she realized Regina reminded her of her own teen self. Regina worshipped her, so much so that when she had to write about the person she admired the most, she chose Sloane. She declared she wanted to go work for her someday at Wilderness Campaign. Sloane had never been so flattered.

She wiped away the tears falling on her shoes, grateful that Chris couldn't see her crying. She should have done more. She should have been more supportive when Regina met Seth. She'd lost count of the number of times she'd ridiculed him and forced Regina to defend him.

The plane drifted lower. They would never know when impact occurred and when their lives could end. She thought of the places she'd not yet visited—Turkey, Morocco and Greece.

She'd planned a trip to Greece once, bought the tickets and then something had happened…What was it? She couldn't remember, but it must have involved work. There was always work.

Why am I so hard on Regina? I need to do more for her.

If they lived, she was going to Greece. *Maybe I'll go there from Jackson Hole.* Not likely. She'd never drop a three-and-a-half-million-dollar deal for anyone or anything. That was why they called her "the bitch."

I can be better. I just want to live.

She chuckled at the ridiculousness of the situation. Her entire life was in someone else's hands, and there wasn't a damn thing she could do about it. She was helpless. She'd never been helpless, not even as a child. Her parents wouldn't allow it. She'd been doing her own laundry at four and cooking at six. A few eyebrows had been raised when she learned to drive at twelve, but nobody bothered to report her father to the authorities. She'd been self-sufficient her whole life, which came down to the next few minutes.

We're close to the ground. I can feel it.

People were sobbing around her, and she heard Chris whispering the Lord's Prayer.

I will be better.

They slammed against the tarmac, but the sound was lost in the passengers' screams as luggage flew out of the overhead bins. They spun sideways, and she jolted into the armrest. A deafening explosion followed and she covered her ears frantically. She waited for the plane to cartwheel and break in half, but it just kept spinning—slowing—until it stopped.

The screams turned to cheers. The flight attendants, tears streaming down their faces, helped the first-class passengers exit the plane quickly, their belongings forgotten for the moment. She and Chris joined the line to exit. Only an elderly couple remained motionless in their seats, the wife buried in the husband's chest.

It's just like any other flight now. We all have somewhere to be. This moment has past. She looked back at the couple. *Except for them. They really get it. They understand.*

They remained in the Jackson Hole Airport for over three hours. The cries and wails had ceased, replaced by threats of attorneys and shouts of frustrations. The airline held them hostage in the tiny terminal as local officials interviewed each one of the distraught and hungry passengers and finally reunited them with much of their luggage.

Chris remained by her side the entire time. She refused to let go of Sloane's hand, although she said very little. She broke down when she called her parents at the airport, and Sloane had to finish the call for her, assuring the worried couple that their daughter was fine.

She called Regina and savored the sound of her voice. She was typical Regina, cool and calm. *That's my girl. I promise to do better.*

They were shuttled onto buses and taken to a posh resort. An army of bellhops appeared, gathered their luggage and escorted them to registration. A sympathetic clerk greeted Sloane and Chris at the counter. She obviously knew why they were there.

"Will you each need a room?" she asked, her fingers tapping away on the keyboard.

Before Sloane could answer, Chris blurted, "No, just one."

* * *

Sloane was always amazed by the silkiness of youth. Skin separated generations. She thought her body looked pretty good for forty-four. She exercised, moisturized and was genetically blessed. Still, there was nothing she could do, no product she could buy and no surgery she could have that would equal the unadulterated skin of *youth*. She would never again look as marvelous as the woman who lay in front of her.

Chris knew this. She stroked her belly and pinched her nipples, bringing them to attention. Her fingers drifted lower— to Sloane's favorite skin on a woman. She touched herself and gazed up at Sloane, who hovered over her, watching and enjoying the show.

"Wanna take over?" Chris asked, her speech slurring terribly. She'd downed another two vikes in the airport to calm her nerves, and her fear, perhaps her entire recollection of the horrific afternoon, was gone.

Sloane imagined how few lovers had touched Chris's body in comparison to her own. Even if Chris had a different partner every weekend, she'd never catch up to Sloane's list of conquests. She was the one with experience. The twenty-year age difference meant hundreds of women had suckled, caressed and teased every part of her. To touch someone like Chris was always a gift, one she treasured each time she bedded a twenty-something. *And aren't they the best?*

She lowered herself against Chris, grateful she'd also swallowed two more vikes. The soft lighting disguised the flaws that betrayed her age.

Chris didn't seem to care as she reached for Sloane and said, "I'm a much better lover than a flyer."

CHAPTER THREE

"Our objective is to make this stretch of road ooze green," Sloane said, dragging her finger across the enormous wall monitor.

From her seat at the long conference table, Regina gazed at the topographical map depicting western Colorado and Highway 550, the road that connected Montrose to Telluride. Sloane owned a home in Telluride and spent most of her free time there, skiing in the winter and hiking in the summer. She lived to be outdoors, which was expected of her as the owner of a sporting goods chain. She'd returned from her recent vacation bubbling with the idea to open a new Wilderness Campaign franchise in Pinedale, the little town that sat on the road to Telluride.

She clicked the remote and the topographical map disappeared, replaced by a pie chart and bar graph with several annotations. Regina read through her hard copy of the slick presentation as Sloane continued, her arguments persuasive and crisp. She could tell she was amped up on Vicodin, and her customary morning Red Bull sweated on a coaster within her grasp.

"R and D has done a full study of Pinedale, which is poised for economic growth. Unemployment is high, but the traffic through the town is significant. They are clearly benefiting from Telluride's reputation as a celebrity hotspot. Since many tourists can't afford or won't pay for the expensive airfare into the Telluride airport, they fly into Grand Junction or Montrose."

She clicked through three more slides showing the statistics on air travel. Regina could only imagine the sleepless nights endured by Roger, Alice and Reece, the entire R and D team, as they scrambled to put together this presentation, which Sloane was slated to present to the board the next day.

"That means they travel through friendly Pinedale. If we put a Wilderness Campaign here, we can scoop up the rental fees on skis and backpacking equipment before the tourists arrive in Telluride. Of course, they would much rather pay our reasonable prices than the exorbitant ones charged by the local merchants."

Regina winced at her verbiage. Despite working for a major chain, she was a believer in small businesses and buying local. Sloane had teased her mercilessly when she'd come to work at Wilderness Campaign, calling her a sellout. Regina knew Sloane didn't hate small businesses. She just hated competition.

As if reading her mind, she added, "Don't worry, Reg, so far there aren't any hiking or camping merchants in Pinedale."

"That's good," she murmured. "Will the townspeople be excited about a WC in the area? Are there other chains?"

As the scout for Wilderness Campaign locations, she'd faced more than a few hostile crowds at city council meetings and groundbreaking ceremonies. She'd learned there was an entire segment of the population that hated chains, especially when they pushed their way into a community, which Sloane was not opposed to doing if it meant a profit.

"There's one other chain on the main drag—"

"Okay," she said cautiously.

"It's a Happy Burger Joint, so it's not like we'd be the only one."

She stared at her in complete disbelief. "A Happy Burger? You're comparing Wilderness Campaign to a *Happy Burger?*"

She held up a hand and took a slug of Red Bull. "Pinedale is optimal. The prime location already exists."

In other words, Regina thought, do whatever it takes to make this work. If they didn't have to construct the building, the company would save millions. "Where is it?"

Sloane pulled out an eight-by-ten photo of a large two-story wooden building with a wraparound porch and enormous windows. "Right now it houses three shops on the main drag—an ice cream parlor, a coffee place and a collectible shop run by the owner of the whole building." She took a breath and changed her tone. "This is Business 101, Regina. The Seven Ps at work."

Sloane lived by the Seven Ps and insisted every decision be governed by product, price, place, promotion, people, process and physical consideration. Regina couldn't fault her logic. While her rigidity might have cost her some deals when one of the Ps couldn't be satisfied and she broke off negotiations, every Wilderness Campaign store was thriving, a testament to her shrewd business sense. "If it works, don't mess with it" was her motto.

She shoved a folder at her. "You need to read this study. Because of their unemployment rate, I'm betting they'll be glad to see us. This is a great idea," she stated emphatically, as if convincing herself.

Sloane credited Missy, her latest fling, with the brainstorm, but Regina knew Missy would be out of the picture before the blueprints were drawn. It was like that with Sloane. She went months without a companion and then magically appeared with a beautiful and fit woman on her arm just weeks before a vacation. Regina surmised she hated to travel alone, and although the lucky woman's heart would inevitably be broken, she'd carry with her memories of mouth-watering meals and amazing experiences as well as several pieces of expensive jewelry. Regina knew Sloane was always honest and never made promises, yet the yearly or bi-yearly fallout that occurred each time she dumped a woman bothered Regina, who often fielded the angry phone calls or mediated the confrontations between the jilted lover and Sloane's doorman. Once she'd even gone with her to court to obtain a restraining order.

She'd witnessed the pattern for many years, first as the niece of Sloane's best friend and now as her employee. Few people were privy to the little amount of time that constituted Sloane's private life, and she speculated her customary eighteen-hour days were a shield to ward off the loneliness she felt when she wasn't working.

Sloane spun her chair and faced her. Her shoulder-length curly brown hair fell wildly about her face much as it would after a day kayaking. A gold clip sat on her desk in the event a board member made an unexpected appearance and she needed to pull it back into a professional style that would match the tailored suit she always wore.

"Didn't you tell me Seth's mother lives around there?" she asked, motioning to the map.

Regina nodded uncomfortably, hoping she had forgotten. "Yes, she and her partner live in Pinedale according to the return address on the card."

"And Seth is estranged from them, right?"

"Yes."

She drummed a rhythm on the desk. Regina was certain she wanted to ask an inappropriate question and was trying to decide how to frame it. "If I sent you to check this out, would you want to invite him along?"

Her eyes widened. That was *not* the question she expected.

She grinned. "Don't look so surprised. Just because I think he's a loser doesn't mean I don't have some sensitivity to family dynamics."

She opened her mouth to protest, but Sloane held up a finger and tapped the Bluetooth earpiece.

"Sloane McHenry," she said, her gaze wandering to a far-off place as the conversation continued.

Regina turned away and bit her lip. Even after eight months of enduring Sloane's petty comments, it still hurt to hear her mentor trash the man she'd fallen in love with.

Seth wasn't a loser. She knew that. He just wasn't good enough for her, according to Sloane. He hadn't gone to college, wasn't in college and had no desire to get a degree—three facts that instantly dismissed him as boyfriend material in Sloane's opinion. He spent much of his time as a volunteer for the causes he believed in, and it didn't help that he *liked* his current job as a bartender at a tavern near Harvard.

While Sloane lectured the unfortunate caller on the right way to handle clients, Regina perused the shelves, which were filled with business and management books, all of which she'd read at Sloane's insistence. Sloane herself had read most of them at least a dozen times, underlining and highlighting the most critical passages. Regina shared her belief that learning and reflecting were keys to a successful career.

Next to the bookcase was Sloane's brag wall, an array of framed photographs showing her hiking Pikes Peak, deep sea fishing in the Atlantic, on safari in Africa, standing over a buck she'd taken down with her bow and arrow in the Canadian wilderness and cycling in France. It was a pictorial résumé, proving she was a capable outdoorswoman and qualified to be the CEO of Wilderness Campaign. Every type of the store's merchandise was depicted—with one exception. There wasn't a photo of Sloane brandishing a firearm. While Wilderness Campaign boasted an extensive selection of shotguns, rifles and handguns, she detested guns and was a member of the NRA in name only. For the most part she was a conservative Republican. She and Regina had argued politics hundreds of times, Regina failing to understand how she could be aligned with a political group that didn't believe she should have any personal rights.

"Your personal life is only part of the pie," she often said. Nothing was more important to her than business, Regina knew, and she'd readily sacrifice the right to marry the woman of her dreams for a fatter profit margin.

The call ended and she turned back to her, continuing the conversation as if it had never been interrupted. "I won't pretend to understand, Regina. I think Seth is a great guy, but he's not for you. Anybody who can spend all night serving beers to some of the most brilliant minds in America and not develop an interest in learning has no drive."

"That argument is completely flawed," she said drily.

Sloane finished the Red Bull and replied. "I disagree, but since when does logic figure into his thinking? How logical is it to move to Boston to become a lobster fisherman?"

She held her tongue. He'd actually moved to the northeast for a much more altruistic reason, but she refused to engage in the same argument again. "Is there anything else you need from me right now? Otherwise I'll get started on these arrangements, and in answer to your question, no, he won't be joining me."

"No, and good," she added. "I'm glad he isn't going."

She started to leave, but she hated giving Sloane the last word. With her hand on the knob of their adjoining office door, she faced her once more. "What happened to your promise? I thought you were giving him a chance. You said that nearly dying changed you."

Without looking up from the report she was reading, Sloane said, "Maybe not so much."

Place

A successful venture must occur in an optimal
environment where consumer needs can be satisfied.

CHAPTER FOUR

Lenny believed mornings were the best part of the day. Hope was a gift that appeared with the sunrise and brought new and exciting possibilities. She couldn't understand why most people clung to habitual routines that destroyed the potential for adventure.

She'd always been an early riser, determined to make the most of each day's fresh start. When she and Pru first moved to Pinedale, she began each morning at a different restaurant or café and sampled every cup of coffee the town had to offer. She'd learned the best cup was at Kate's Place, which became their favorite haunt, and the worst was at the gas station on the highway. Pru chided her for learning the obvious, but she challenged stereotypes, and once in a while—not often—she was pleasantly surprised. Pru had refused to accompany her on her early morning jaunts, content to stay in bed for an additional two hours of sleep.

Ironically, since Pru's death she'd been craving normalcy. As the sun peeked over the horizon, she climbed into her old Jeep, and her dog Rocket jumped in the back. His little brown face looked concerned.

"It'll be all right, boy," she said, scratching the white tufts of hair that hung around his ears.

Once they were on their way, she checked her watch. It was only twenty minutes to the parking area and the three-mile Blaine Basin hike that ended at an alpine lake. It would be an incredible way to start the morning.

I will really enjoy this hike. Pru would want me to go.

Pru's death was her fault. Instead of pressing her to see a doctor when the minor pains had started, she'd agreed with Pru's rationalizations in order to keep peace in the house. She acquiesced to her fear of doctors and hospitals. When the pain worsened, she half-heartedly coaxed her to see Dr. Singh but quickly backed off when Pru protested. Eventually it was too late and Pru's first doctor's visit ended with a transfer to hospice care.

She glanced at the passenger seat—Pru's seat—imagining her leaning out the open window, her hair flapping against the breeze. Deflated, she pulled onto the shoulder and turned off the Jeep, wrapping her arms around the steering wheel. She didn't cry. The tears had ended months ago, but loneliness and futility remained like squatters who refused to leave. She'd finally gotten over her death, of this she was sure, but she hadn't resumed her life.

"I can't *find* my life," she muttered.

Rocket whined and sailed into Pru's seat. He planted his chin on her bicep and nuzzled her. When she didn't respond, he offered a low growl and she laughed.

"You really should be a life coach, you know that?" she said. He wagged his tail and looked at her quizzically. They'd found him as a puppy outside a grocery store in a box a month before they moved to Colorado. Pru figured it was fate since all three of their dogs had passed. He was a full-fledged mutt with an indescribable genealogy, and they always shrugged when people asked what kind of dog he was. Most distinctive were his ears. White tufts of fur hung from their edges, and they always seemed pitched for listening.

She sighed and pulled out a pen and a map of western Colorado from the glove box. Peering through the windshield, she saw mile marker eighty-six in the distance. She wrote the number on the line indicating Highway 62. "Three miles further than last time." She showed him the map as if he could read, proud of her accomplishment. "We'll get there again eventually, even if it is without Pru this time."

She threw the Jeep in drive and U-turned back to Pinedale. It was seven o'clock, and there was still time to grab a cup at Kate's Place before she headed to the animal shelter for an hour or two of volunteer service. Before she opened the shop, she'd stop in quickly at the library, which served as the makeshift town hall. As Pinedale's mayor, she had few daily duties to perform, but she always liked to check in with Maddie, the town clerk and only paid employee. In her mind, Maddie was the one who really ran things and she just signed stuff.

Kate's Place was buzzing with Monday morning commotion. All of the tables were full and a to-go line formed near the cash register. She waved to several townies as she stepped behind a woman who smelled like rain. She rarely noticed such things, but the lady's scent reminded her of being outdoors in happier times. Even from the back she knew she was a stranger with money. She shifted her weight from side to side, obviously impatient. Definitely an out-of-towner. While she was dressed casually, her L.L. Bean plaid shirt was freshly ironed, her black boots polished, and the designer jeans she'd chosen clung to her bottom perfectly.

She blinked and stared at the floor. She knew the color was rushing to her face.

"Hello, Madame Mayor."

She looked up at Jimmie, an enormous African-American waitress toting a paper cup of coffee. "Good morning, Jimmie, and you don't have to call me that."

Jimmie's curls bobbed with her head shake. "Nuh-uh. You're the mayor and worthy of the respect. I saw you come in and I just poured this. Nice and hot. Two sugars."

She smiled and handed her the coffee, which seemed miniature-sized in her enormous hands. She knew Jimmie was a former shot putter in high school, and while much of her bulk had turned to fat, she could fly across the restaurant in a matter of seconds to break up a fight or grab a meal jumper headed out the door.

"Thanks, but I could've waited in line like everyone else."

"You shouldn't have to, and that's Kate's rule, not mine."

She realized the attractive woman with the nice rear end had turned around and was listening to the conversation. She glanced at her and was struck by the blueness of her eyes. Of course, Pru's blue eyes were still the prettiest she'd seen, but this woman was handsome with striking features that commanded respect—aquiline nose, high cheekbones and full lips. Her curly brown hair twisted over her shirt collar, suggesting a wild side.

"You're the mayor?"

She nodded and Jimmie added, "She's the *best* mayor this town has ever had," before she hustled back to her tables.

"I think you're the person I need to speak with. I'm Sloane McHenry, CEO of Wilderness Campaign." From thin air a business card appeared between her fingers. "I have a proposition for you that could potentially wipe out unemployment in this town."

She raised a suspicious eyebrow. "Really?" Now she had her attention. She scanned the gold print on the card and asked, "So, Ms. McHenry, where do you want your store to go?"

Her broad smile cracked for a split second, but she regained her poise and glanced around the busy diner. "I don't do business in a coffee line, Madame Mayor."

She scowled and said, "Just call me Lenny, please. Lenny Barclay."

They shook hands and she was impressed with Sloane's grip and the calluses on her palms. She obviously wasn't afraid of hard work.

"Is there a more convenient time when we could discuss this matter? When might you be in your office?"

She grunted. "Try never. There isn't an office, and I didn't even run for the damn position, not really."

She looked confused, and Lenny could tell she was uncomfortable. The conversation wasn't going as she planned, which pleased Lenny immensely. Although she'd never asked to be mayor, the town had placed an enormous amount of trust in her, even if it was out of pity over Pru's death. They figured she needed something to take her mind off her troubles. Being mayor of tiny Pinedale seemed like a manageable distraction, and on most days it managed itself, except whenever carpetbaggers like Sloane McHenry appeared, wanting to worm their way into the Pinedale economy. More than a few slick operators had treated her to a steak dinner at the Chatsworth Hotel, hoping to gain favor with the town council. *Of course, none of them was this attractive.*

"Well," Sloane said slowly, "you name the time and place."

"How about there?" she asked, pointing to a window. "Say two o'clock?"

She watched as Sloane realized what was beyond the window. "You want to meet on Mt. Sneffels?" She grinned. "Fine by me."

Lenny stiffened. She'd assumed the well-heeled, refined lady wouldn't want to get her expensive leather boots dirty. *She's called my bluff, and I can't even bring myself to drive to the trailhead yet.*

Sloane grinned and leaned closer, and the smell of rain filled Lenny's senses. "Didn't think I'd agree, did you?" She shook her head. "I'm very familiar with the trails in this area, and I'm the CEO of an outdoor company. To keep my board of directors happy, I have to hike, fish, camp, ski and kayak, preferably all at the same time. So, do you want to meet here or at a trailhead?"

She felt what little pride she had slink out the door. She was in over her head, and she sensed this woman posed a threat to the town. She'd need to be careful and she probably needed help. She needed Pru.

"I could pick you up here?" she found herself saying as Sloane stepped up to order her coffee.

"Sounds great. I'll be outside at two."

She waited until Sloane paid and they left together. "Do you have hiking equipment? If not, I could loan you a backpack or some poles."

Sloane lifted her blue eyes from her cup and Lenny's pulse raced. "I think I'm covered unless we're planning on rappelling or possibly staying overnight?"

She nearly spit up her coffee. It wasn't a question. It was an invitation. "Um, no, this is just a nice three-mile hike to an alpine lake. Should only take us about two hours or so."

"The Blaine Basin trail?"

"Uh, yes. Have you been there before?"

She nodded. "It's lovely, don't you think?"

She looked away. "Yes," she said quietly. "It's beautiful."

The long pause that followed was almost enough to make her blurt an excuse and cancel the invitation. Although her adventurous nature was slowly returning (*three miles further down the road that morning*), this was a *commitment*. She'd have to make it all the way there without having a breakdown on the trail in front of a stranger. *Can I do it?*

Sloane obviously recognized the shift in her mood and said kindly, "Well, I love it. It's one of my most favorite places in Colorado."

Her defenses slipped a notch when she heard the admiration in her voice. "You really know the area?"

"I have a house in Telluride, and of course, there are Wilderness Campaign stores throughout the state. I come here as often as I can, although I call Boston my home."

"Never been there."

"It's a great city, not my favorite," she quickly added. "That would be Geneva, followed by Quito. Fabulous climbing in Switzerland and Ecuador."

"Haven't been to either of those places," she said with a shrug. "My life is west of the Mississippi, always has been, always will be."

The definitiveness of her tone ended the conversation. She hated ostentatious people who flashed their wealth by what they wore, what they did or what they said. Yet she'd learned to temper her disdain since Pinedale needed them to survive.

"You never wanted to travel," Sloane probed, "or you just haven't had the opportunity?"

"Both," Lenny said, annoyed at her intuitiveness.

Sloane stepped off the porch and tripped over the uneven pavement that Lenny had fought unsuccessfully to repair. As she fell forward, Lenny reached out with her free hand and caught her. She steadied herself in Lenny's embrace, her face crimson. For the briefest moment she looked...*vulnerable*. In a second, the cool demeanor returned.

"Good hands, Mayor Barclay. I see neither of us spilled a drop of our coffee. Did you play sports in school?"

She stepped away and shook her head, completely flustered. *I haven't been that close to any woman in a year.*

"Well, I'll see you at two," she said, heading toward a large black Range Rover. Lenny felt her disdain returning at the sight of the huge machine.

She crossed the lot to her old Jeep. She could still smell Sloane's cologne on her shirt. *Rain. She smells like rain.* The Range Rover pulled up beside her. The passenger window rolled down and Sloane handed her a leather portfolio. *Pinedale Proposal* was visible through the oval window in the center of the cover.

"I'll give this to you now," she said over the hum of the engine. "I'm guessing there's only a fifty-fifty chance you'll show up this afternoon."

"Why would you say that?" Lenny said in disbelief. *Is she reading my mind?*

"Something's up with you, Mayor Barclay, and I've possibly pissed you off as well by sounding snotty." She sighed and said, "Damn, I can't believe I've screwed this up so badly."

"What?"

She raised her chin and gazed at her, all business. "I apologize if I've said anything to offend you. I would very much like us to take a hike together and discuss this proposal along the way. Would you be amenable to such an arrangement?"

Her smile was incredibly persuasive. *I'll bet she gets whatever she wants most of the time.* She imagined this persona was the one most people saw: a cool, well-spoken, detached ice queen who was never surprised, but it was too late. She had already seen her lose her cool, be a klutz and fumble for words. She liked that woman better, and she definitely wanted to see her again.

"Amenable?" she said with a slow grin. "Why, I don't think I know that word, Ms. McHenry."

Sloane threw her head back and laughed. Lenny's gaze followed the curve of her chin to the base of her lovely neck before she drove away.

CHAPTER FIVE

Although the gas gauge's needle sat on the top of the E, Regina flew by the last gas station in Montrose, supremely confident in her math skills. She'd rented a Jetta, the same car she owned at home in Boston. It held fourteen-point-five gallons and averaged twenty-seven miles on the highway. She'd methodically recorded her fill-ups for the past three years, comparing the gauge to the gallons she pumped. She knew two-point-one gallons remained in the tank, and since she was only nineteen-point-six miles from Pinedale, she would arrive at the lodge with one-point-three gallons to spare.

"Plenty to find a gas station," she said to herself. "Even if a slight wind picks up and Mother Nature tinkers with my calculations."

She was not fond of unpredictable variables that skewered her statistics, especially nature and human behavior. She regarded both as the complete nemeses to mathematics. One needed only to review the devastation caused by the Japanese tsunami or the shooting of former U.S. Representative

Gabrielle Giffords to recognize the fragility of statistics. Who could plan for a 9.0 magnitude earthquake or the appearance of a deranged gunman at a shopping center? She knew the chance of either happening to her was several numerals to the right of the decimal point. Yet close to two thousand had lost their lives at Fukushima and while Gabby Giffords had survived the attack the severity of her wounds required her to resign.

While she hated outliers, she knew they were just pesky twists of fate and their effects could be avoided or minimized through research and planning. She downloaded several weather applications for her phone, watched the Weather Channel religiously and studied storm patterns the week prior to any trip. She knew sunshine and comfortable temperatures were expected for the next three days, which was common for the beginning of June.

Sloane had said they could swoop in and out of Pinedale but had provided no timeline. So when she was caught on the phone with her travel agent, who'd needed a return date for her plane ticket, she'd blurted, "Thursday," knowing she had meetings scheduled for Friday morning. For absolutely no reason other than its convenience, she'd decided the remains of Monday and three full days would be enough time to scout the location and attend to her personal business.

She shifted in her seat, uncomfortable with the number three. It was a random choice with no statistical evidence to back it up. It was a most common and friendly number, symbolizing the parts of the Trinity, pi (if it were rounded) and the number of strikes given to a batter.

Yet as she thought more about it during the flight from Boston to Denver, she feared the time in Pinedale couldn't be accurately calculated and, more importantly, that there wasn't a formula to ensure a positive outcome. She knew she was a great salesperson with a handful of awards atop her credenza at work, but this could prove to be the hardest sell of her life. The fact that Sloane would be hovering over her shoulder put pressure on *both* situations, which were inextricably connected. Sloane coveted Pinedale and probably was already planning the store's grand opening, but Regina's objective was different: to meet Lenny, the woman who might become her mother-in-law, and to reunite Lenny with Seth.

She sailed down Highway 550, passing a yellow caution sign with a leaping deer. She tightened her grip on the wheel, grateful it was daytime. She rarely drove at night, which was when forty percent of highway accidents occurred. The statistic was disturbing enough, but more than likely her anxiety stemmed from the death of her parents at the hands of Steven Wade Pearlman, the sleepy and somewhat inebriated semi driver who'd crossed the double line and plowed into them eight days after her twelfth birthday. Her Aunt Mimi and Sloane, Mimi's best friend, had raised her.

It felt good to be out on the open road surrounded by the San Juans, a rugged mountain range in the Rockies and a part of the Colorado mineral belt. Telluride, Ouray and Silverton had begun as mining camps and burgeoned into cities when gold and silver was discovered during the nineteenth century.

She chuckled at a homemade sign by the side of the road: *Welcome to Pinedale. What we lack in wineries, we make up for in whining.* At least one person had a sharp sense of humor, but if she were the marketing director, she'd be telling the mayor to implore the landowner to take down the sign. Portraying the citizens as whiners was *not* good PR.

Pinedale was a blip between Montrose and Ouray. She'd spent hours researching the town and downloading photos. She glanced at the picture of the Pinedale Lodge on her phone, made a few turns and pulled into the stone entry.

Three of the twenty-six reviews on Trip Advisor had mentioned Kirby the innkeeper and commented on his superior customer service skills and friendliness. Only one former customer, TravelerBetty, had described him as nosy and overly attentive. Since Betty had also complained about the quality of the toilet paper, she had chosen to ignore the review. Overall the Pinedale Lodge scored four-point-three stars out of five. After poring over six other travel websites and blogs, all boasting at least eighty percent favorable reviews, she'd made two reservations, one for her and one for Sloane. No one was to know they were together, at least not at this point.

The main room was empty, but she heard voices in the back. The overstuffed chairs and deep burgundy leather couch reminded her of Aunt Mimi's den, complete with a fire in the fireplace. A coffee cart sat in the corner, and she recalled espressos and lattes were mentioned in one of the most complimentary reviews. The manager obviously realized it was the little things that counted.

"Hello," a voice said.

She jumped and faced the older gentleman who'd slid into the room without her realizing it. His face was like butter, with kind brown eyes and hound-dog cheeks that lifted when he smiled.

"I'm sorry I startled you," he said apologetically. "I'm Kirby and I'm guessing you are Regina Dewar?" When she nodded, he added, "We're so glad you're here."

His sincerity lived up to the reviews. She completed the registration paperwork and he escorted her upstairs. "We were able to give you Room Two-Fifteen as you requested."

She'd studied each of the floor plans online, determining that 215 was four square feet larger than the other units, had two extra windows and faced the mountains. While she doubted the extra square footage would make much of a difference to her comfort level, the room came with a king-size bed instead of a queen. Since Seth had moved in with her, she'd become aware of her "nightly thrashings" as he called them, which resulted in bruises to his calves and the covers being twisted into a knot like a licorice whip. After a few weeks together, they'd made a trip to IKEA for a king-sized futon. It became their first purchase as a couple.

Kirby opened the door and turned on the light for her. She opened every drawer, tested the windows, pulled the drapes, examined the smoke alarm, scrutinized the shower curtain for mold and yanked down the bedspread to check for bedbugs. He watched silently, an amused expression on his face.

Satisfied, she nodded and withdrew a five-dollar bill from her pocket. He politely refused with a wave of his hand. "Can't take that, ma'am. Coffee's on by seven and I'll be available to answer any questions you may have about the area. If you have a problem, just dial zero." He smiled again and left without further chitchat.

She headed into the spotless bathroom and took a quick shower. She'd received a text from Sloane stating she'd already made contact with Lenny Barclay, but she wanted Regina to check out the location before noon, so she'd have to hurry. Seth's ringtone filled the room, and she steeled herself for the lie she was about to tell. Actually she'd already lied when she'd told him she was going to Denver for a convention. She rationalized that anything else she said now was just an extension of the same lie.

"Hey, babe," she answered.

"Hey," he said. "How's Denver?"

"Great." She propped herself on the bed, still wrapped in the bath sheet. "I'm getting ready for the second session right now. Did you just wake up?"

He groaned. "No, I've been up since seven. Rosemary's car wouldn't start again."

She was glad he couldn't see the jealous look on her face. Rosemary was the twenty-one-year-old cutie who lived two houses down and always seemed to need help with everything.

"It was nice of you to help her," she managed to say.

He chuckled. "I can hear the sarcasm in your voice, Reg."

"Was it that obvious?"

"Only a little. The dogs say hello."

She grinned, picturing their menagerie sitting at attention and wagging their tails. "I'm sure you're taking great care of them."

"Do you know how hard it is to walk five dogs at the same time?"

She laughed. She'd done it herself and it wasn't easy. When they barreled through the door, each one had an agenda and she'd been pulled in multiple directions.

"Well, I'm off to the hardware store to get the materials for your porch swing," he said.

"Really?"

They had found an old porch swing during a weekend tour of yard and estate sales, one of their favorite Saturday activities. He had been promising for a month he'd refinish it for her, but there was always a favor to do for a friend or an extra shift to work for a sick colleague. He was always helping others, and he couldn't say no.

"Uh-huh. When you get back, we'll cuddle up and make out in front of the neighbors."

"Hmm, I don't think so."

"I do," he teased. Changing the subject he said, "I also got a call back from the food bank. They need me to deliver some care packages this afternoon."

"That's great, babe." She sighed and glanced at her watch. She needed to get moving. "Okay, I'm not jealous anymore. Go see Little Miss Helpless."

"Hey, my dad called. We had a nice chat."

"Did he try to convert you again?"

Seth chuckled. "Only after two full minutes of conversation unrelated to religion. Then when he started ranting about the two of us living in sin, I cut him off just like you suggested."

"Well, two full minutes is something. I've got to run, but tell me about it tonight, okay?"

They said their goodbyes, and she closed her eyes, picturing the two of them sitting on the swing, watching the neighborhood children play in the nearby yards. It was just so *domestic*.

She grabbed her purse and smiled. She was lucky to have him. He was the most gentle and thoughtful man she'd ever met. Even on his day off he was helping others. It was typical for him, but so unlike his father.

She knew he had moved to South Carolina, longing for a change, leaving Lenny and Pru behind in Arizona. But life in South Carolina proved less than ideal. He'd been brainwashed (his term) by Jenny, his very first girlfriend, an ultrareligious crazy who had convinced him to cut off all ties with his going-to-hell lesbian mother and her partner. The last straw, though, had been when she had tricked him into attending his own baptism at the creek. He'd balked at getting naked in front of two hundred people, and their relationship ended in a very public way. His father and stepmother had been baptized that day, however; they had been quite enamored with Jenny.

Life became unbearable, he'd told her during a tipsy confession one night. He'd clearly hated listening to Philip discuss Lenny and Pru's damnation, although he couldn't bring himself to reunite himself with his mother, a situation he had yet to explain to Regina.

He found a lifeline when an old friend in Boston called him. He was dying from brain cancer and needed help. Seth moved right after his twenty-first birthday.

He was so amazing. She hated lying to him. She rubbed her empty ring finger and imagined an engagement ring on it. They'd playfully discussed marriage and a wedding, agreeing they wanted a small ceremony outdoors. She only had one concern: statistically they were headed for divorce before they even said, "I do."

She was twenty-eight and he was twenty-four, although he was very mature for his age. Nevertheless, marriages between an older woman and a younger man were more likely to end in divorce than marriages between an older man and a younger woman.

Money was the next most influential factor for success, and partners who made similar amounts were much more likely to stay together than couples who experienced great disparity. Without a college education, she doubted he could compete with her current six-figure salary.

Finally, religion and family were other factors warranting scrutiny. Neither of them was religious, so she considered it a nonissue. Family, however, was their Achilles' heel and the most statistically significant detractor to their potential success. She was glad he was reconnecting with his dad, but she was equally concerned about his nonexistent relationship with his mother and Pru. It disturbed her that he wouldn't confide in her. Couples without strong family support were statistically doomed. She only had a sliver of a family and he wasn't faring much better.

She calculated a marriage with Seth had a thirty-seven percent chance of failure, and sixty-eight percent of that thirty-seven percent could be attributed to familial issues.

Consequently, she'd decided to be proactive and improve their chances, but the spark of his anger, which could burn as brightly as his father's, would surface once he learned she'd come to Pinedale to confront the woman his father had called "an awful mother whose soul was damned to hell."

In her mind, though, the meeting was inescapable in order to improve the odds. If their marriage was going to stand a chance, she had to face his mother.

CHAPTER SIX

Life looked different when you were only two feet from the ground and all of your senses were acutely sharp. Rocket wasn't sure what "acutely" meant, but he'd heard Pru use the word many times when she was talking about his ability to sniff and hear.

Over the years his vantage point had led him to draw several conclusions about humans: they were creatures of habit, constantly using the same routes through the house to get from one room to the other; they were suckers for a good sit and a tail wag and none of them ever vacuumed enough, although Pru was better than most—and certainly better than Lenny.

He missed Pru. She was the one who always remembered dinner was at five o'clock, *not* five thirty. She was the one who knew he liked to be scratched behind his ears, and she always thought to toss him an extra dog biscuit each night when they closed up the shop.

He couldn't blame Lenny. She was a pile of sadness. She wandered through the house without going anywhere after it was dark. Sometimes she'd drop onto a barstool at the kitchen counter, while other nights she'd slip out to the deck and fall asleep in Pru's lounger. Most nights, though, she'd curl up on the overstuffed chair that faced the enormous glass windows and Mt. Sneffels. He liked those nights best. Then there was room for him to snuggle next to her. He knew it was his job to take care of her. Pru would want it that way.

He could tell she was making changes. She wanted to hike, and each day when they drove down the road, he saw the mountain draw nearer. His tail wagged frantically and all of the happy memories returned of them exploring the trails, the woods and *the smells*. There was nothing better than that except Mrs. Willoughby's Homemade Dog Tasties. Those were the best!

He loved Lenny, but it had always been Pru who was "the dog person." Lenny didn't seem to notice when he cocked his head to the left, hoping for an extra dog biscuit, a scrap of table food or a longer walk. She never stopped to look down at him, and unless they were snuggled on the overstuffed chair or riding in the Jeep, he rarely saw her face. He only *sensed* her sadness from the shuffle of her feet or the heavy sighs that filled the air above.

He glanced at her curiously now. She was talking to herself. That wasn't unusual, for she often talked to Pru even though she was gone. He knew when that was happening since she sounded exactly as she had when Pru was alive. Sometimes she'd even laugh. But she wasn't laughing now. In fact, she sounded angry.

"If you think you can barge into this town, you are sorely mistaken, even if you do have incredible lips and a great ass." She stared out the windshield and pointed her finger. She wasn't looking at him or using his name, so he wasn't in trouble.

He gazed through the windshield but only saw the stores along Harrison. He couldn't imagine who was in trouble with Lenny.

They were on their way to open Pru's shop. His tail wagged in anticipation. People would wander through the aisles, and most would stop to pet him or scratch him behind the ears. It was endless doggie massages all day!

Even better was all of the food. They had never enforced a No Food or Drink policy in the store, and at least a few people would drop a part of a cookie or a scoop of ice cream on the floor. Some would offer him little snacks, although Pru had put up a sign telling customers not to feed him. He was still trying to figure out how to make that sign fall down.

They pulled into their usual spot and he bounded out of the Jeep. "Hurry back," Lenny called.

While she headed for the front door, he sniffed his way to the busy intersection, checked both ways and trotted across the street to the public park. It was early and the ground teemed with the unusual smells of night. He made a lap around the perimeter, veering off-course twice when he couldn't resist the pungent odor of *wild* animal. His nose sank deep into the ground as he followed the scent past the picnic tables to the large wooden sculptures. It ended near the trashcan. He lifted his leg and made his mark.

Twice a day he came to the park—when Lenny opened the store and when she closed it. The second time she came with him to clean up his messy business, but in the morning, he got to explore by himself *without a leash*. He enjoyed his free time, which had begun after Pru was gone. Pru never would have let him wander around the park alone, but Lenny was different. He'd always known that about her. She smelled different. She smelled free. Pru had always smelled...cautious.

"Hey, Rocket," a voice called.

He glanced at the picnic table across from the swings. His friend John Snyder was enjoying his morning breakfast burrito. Rocket loved John because he smelled like chicken, pork and cookies. He owned the True Grit Bar and Grille and ate breakfast at the park before he opened every day.

He waved a piece of the burrito, and Rocket galloped to his side. He sat politely until John held out the food. "That's a good boy, Rocket. Now, don't tell Lenny I'm feeding you. She'd skin me."

He wagged his tail and John leaned forward, a deep wheeze escaping his lips from the effort.

He could smell the sausage and his mouth started to water. He gobbled it up quickly and John laughed.

He worried about the huge man. Mixed with the food smells was the smell of sickness and disease. As people went, John was enormous, and some animals were afraid of him, but not Rocket. He knew John was friendly and each morning would offer him a little taste of his breakfast.

John gave him a pat on the head and said, "Have a good day."

He trotted back across the street. He darted through the pet door at the back of Books and Beans, ignoring Pugzie's hiss from her chair. Pugzie belonged to Sue, the owner of Books and Beans and of Two Scoops Ice Cream Confectioners, which shared the building with Pru's Curious Curios.

Unlike Rocket, who lived with Lenny, Pugzie lived at the bookstore and rarely ventured from her chair except to visit her litter box and food dish. He thought she was useless. All she did was sit like royalty on a throne. She didn't work like he did, and she wasn't even friendly to the customers who made the effort to pet her. She *endured* their touch, and while she didn't hiss at them like she did at him, he knew she hated them. She hated *everyone*, including Sue. Once she'd bitten Sue when she tried to put a Christmas jingle bell around her neck. He didn't understand cats and normally steered clear of her except when he had to pass through the pet door that was next to her chair.

"Ready to go to work?" Lenny asked from behind the register.

He climbed up the three steps to an upper platform. He knew that was his spot. He watched the customers, and if one of them, usually a child, started to mishandle the merchandise, he strolled over and started whining. The customer set the item aside and gave him affection instead. Pru used to call him Mr. Distractor.

"I'm guessing you've saved us hundred of dollars in broken merch, Mr. Distractor," she often had said.

Lenny unlocked the front door and flipped the little window sign from Closed to Open. He watched expectantly for the first customers, but no one entered. It was like that lately. Before Pru died there were always one or two people waiting outside when she opened the door each morning, but now it took a while for anyone to come by and there were fewer customers throughout the day. For him, that meant less petting and less dropped food.

Lenny didn't seem to notice. She went behind the cash register and fiddled with her cell phone. The bell jingled and he jumped to attention, until he saw it was only Toby, the college kid who helped her.

"Hey," he said, grabbing a few pieces of furniture to set outside as a way to lure customers into the store. "Sorry I'm late."

Lenny shrugged it off, but Rocket knew if Pru were here, she'd lecture him about his constant tardiness. She had been like that. He gazed around the shop, which looked a lot different since Pru had died. It wasn't pretty the way it used to be. Nothing was the way it used to be.

He lay down with his nose between his paws and waited for that first customer.

People

A successful venture depends on involving people with the right motivation and skills, positioning them in the correct roles and creating a mix of personalities that will realize the organization's vision.

CHAPTER SEVEN

Guilt nagged at Sloane. She wasn't accustomed to questioning her motives when it came to business. She was struggling so much, in fact, that she had to escape Pinedale and Regina. She'd neglected to mention two critical pieces of information to her: Lenny's partner was dead and the location Regina was scouting for the Wilderness Campaign was Pru's Curious Curios, the business that was Pru's legacy.

She'd deliberately removed Pru's death certificate from Regina's dossier, which seemed to be the only evidence that she was gone. Apparently Lenny had filed as little paperwork as possible. If Regina knew of her death before arriving in Pinedale, she would have approached the takeover differently. *And I can't have that. We need to stick to the plan.*

Still, she needed to tell her soon. She knew Regina would flip out and most likely U-turn back to Grand Junction and the jet bound for Boston via Denver. Sloane would threaten to fire her, but Regina wouldn't care, knowing she would never do it given the circumstances and their personal relationship.

She was the closest thing she had to a daughter in her life. She couldn't can her.

She had a few hours until her hike with Lenny Barclay, plenty of time to motor ten miles up Highway 550 to Ouray, the county seat and a mining town made famous as the movie location for John Wayne's *True Grit*. As the speed limit slowed and the highway morphed into Main Street, she leaned back and relaxed. She passed the Hot Springs Pool, which wouldn't open for another few hours, and pulled up in front of the Backstreet Bistro, her favorite coffee haunt.

Ouray was in a valley nestled in the San Juans, and some of the best hikes provided a bird's-eye view of the entire town. She found it quite charming and had inquired about several of the old Victorian houses there, but she couldn't bring herself to buy one. Ouray wasn't a place for singles. It reminded her of her hometown, Hendersonville, North Carolina, a place of warmth and closeness. Her life was better suited to cosmopolitan Telluride, where everyone and everything was only for the season.

Armed with her second cup of coffee for the day, she pulled a thick file from her passenger seat and walked back up Main Street to Fellin Park, the heart of the town. Bordering the Hot Springs Pool, it was a hub of activity. She'd attended many art festivals and wine tastings there over the years, but most of all, she loved the Friday night music performances in the summer. She and her chosen honey would roll out a blanket, crack open some beers and enjoy the concert, surrounded by tall cliffs.

The park was already busy. A group of seniors enjoyed a softball game on the well-tended diamond, and mothers watched their children scramble about the play equipment. She found a picnic table under a tree, determined to peruse the thick file on Lenny Barclay and Prudence Cavender. Instead her attention drifted to the squealing children as they soared on the swings or hung upside down on the monkey bars. For a fleeting moment she yearned for a child and a re-do of her life. Then her iPhone vibrated with a text from her assistant. She tapped in a response, and they exchanged messages back and forth three times until he understood what to do. When she once again looked at the children, the feeling was gone.

"Thank God," she murmured.

Since the plane crash she found herself occasionally questioning her life and decisions—something she'd never done before. She'd never looked back, always confident in her choices when she made them and also recognizing there was no point in belaboring decisions that were in the past. All that mattered was moving forward. She had no idea what was over her shoulder in the dust, and she couldn't comprehend the concept of regrets, which she found maudlin and sissy-like.

Still, sometimes she remembered sitting in crash position, spinning. She'd never forget the spinning, and she'd come to realize life moved in many directions, not just forward.

She pulled up her iTunes and opened the file. In less than a minute Melissa Etheridge's painful wail drowned out the children, and she focused on the carefully prepared research.

Pru's life was a straight line. She'd become an accountant and spent her entire career building a business and sound investments. She'd met Lenny when she was thirty-eight and Lenny was only twenty-one. They moved to Pinedale in 2010 after Pru retired, but she wouldn't enjoy it for very long. She'd died in 2011 from pancreatic cancer. She'd had solid credit, no criminal record, and had given to numerous charities. Clearly a model citizen.

"I would've hired her," she murmured as she read through Pru's many accomplishments and the large nest egg she'd accumulated for retirement.

Lenny was a different story. The research team had managed to pull her college transcripts, which went on for twelve pages and ended with no degree. Her credit history was a mess, including a bankruptcy in her thirties. Apparently Pru had been smart enough to keep their money separate, as Lenny's résumé was a patchwork that included blackjack dealer, professional clown, welder and ride operator at an amusement park. Along the way there was also a misdemeanor for inciting a riot outside a university animal testing lab when she was eighteen and a DUI at twenty-six.

"And yet you're still the town mayor," she added sarcastically.

Also included were six pages detailing her community service. The list of causes, charities and organizations varied greatly, and there seemed to be no theme. She helped everyone including such interestingly named groups as Save the Redwoods, Free Sex Nevada and Arizona Guinea Pig Rescue. Sloane's personal favorite was a cryptic unexplained acronym: K.E.R.F.U.F.F.L.E. She could only imagine what they advocated.

There was a colorful segue of eight paragraphs detailing her son Seth's difficulties in school, including a string of suspensions tied to his own activism and refusal to follow certain policies. He had poor grades throughout high school and had opted to move to South Carolina instead of attending college. After shifting from job to job, three years later he'd abruptly moved to Boston and worked on a fishing boat before taking a job as a bartender. Regina had said he'd moved to help a friend, but Sloane couldn't remember the details.

"So much like his mother."

The dossier concluded by listing his girlfriend as Regina Dewar, vice president of new accounts at Wilderness Campaign, LLC.

She closed the file and shook her head, unable to comprehend the lasting relationship between Lenny and Pru. Clearly they were complete opposites, and she imagined it was Pru who provided Seth with a modicum of stability. Lenny seemed to be an adult child, incapable of caring for anything but herself, which would explain why the shop owed several thousand dollars in back taxes. Perhaps Lenny would be inclined to sell, knowing she was in over her head.

"And so it begins," she said triumphantly, dropping her cup into the trash and heading back up Main Street. People like Lenny didn't belong in the business world, and Sloane's competitive nature fueled her desire to overtake them.

The town was coming to life as more shops opened and early season tourists, most of them elderly couples, wandered in and out of the one-of-a-kind stores, making her cognizant of her own singularity. An image of Chris flashed in her mind—the kisses, her flawless skin.

It felt weird being in Colorado without someone. She'd always brought a companion to hike and fish with. Missy, her previous fling, had proven to be the best. Although she was only seven years younger, she was inexhaustible. Sloane had struggled to keep up with her, especially at eleven thirty at night when Missy wanted to bar hop through the Telluride saloons and she wanted to curl up in bed. She'd relished the challenge, and in retrospect, it had been a wonderful two weeks.

Her thoughts drifted back to Regina and the lies she was telling her. She hated fighting with her. She understood her perspective and, more importantly, her need to control everything, which stemmed from the death of her parents. She hated unknown variables and did her best to temper her emotions and planned her calendar weeks ahead to ensure nothing unforeseen tripped up her life.

Learning that Pru was dead and that the property in question belonged to her potential mother-in-law would send her world into a tailspin, but maybe it was time for the girl to see life for what it really was: a daring adventure or nothing at all.

"Speaking of adventures..." she said, as she cruised down a side street and stopped in front of an old Victorian home. A large wooden sign hung above the porch, *The Carnation B&B* in bold red letters. Carnations bloomed everywhere, and she thought it was a pity there weren't more tourists to enjoy them. The summer season had barely begun, and until then, Riya, the owner, had the place—and the hot tub—to herself.

She found the front door unlocked as Riya had said it would be, but she engaged the deadbolt before strolling through the homey front room and into the kitchen.

"Riya?" she called.

"Out here!"

She saw the open patio door and found Riya enjoying the hot tub's jets. She had stacked her dark hair onto her head and wore only a hint of lipstick. A natural beauty, Riya spent little on makeup, and although she was approaching sixty, she still looked forty-five.

"It's been a while," she said, stretching out her legs.

Sloane stared into the foam at her naked body, growing hot with desire. "It's great to see you. I'm sorry I didn't stop by when I was here earlier this year."

She snorted. "I'm glad you didn't call," she spat, her Indian accent thick. "I've got no interest in sharing you or having threesomes. Our time belongs to us. Who was she, anyway? Anyone of importance?"

She looked away and shrugged. "Are they ever?"

"So, she's already gone?" Riya slowly caressed her large breasts, hidden by the pulsating jets. "She's not waiting for you back at the hotel or, worse, out in the *car*?"

"No," she laughed, kicking off her boots. She peeled off her clothes, waded into the hot water and straddled her.

"How long do we have?" Riya asked, her fingers stroking Sloane's inner thighs.

"About an hour. I have to…"

She never finished the thought. Her voice turned to gasps from Riya's touch.

Riya offered a stony stare and said, "I don't care what you *have* to do, remember? That's why you're here."

"No," she whispered, but she knew Riya couldn't hear her over the jets, and she wouldn't care anyway.

"I'm your escape. I'm the only lover who really matters and the only woman over thirty you sleep with, yes?"

"Yes," she managed to gasp, before the first orgasm ripped through her.

"I'm the only one you return to. You throw everyone else away like trash but not me, you selfish narcissist."

She closed her eyes and endured Riya's tirade. It was part of their ritual and the only condition Riya had placed on their periodic encounters. If she wanted the sex—and it was the hottest sex she'd ever had—she had to allow her to unload her anger and frustration. At one point Riya had made the mistake of telling Sloane she loved her—and Sloane had laughed.

Riya's finger plunged deeper inside her.

"Not so rough," she cried.

She chuckled and grabbed her chin with her free hand, forcing Sloane to meet her metallic gaze. "You wouldn't want it any other way. You don't want tenderness." When she looked away, she said, "Look at me. You want to forget about everything you don't have in your pathetic life, you rich bitch."

She ignored the insults and her cruel declaration of the truth. She rode her, bobbing in the water, getting exactly what she needed.

CHAPTER EIGHT

Regina gazed at the San Juan Mountains from her room window. She decided it was one of the most beautiful sights she'd seen in a long time. The tallest peak, Mt. Sneffels, was still brushed with snow in summer. It was a "fourteener," meaning it was at least fourteen thousand feet high.

She'd been brought up in Missoula, Montana, just a few hours from Glacier National Park, and she'd spent her summers hunting, fishing and hiking in the Northwest or Canada with her parents. In the short twelve years they were in her life, they'd sealed her love of the outdoors. When they were gone and she'd been forced to move east, her Aunt Mimi and Sloane broadened her horizons with several wonderful trips during her teenage years, including one to Rocky Mountain National Park.

College and graduate school had ended their adventures, and weekends spent traipsing through the wilderness and huddling around a campfire gave way to library study rooms and extra shifts at the diner where she worked. Love of the outdoors was something she had in common with Seth, but they'd only ventured out of town three times during the course of their eight-month relationship. She was usually too busy, and he was either working or helping friends.

It was actually a conversation about Colorado that had ignited their courtship. She'd gone out with friends to the bar where he worked and noticed a picture of the Rockies taped to the back wall. She'd asked him about it as she fetched another round. He'd smiled broadly and they exchanged pleasantries about their hiking adventures. She'd gone back to the bar three more nights in a row until he asked her out.

She lingered at the window. She thought she could reach out and touch the San Juans, and she felt a strong desire to grab a backpack and head for the top of Mt. Sneffels. Of course, the statistics for ill-prepared hikers were dismal, and if she were ever to undertake such a challenge, she'd engage in weeks of research prior to the trip. No, she was in Pinedale for a purpose and falling off Mt. Sneffels wasn't it.

Besides, she would never hike the Rockies again without Seth. They'd been to several of the same places like Glacier, Yosemite and Yellowstone. When she'd asked him where he learned about camping, he'd shrugged and said, "With friends. Boy Scouts. The usual."

For the first two months of their relationship when everything was new, she didn't press him about his biography. Of course questions about parentage had come up quickly on their second date, and he'd just said, "I'm not close to my moms," and they'd moved on.

When their relationship progressed, he freely shared the story of moving to South Carolina, his ill-fated relationship with a religious zealot and his father's subsequent born-again status that drove them apart. Yet, he still avoided discussing his mothers.

"Why won't you talk about them?" she'd pressed one night when they were doing the dishes.

"There's nothing to say," he'd said, staring into the soapsuds. "We just drifted apart."

"I can't believe they never call you or write to you."

He'd stiffened and said, "Leave it alone, Reg."

So she'd left it alone for another two months, but it nagged on her. One Saturday night his father showed up unannounced at Seth's apartment. He was in town for a business meeting and wanted to make amends.

They'd spent the awkward evening together, and in those few hours Regina learned how much Philip hated Seth's mother, a woman he'd bedded and impregnated on her eighteenth birthday, a woman who was too crazy to continue seeing. By the time he'd left Regina didn't know what to think. He'd portrayed Lenny and Pru as evil shrews damned to hell and castigated them for never reaching out to Seth.

Regina thought he might be right about that part. It seemed Seth's mother and partner had done nothing to rebuild their relationship with their son, whereas Philip had shown up on his doorstep. Regina found herself becoming quite judgmental of them—until the weekend they'd packed up Seth's apartment and he'd moved in with her.

She'd been packing his closet and found a shoebox on the closet shelf. Inside she'd found a photo of him with his mother and another woman. He was petting a rangy mutt while the two women knelt next to him, their arms wrapped around each other—like a family. She'd immediately seen his eyes and smile in Lenny's expression. Both women wore Life is Good T-shirts, and she finally understood where he'd learned to love the outdoors.

Underneath the pictures were dozens of unopened greeting cards addressed to him. The postmarks went back four years and the sender was noted as Barclay/Cavender. The address changed from Phoenix to Colorado at some point, indicating Lenny and her partner had moved. She'd also found several opened cards with lovely sentiments inside that referenced enclosed money or gift cards. All had been signed *Mom and Pru*. The last handful had FORWARD written on the front along with Seth's Boston address. The handwriting clearly belonged to a woman and Regina had realized two facts: Lenny probably didn't even know her son had left South Carolina and, despite her religious conversion, it seemed likely that Seth's stepmother had continued to forward mail from his "headed to hell" mother.

She stared at the postmark of the last card—2011. For some reason, the cards and letters had stopped over a year ago.

A few other mementos such as a pencil from the Redwoods and a bear keychain from Glacier had been littered amongst the cards and pictures of him on various vacations and at various birthday parties.

What happened?

She'd heard him on the stairs coming in for another load and quickly had grabbed the most recent unopened card before replacing the box in the closet and ducking into the bathroom.

She'd kept the card at work, sometimes pulling it from her desk drawer and staring at the red envelope. Sloane had seen her studying it one day, and she'd told her the story, but as usual, Sloane hadn't seemed surprised or interested. As each week passed and Seth said nothing about his mother, Regina grew more anxious about their relationship. Couples who kept secrets statistically struggled.

Left to her own imagination, she had created endless fictions about him and his family. She'd pictured a violent blowup, Jerry Springer style, with thrown chairs, obscene gestures and screams at a fevered pitch. She could imagine Philip in such a state, but Seth only had flashes of anger. He was much more even-tempered, and she had wondered if his balanced personality was the result of his mother's influence over his formative years when Philip was the absent parent. She'd found it quite interesting that he carried his mother's last name and not his father's surname of Meeks.

Maybe that was why she was here. She had to know about the women who were fifty percent responsible for the man she might marry. She bit her lip, torn between the optimism that Lenny and Pru were not the shrews Philip had depicted and the dread that he was at least partly correct. She wasn't sure what she'd do if she hated them by the time she left.

She realized it might not matter. Seth didn't seem to care that his mother wasn't in his life. If the status quo continued after their marriage, there would never be any fighting over whose parents to visit or where they would spend Christmas. Yet in recent months she'd found him sitting on the porch in the middle of the night staring into the darkness. He would reveal nothing and mutter that he couldn't sleep. When she'd confronted him about the insomnia, they'd had a fight. She was debating whether to move out when he finally sat her down and told her the insomnia had nothing to do with her.

"I'm just sorting out some things from my past," he said cryptically. He'd refused to say more but had agreed to see a doctor for a sleeping pill. They both knew sleep was critical to their busy lives and already a rare commodity. After he'd started taking Ambien the insomnia stopped, but she knew they hadn't addressed the issue and it would resurface again. It was a threat to their relationship, and she could handle avoidance for only so long. She needed to see the big picture, and if her future mothers-in-law were just two steps to the left of Lady Macbeth, she wanted to know.

She turned away from the window, grabbed her messenger bag and headed out to Harrison Road, Pinedale's main drag. Sloane had texted her stating she'd already made contact with Lenny. Apparently they were going hiking. Regina knew Sloane would save her pitch for just the right moment. Very few people ever said no to her, which meant Regina's mission was to scope out the property Sloane believed was an optimal location for the store. If she met Lenny, she was not to divulge her relationship with Sloane.

It felt good to walk after the long plane ride and the drive. The Pinedale Visitors Center sat adjacent to the train museum on her left and a string of businesses on the right. The buildings varied greatly in their shape, size and color. Some were old while others were newer but built to look rustic in the spirit of the mining community that had birthed the entire area. An old stucco box-like structure sat on a block by itself next to a sign proclaiming God's Rods. She guessed it was a fishing store.

A shuttered building separated God's Rods from the one franchise in Pinedale, Happy Burger Joint. The parking lot overflowed with cars, most bearing license plates from out of state. The fast-food restaurant bordered one of the few stoplights on Harrison, and the drive-through patrons took advantage of the left turn lane that gave them an easy way to rejoin the parade of vehicles on their way to Telluride.

Regina gazed at the shuttered property between God's Rods and Happy Burger Joint. It was rather spacious and she guessed it had been some sort of clothing shop or gift shop in its prior life.

A Chinese restaurant, a real estate agent and the local post office were sandwiched together on the next block, across from an enormous church. She could see the steeple of another church a block over, and she guessed Pinedale was serious about its worshipping. It was also the only competing interest she'd seen after walking six blocks. There was only one medical plaza, one pizza place, one vet and even one market. It was as if everyone sat down and agreed to legalize monopolies. When she ventured up a side street and saw a second tavern, her faith in capitalism was restored. No town could operate with just one bar.

She passed the Chatsworth Hotel and detoured into a residential area to get a feel for the community, finding the homes as eclectic as the businesses. The same block housed a dilapidated mobile home that looked ready to fall off its foundation, a log cabin with a dirt yard and a gorgeous three-story Victorian. The fresh yellow paint, white picket fence and lush green lawn compelled her to pull out her camera phone—definitely Cinderella next to the stepsisters.

She returned to Harrison Road and the loud rumble of engines. An array of six Harleys drove past followed by nine Lamborghinis of various colors. She stopped and gaped at the beautiful cars snaking down the street. They cut through town and made the curve at the top of the hill on their way to Telluride. Pinedale survived because of the Telluride and Ouray tourists who needed to eat or wanted to stretch their legs in the quaint park bordering the community center. A large wood carving of a bear and her cubs stood next to the sidewalk. She marveled at the intricacy of the detail. Several other carvings of various sizes lined the one block park and she resisted the urge to tour all of them.

She pulled out the sheaf of papers the R and D department had thrust in her hands as she'd hurried out of the office. She chided herself for not reviewing them carefully on the plane, but she'd been so tired, having been awake much of the previous night. She was too nervous about the trip to sleep.

She scanned the information for an address, annoyed with the R and D team for the haphazard collection of information. The front page only mentioned a parcel number, and it wasn't until she skimmed through three pages of the narrative that she found the actual address. She cocked her head to the left and read the street sign.

"It should be right here," she murmured. She gazed across the street at a clapboard strip mall. "That's it?"

She was surprised that Sloane viewed the property as optimal. It wasn't as large as she expected, but it was airy, fronted with large bay windows and it appeared solid but drab. The dirt parking lot was mostly empty, save for one of the Lamborghinis which had broken ranks and was parked in a corner as far away as possible from the handful of cars in the lot. Three wooden signs hung from the eaves identifying the merchants as Two Scoops Ice Cream Confectioners, Books and Beans and Pru's Curious Curios.

She blinked and leaned forward, certain she was misreading the sign. "That can't be right."

She shuffled through the papers becoming more frustrated by the minute. Nowhere was the location named. She skimmed R and D's narrative once more and realized it was only referred to as "the property." Something was fishy about this, but she'd take that up with Sloane later. She crossed the street and faced the building. Pru's Curious Curios *was* "the optimal location." How could she not know this? How could Sloane keep this from her?

A little girl giggled incessantly as she galloped on the electric horse that sat on the long front porch all three businesses shared.

An elderly couple who seemed to be her grandparents shared an ice cream and watched from a bench nearby.

She took a deep breath and climbed the cement steps, noticing weeds protruding from the web of cracks. A bell above the door announced her entrance, but she doubted anyone heard it over the jazz piano that echoed loudly—too loudly—through the store. She strolled through the aisles, noting the unimaginative displays. Much of the merchandise lay on tables in simple rows similar to a swap mart. There didn't seem to be any logic about placement. Kitchen items shared space with handmade mufflers, old records sat next to jewelry, and novelty cards, usually a huge seller, were scattered throughout the store in bins and on racks. Someone looking for a special sentiment would become easily frustrated trying to find a particular message of sympathy or thanks.

She gazed into the second-story loft, trying to decide if she was curious enough to trek up the rickety spiral staircase that looked as if it might fall over at any moment. The skylight illuminated stacks of boxes, a half-dressed mannequin, racks of paperback books and some large metal signs that looked as if they belonged in a grocery store. From her vantage point she couldn't tell if the second story was part of the store or a storage area, although the staircase wasn't closed off. She decided, like the rest of the current customers, to forego the climb.

It's not good if people don't know where they are supposed to go.

The walls were practically bare, and Regina restrained herself from finding a ladder. If merchandise was in the air, it wasn't cluttering the walkways. That was the most significant problem, she decided. There was too much *stuff.* Price tags were in different handwritings, suggesting Lenny and Pru worked on consignment with multiple sellers who were allowed to bring in anything they wanted. When she tripped over an old box of electric cable labeled "Make an Offer," she realized she'd wandered into an ongoing yard sale.

She surveyed the handful of customers and immediately pegged as the Lamborghini owner the guy with an expensive black leather jacket and a girlfriend wearing four-inch heels and expensive jeans. Three other gray-haired couples trolled the aisles—tourists. The only other people in the store were a pre-teen girl who was fascinated with a jewelry rack and a bored young man sitting at the cash register playing a game on his cell phone.

The Lamborghini riders exchanged a look and quickly departed without making a purchase.

That's a loss. They had big money to spend.

A loud clatter made her jump and she turned to the source, a toppled display of earrings. The girl immediately dropped to the floor and began collecting the bright turquoise droplets. She moved to help, righting the metal tree that held the earrings.

"I'm so sorry," the girl whined.

"It's okay," she said quietly.

"No, it's not okay," a voice disagreed.

She glanced up into a stern face. The woman's arms were crossed and her gaze focused on the girl.

"Lenny, I—"

She pointed a finger at the door. "Out," she hissed.

"But—"

She pointed again and the girl slunk away. The woman noticed Regina's horrified expression and rolled her eyes as she bent down to help. She whispered, "Shoplifted from me three times. Finally had to kick her out. Only trouble is I don't think she can control it."

She blinked. "Her? Really?"

"Hard to believe, huh?"

Once the earring tree was reassembled, they both stood.

"Thanks for the help. I'm Lenny Barclay," she said, extending her hand.

"Regina Dewar."

The face that greeted her was warm and friendly like the picture from the shoebox. *Seth looks so much like his mother.* Dark brown hair, without a hint of gray, draped over her shoulders. She wore cargo shorts, and her toned body suggested she spent her leisure time hiking the Rockies. *She certainly doesn't look old enough to have a son in his twenties.*

"Where are you from, Regina?"

"Originally Montana, but now Boston. Have you ever been there?"

She shook her head. "No, I'm not particularly well traveled, but I've been to Montana, Wyoming and California a few times."

"Glacier?"

"That and some other places, Granite Peak and The Beaten Path. Do you like to hike?"

"Love it, but I don't get a lot of time to do it right now. My job eats up most of my life."

She raised an eyebrow. "What do you do?"

"I'm in marketing," she hedged, wondering if Lenny would ask her more questions. Sloane wouldn't approve of Regina exposing her connection to Wilderness Campaign, but she found herself tempted to since Sloane had kept her in the dark about the optimal location.

She made a sweeping gesture. "Well, I'd love your feedback about Pru's, and if you have any ideas to help us, please tell me. I don't shy away from constructive criticism."

Regina's gaze strayed to a father holding a little girl over his head so she could grab an item from a high shelf. She inwardly cringed until the little girl's feet were back on the ground.

She must have telegraphed her dismay for Lenny said, "I know there's a lot that could be improved. I haven't really done much with it in the last year." She sighed. "Just haven't been motivated."

"What about Pru? Is she a real person?" she asked innocently.

Lenny bit her lip and dropped her gaze to the concrete floor. "She was, but she's gone."

"Gone?"

"She died."

She felt her face crumble. "I'm sorry," she whispered.

"It's okay. I'm finally used to saying it. A lot of the visitors always ask. For the first three months after I reopened the store, my friend Sue, who runs the coffee shop and the ice cream store, pretended she was Pru so I wouldn't have to answer any questions. I'm not sure how convincing she was, but I couldn't handle it. Thought about changing the name, but I couldn't do that either. Now it's mine and I have no idea what to do with it. That's the truth. This was Pru's idea, her way to spend retirement. I was just supposed to be the help. Not how it turned out," she said softly.

Regina managed a little smile, although she thought she might faint. *File that away. That's your personal life. You're here to talk business.* "Well, it's a great location and a terrific building."

"You think? Pru always said it was the second best one on Harrison, after Schoolhouse Emporium."

"What's Schoolhouse Emporium?"

She scowled. "The competition, and if I'm being honest, the *better* store, at least since Pru's been gone. Come here and I'll show you."

They wandered behind an enormous screen and into a hallway filled with antique doors. There was barely room to walk as the doors severely angled into the pathway. She kept her eyes down, concerned about a broken ankle, until they reached a back room she assumed was the office.

The clutter and disorganization extended to Lenny's private space. Regina's mom would've said the place was "packed to the gills," and it would've been the truth. Buried underneath a stack of mail was an ancient laptop.

The computer slowly whirred and beeped to life. Lenny went to her favorites and pulled up a website. *She knows how to use the computer. She just hasn't joined the twenty-first century.*

"See?" she said, gesturing to Schoolhouse Emporium's colorful home page. "Carlotta really puts me to shame."

"Carlotta?"

"Carlotta Ochoa is the woman who owns Schoolhouse Emporium *and* La Casita, the Mexican restaurant, *and* her bar, Charlie's. She practically owns the town."

Regina slid into the desk chair and surfed through the Schoolhouse Emporium website. It was slick and easy to navigate. Carlotta had incorporated several bells and whistles, including photo sliders, printable coupons and a virtual tour through the store. She sold dozens of items online and was linked to Facebook and Twitter, boasting over a thousand followers on each.

The building itself was impressive, complete with multi-levels and an extensive square-footage. She imagined her inventory must be triple whatever Lenny could possibly sell. The place was at least twice as big. *Now, that's an optimal location.*

She scrolled to the bottom of the home page and read the fine print. "Wow, she must be doing okay if she can afford to have Baseline Advertising Group design her website. They're national."

"She's loaded," Lenny said with a sigh. "All three of her businesses make money, and she lives up near me, only higher on the mountain. She's the Dollar Mart CEO, or at least she's a figurehead. After her geriatric husband died she sold it to a corporation but still maintains some power."

"Is she looking to run you out of business or buy you out?"

"I don't know. She just bought the building next to the Happy Burger."

She heard the disdain in her voice. "Not a fan of chains?"

Lenny slowly shook her head. "Not in Pinedale. Not here. Chains have their place. Just not in a small town. Here, we all keep each other fed. Even Carlotta shares that view. She just wants to own everything herself, at least that's my opinion."

She imagined Lenny and Sloane's hike would be quite interesting. She was so angry with Sloane for withholding the information about Pru's death that she hoped Lenny pushed her down the mountain.

"So what would Carlotta do with Pru's?"

She shrugged. "I've heard rumors. I imagine she'd gut all three of our stores and turn the whole place into some kind of Western wear place. Or maybe she'll open a dance hall. I don't know what she'll do, but I know that I will lose Pru's dream. So, if you've got any ideas that might revitalize this place, I'd love to know. In any case, it was nice meeting you."

Several feelings rushed through Regina's mind at once— her anger with Sloane for not telling her about the location or Pru, anxiety about Seth's anger with *her* when he learned where she was and why she was here and the thrill of competing with Carlotta Ochoa. Sloane clearly didn't know that another powerful woman was looking to purchase Lenny's business—possibly her future *mother-in-law's* business.

Her decision made, she squeezed Lenny's arm and said, "Don't worry. We can fix this."

Promotion

A successful venture depends on accentuating its
benefits through persuasive tactics.

CHAPTER NINE

As Lenny's Jeep turned into the parking lot of Kate's Place, Sloane quickly reviewed her strategy: engage, entertain, encourage, entice and excite. This was her version of the Seven Ps, which she'd vowed someday to publish in a business journal. She had read Lenny's biography, and her confidence was strong. Lenny was emotionally vulnerable and lacked business savvy. She was no match for her.

She opened the door and climbed into the Jeep, wearing a broad smile. *Engage.*

"Hi," she said. "I'm glad we're doing this. I haven't been to Blaine Basin in a long time."

Lenny nodded and pulled onto the road. Her hands gripped the wheel tightly and her brow furrowed in deep concentration. It was difficult to engage someone in conversation when her mind was so clearly focused on other things. She needed to break the ice—carefully.

Rocket shifted in the backseat and she turned to greet him. "Hi there, boy. So you're a hiker, too?"

"He loves to hike," she said.

"I wish I had a dog who'd hike. My little Fergie much prefers sitting in her chair at home."

"What kind of dog do you have?"

"A Maltese. She thinks she's a princess, complete with her throne and tiara. One of my friends actually found a little doggie tiara and scepter online. She looked hilarious."

Lenny laughed and said, "I've had a dog or two like that over the years. Rocket's a lot more fun. He goes everywhere with us...I mean, me."

Entertain. Don't ask her about Pru. Keep it light.

She regaled her with three more stories about Fergie, the fictitious Maltese who was constantly in trouble. By the time they turned off to the dirt road that led to the trail, Lenny was laughing heartily, her grip on the steering wheel had loosened and she was casually leaning back in the seat.

Sloane could never own a dog, not with her busy schedule. She rationalized, though, that the stories helped Lenny relax and forget her troubles. It didn't matter that Fergie's escapades were really a collection of dog stories depicted in a *Cesar's Way* magazine she had found abandoned on the airplane that took her to Denver.

She let the conversation fall into a lull, waiting to see if Lenny would initiate the discussion that brought them together.

"Is that 'Precious Time' by Van Morrison?" Lenny asked.

She realized she'd been drumming on the door frame and humming out loud. "Oh," she said, surprised, "Um, yeah, it was. You recognized it?"

"I'm a big fan of Van."

"Me too," she said. "Have you seen him in concert?"

"Many times. My favorite was at the Hollywood Bowl in 2008."

"I heard that concert was amazing."

"It was," Lenny agreed. "I went with a friend, and we climbed a tree in a nearby yard to see it."

"Uh, not exactly the way I'd want to see a concert. Sounds a little uncomfortable."

"Well, we hadn't exactly planned on attending. It was a last-minute thing." Their eyes met and she added, "You've got great rhythm. Do you play an instrument?"

"A few, but I like drums the most so I tend to drum anywhere I am. Probably a nervous habit."

"Are you nervous now?"

She blinked. Lenny's gaze was focused on the road, a little smile on her face.

"A little, I guess. I've never been on a hike with someone as important as a *mayor*."

Encourage.

Lenny snorted and waved her off. "It's not a big deal, believe me."

They pulled into the trailhead parking area. Lenny killed the ignition but remained motionless, deep in thought. Her grip once again sat at ten and two o'clock on the steering wheel, and she gazed through a thicket of trees that surrounded the parking area. Sloane was hesitant to disturb her. She was far away, probably thinking of Pru.

Rocket slid between the seats and nuzzled her arm with his nose, but she remained still. Sloane tapped the dashboard as she softly crooned the opening lines to "Moondance."

By the time she got to the chorus, Lenny had joined her with a voice that was twice as good as her own. The chorus ended and they stumbled into silence. If she had been with one of her flings on vacation, she'd be all over her at this point, and they would have crawled into the backseat for a quickie. But this was business. *Or is it? Why are you staring at her? Why does this feel so awkward?*

Rocket whined and shifted his head back and forth between them. To escape the moment, she visualized herself in her Boston office, ensconced behind her desk on the phone.

"Did you have a chance to review the report I gave you?" she asked out loud, still imagining she was on the phone.

Lenny coughed and shifted in her seat. "Uh, well, I only had time to skim it, but I have some questions."

"Should we walk and talk at the same time?"

Lenny looked like she might throw the Jeep in reverse and abandon the hike, until Rocket let out a sorrowful howl. She looked at him lovingly and scratched his funny ears. "Okay, boy, you win."

I owe that dog an entire box of treats.

They pulled their packs from the back of the Jeep and headed down the trail. Lenny kept a quick pace while Rocket bounded ahead, smelling every log and plant in sight. The trail meandered through clearings overflowing with blossoming flowers and deep into the woods of the north face of Mt. Sneffels. Periodically the trail turned muddy as small streams crossed their path and disappeared into the depths of the mountain.

"Isn't it amazing how the landscape changes so much?" Sloane mused.

"It's because we're at the edge of the Colorado Plateau."

"What's that?"

"It's actually a region that encompasses the Four Corners area and includes the Canyonlands in Utah and Lake Powell in Arizona. The San Juans are the eastern border."

"The Canyonlands are great," she said, remembering a particularly fun weekend at Bryce Canyon with Jericho, a woman who loved sleeping naked on the ground and staring up at the stars.

"The whole plateau spans a hundred and thirty thousand square miles and is over five hundred million years old," Lenny continued. She stopped and pointed between two spruce trees at a meadow of blue columbine wildflowers. "What's really impressive is when you think about what was going on during the continental drift. Everything was shifting, and eventually when the mountains rose up about ten million years ago, the plateau stayed put. They think it was floating on a surface of molten rock."

She was impressed. She loved hiking but she certainly couldn't articulate any trail's biography—even with a college degree.

"How do you know all this?"

She shrugged. "I took this course on the geography of the western United States. It was fascinating."

"Apparently. Did you ever think about becoming a forest ranger or a geologist?"

She chuckled. "I considered both of those—as well as topographer, archaeologist and animal behaviorist. I thought about becoming a *lot* of things, but nothing ever seemed to stick for very long. Work was something you did so you could play."

"How many jobs have you had?"

"Couldn't tell you, but I've only been fired five times and once was because I wouldn't sleep with the boss."

"That doesn't count then. That's justified."

"They were *all* justified. Once I got fired from a sports bar because I didn't fill out my T-shirt well enough."

She stopped walking. "You're kidding."

"No, my bra size wasn't large enough."

Her gaze automatically traveled to Lenny's chest. "I don't see anything wrong with your breasts or any other part of you, for that matter."

She lowered her eyes and plowed ahead quickly. "Were *you* ever fired?"

"Yup, from my first job at an ice cream shop—because I wouldn't work a double shift without overtime pay. I threatened to file a grievance and my boss called me a bitch."

They had come to the creek bank, a natural place to take a break before they crossed the two planks that served as a makeshift bridge. They perched on a cluster of boulders and sipped from their water bottles. Sloane listened to the soothing flow of the stream.

Lenny pulled a PowerBar from her pack and offered Sloane half.

"Thanks, I love these. Sometimes they're my dinner."

"Mine too. I'm not a very good cook. Pru did all of the cooking."

She sensed Lenny's sadness returning, so she said, "In case you're wondering, I never filed the grievance. I let it go. I was only fourteen. I could talk a good game, but I really didn't know anything."

"I have a hard time believing there was ever a time when you were uninformed."

"Oh, I was informed. I just didn't know how to wield my power."

"Is that what's most important to you? Power?"

She pondered her answer carefully, knowing Lenny was testing her. "It helps." She could tell from her expression that she didn't agree. "What about you?"

She stretched her arms above her, seemingly unaware that Sloane's gaze had returned to her chest. "I have no idea, but I want to know what you think is *most* important."

"Most important? In life?"

"Yes," Lenny said, laughing. "If I'm going to do business with you, if this *town* is going to do business with you, I have to know who I'm dealing with." She slid off the rock and put her hands on her hips. "I need to know that the greater good will be preserved as you set out to make a small fortune on the back of Pinedale."

She was speechless. *I never have conversations like this with anyone. This isn't how a proposal meeting should go.*

"Why don't you chew on that for a while," Lenny said over her shoulder as she shuffled across the bridge and headed up the trail.

They continued toward the lower basin, crossing two streams and cutting through a meadow of bluebells. Sloane particularly enjoyed the Blaine Basin hike because it was surprising and ever-changing. Unlike Lenny, she wasn't versed in geography, topography or forestry. She couldn't read the clues in the landscape, which, like foreshadowing in a book, hinted at the foliage beyond the next turn or predicted the route of Wilson Creek. She relished the challenges they faced, including tiptoeing over the log that sat above turbulent water or exploring one of the abandoned mines she knew awaited them near the upper basin.

They heard the waterfall pouring from the side of Mt. Sneffels before they saw it.

"How much further to the lower basin?" Sloane asked. "I can't remember."

"It's about a mile but it's going to be steep and rocky," Lenny said. "We also could encounter some problems because of the erosion from the runoff, but it's worth it."

She nodded eagerly and they climbed upward.

Entice.

She'd decided to avoid discussing business until Lenny's thirst for adventure had been satisfied. It was all about timing, and a few deals had fallen victim to her youthful impatience years ago. She'd learned.

And the view wasn't bad either. Lenny forged ahead, allowing her to openly gawk at her fine derriere and toned legs. Periodically Lenny would stop and marvel at the shocking color of the flowers or stare at Sneffels' peak, and she found herself enjoying the hike because *Lenny* was having a good time.

As they passed through the narrowest part of the trail, Rocket bounded ahead and disappeared amidst the tall grass. They entered a sprawling green meadow, surrounded by steep walls punctured with cascades descending into parts unknown. She glanced at Lenny who turned circles, a smile on her face.

She's gorgeous when she smiles.

They dropped onto the soft grass and enjoyed the natural beauty privately. Lenny laughed as Rocket attempted to catch a butterfly, and she snuck a quick glance at her. She was calm, nearly serene. Sloane hadn't noticed her pale blue eyes before, but they were everywhere at once and matched the blue columbine wildflowers that surrounded them. She was an All-American girl, and while she wasn't striking enough to grace the cover of a Wilderness Campaign catalog, she had a friendly smile.

"Are you staring at me?" Lenny asked, her gaze fixed on Mt. Sneffels.

"No, I'm thinking," she said embarrassed.

"About how to gracefully change the subject to business?"

"That's why we're here."

"No," she disagreed, "that may be why *you're* here. I wanted to prove something to myself."

"What?"

She shook her head. "Forget it. I shouldn't have said that. It's personal."

Suddenly she very much wanted to know, and it had nothing to do with gaining any leverage. "You can tell me," she said coolly. "I make it a point never to mix business with pleasure, so you can tell me anything and I won't hold it against you."

"You mean, you won't *use* it against me should we engage in business negotiations."

"Uh, well, no," she sputtered. "Of course not." Lenny's sharp look told her not to push it. "Okay, fine, let's get to it." She pulled a copy of the report from her backpack and presented it to her. "I wanted you to have some visuals while we spoke."

She hesitated before accepting the thick, coiled stack of papers. "Why don't you just tell me the bottom line?"

"You don't want to read it?"

"I'll read it, just not at six thousand feet."

Excite. Make her want this for the town.

She faced her and said, "I can jump start your economy. If a Wilderness Campaign comes to Pinedale, you'll easily inject a million dollars into the treasury each year. That's not counting the number of people who will also benefit from the fifty or sixty jobs that will be created from opening the store. It's a total win for your community."

"A total win," Lenny repeated. "No negatives?"

She shook her head. "I don't see any. You might have some extra traffic congestion," she added quickly, "but think of the potential when those tourists decide to grab a meal at Kate's Place or have a beer at the True Grit Bar and Grille. *All* of your businesses will profit from the presence of the store. There's no competition."

"Donny Beck at God's Rods might disagree with you," she countered. "You sell fishing gear, don't you?"

"Well, yes."

"Don't most of your stores have a café, too?"

"Most do, but some don't."

"Those tourists who desire convenience might just as easily decide to chow down on a buffalo burger at your place rather than walk up the street to the Adobe Inn."

She narrowed her eyes. "I would agree to forego the café and start a conversation with Mr. Beck about his fishing store. Perhaps he could consign with us."

"No *perhaps*. If we do this, I'll expect a non-competition clause in the contract for every existing business in our town. I'll make you a list, and you'd better not bury it in a bunch of bullshit."

She smiled, invigorated by the exchange. Her hunger for the deal had been fed, and Lenny was clearly a formidable opponent. She should be satisfied, but instead, she wanted to lean over and kiss her. *Why am I turned on right now? She is so surprising.*

"I have to ask you something. I've read your résumé—"

"All sixty-eight pages of it?" Lenny laughed.

"You're shrewd. How come…" She stopped, unsure of what to say and not wanting to offend Lenny again.

"How come I never found a career? Why didn't I stick with anything?" She jumped up, the proposal falling out of her lap. She stepped onto a tree stump, her hands on her hips and her face contorted into a grimace. "Why don't I have any motivation?" she asked mockingly.

"I'm sorry—" she sputtered.

Lenny threw open her arms and cried, "Because of this!"

She looked around, stunned by her extreme mood swings and antics. "The forest?"

"No, the world. Every time I pointed myself in a direction and started walking toward a goal, something else popped up, another opportunity, another cause that seemed more important."

She jumped off the stump and dropped back to the ground. She thumbed through the proposal, and Sloane shook her head. *I clearly have no control over this conversation, but she is fascinating.*

"So if you love causes, why not specialize in nonprofits?"

"I thought about that too." She looked up and grinned. "For about an hour."

Sloane burst out laughing. "I don't know anyone like you."

"Good, maybe that gives me the advantage, because I've known a lot of people like you."

Her face fell. *That hurt. Why did that hurt?*

Lenny obviously noticed her reaction. "I'm sorry. That wasn't nice. You asked why I didn't specialize in nonprofits, and the reason is because I wanted to help *everyone*, not just one group. And I know how naïve that sounds. I get it."

She couldn't believe she was real. She was so genuine and forthright. *I doubt she's ever told a lie.*

"You're a wonderful woman," she whispered, leaning toward her.

I can't help myself. I need this.

Lenny automatically closed her eyes. She took advantage. Her lips trailed up Lenny's jawbone and wandered down the side of her neck, until Lenny tensed and she pulled away.

"I thought you didn't mix business with pleasure." Lenny's tone suggested she was shutting down.

Shit. I need to do something. I'm ruining this. "I don't usually. I'm sorry. I shouldn't have done that. If it makes you feel any better, I found the touch of your skin completely revolting, and to be honest you smell a little."

Lenny chuckled, and Sloane sighed quietly. Lenny flipped through the proposal and asked, "Where did you want to put this thing?"

"I thought you said you skimmed it," she said slowly.

"Well, not really." When she didn't answer right away, Lenny pressed. "Well?"

"Your building." Lenny blinked and she said, "It makes the most sense. You have excellent square footage, you're on the main drag, there's room for a parking lot in the back, and there are several points of entry."

Her expression was unreadable. Sloane remembered she'd been a blackjack dealer and certainly had learned to give away nothing. She decided to stop babbling and wait her out. She wasn't expecting her to jump up and sprint across the meadow into a cluster of trees, Rocket immediately at her side. Sloane glanced up at the dark clouds advancing toward them. It wasn't a good idea to get stuck on a mountain in a lightning storm. She stood and headed toward the trees, eager to see where Lenny had gone.

Why did I kiss her? I hardly know her. "Get a hold of yourself, Sloane. This is too important to screw up."

A light drizzle began to fall, a precursor to the heavy rain that was soon to come. She found her standing on top of a fallen tree whose diameter was at least six feet. The tree spread across a muddy bog, and she suspected the water had uprooted it.

She jumped as thunder pitched from the west. "We need to get out of here. It's starting to storm."

Lenny remained on the log, her arms folded. "It sounds like you've given this location a lot of thought."

"Yes, we've spent a lot of time and money studying this idea," she conceded. "We wouldn't just swoop into a place without thoroughly vetting it. I don't want to waste anyone's time, including my own." When another strike of thunder sounded, she added, "Let's discuss this on our way down the mountain, Lenny. The rain's picking up and the lightning is going to follow."

She looked up at the sky. "I like lightning."

"I don't," she replied sharply. "C'mon, let's go."

She ignored her and walked the length of the tree. "I tell you what? You want to leave but I know you're a businesswoman who loves a deal, so I'll make you a deal. You get on this log with me, jump up and down three times, and if you don't fall off, I'll *give* you the store. *Give* it to you," she said again.

She stared at her. "You can't be serious. That's ridiculous."

"No, it's not."

She jumped up and down three times to make her point. "See? It's not so hard."

"You're insane! And I don't believe you'd ever give me your store just for jumping on a log."

"I would if that were the wager."

There was sincerity in her voice, but Sloane was convinced it was a trick. "Seriously, you're prepared to lose your partner's store. What do you get out of this?"

She jumped up and down three more times. "From your perspective probably very little, which means it's a great business deal, right?" She jumped up and down again. "What have you got to lose?"

She couldn't believe the surreal situation. Lenny must be crazy to propose such a wager. Sloane had wondered about her mental stability. Even if she won, which was highly likely given her exceptional agility, she doubted Lenny would relinquish the deed to the building—but maybe she would. Sloane decided she'd be an idiot not to take the bet.

She wiped the rain from her hands and pulled herself onto the giant log. It was slick and she struggled to gain her balance on the rough bark. Only after she'd taken three steps did she realize she was still wearing her daypack. *Oh well.*

She joined Lenny at the middle of the log. She looked down into the muddy center of the bog, guessing it was at least three feet deep. The drop hadn't appeared as menacing from her vantage point on the ground where the tall grass had blocked her view. If she fell, it would *suck*. Thunder clapped again as if telling her to hurry up.

She checked her stance and the location of her feet. She wanted to make sure she wasn't standing on a knothole or a piece of broken bark. "Okay, so I jump three times, right?"

"Yup. Let's see it."

"One, two, three," she said before she gave a little hop, just enough for her feet to lift off the log. She held out her arms and caught herself before she fell off.

"That's one."

"It is," Lenny agreed. "Two more."

Lightning shot across the sky as the storm moved closer. She took a cleansing breath, counted to three and jumped again. While her landing was a little hard, she twisted to the left and regained her balance. "That's two. One more and you'll have to pay up!" she said in a giddy voice.

Lenny seemed entirely amused by the whole thing. She'd moved to the far edge of the log, bent over, a hand on each knee. The rain was soaking them both, and she looked *good*.

Sloane checked her feet. She needed to stay focused. "Okay, last time. One, two, three!"

From the corner of her eye, she saw movement. Lenny wasn't on the log anymore. Sloane's feet came down—and slid forward. She was falling backward, away from the log into the mud. She sank as if being dipped in chocolate and then bobbed to the top. She flailed her arms, and her fingers grasped the tall grass. She pulled herself out of the bog and tried to wipe the mud from her eyes but only succeeded in blinding herself.

"Here," Lenny said.

She snatched the wisps of tissue that trailed across her fingers and wiped her eyes and mouth. Lenny stood over her, smiling.

"You tricked me!" she screamed. "You made the log move!"

"I didn't trick you, and *you* moved the log, not me. I merely jumped off, and when you came down on it, you moved it forward, which propelled you backward. Simple physics. For every action, there is an equal and opposite reaction."

"I don't give a shit about physics!" she screamed. "Why the hell didn't it move when you were jumping up and down on it, huh?"

"There wasn't enough weight on it yet. It took both of us to move it. You probably didn't even realize that the log was already slipping when you jumped the first two times. Then when you jumped up and I jumped off, well…"

"Then you shouldn't have jumped off! Why the hell did you do that?"

She shook her head. "I never said anything about what I was going to do. This wasn't about me. This was about *you*." She pointed at her and whistled for Rocket. Thunder rolled over them. "You're right about that sky. We need to get moving."

She attempted to stand and fell back on her bottom. Lenny stifled a laugh and she flung some mud on her.

"Hey!"

Lenny turned to leave, and she said, "I'm sorry. Just help me up."

Lenny stuck out a hand and pulled her to a standing position. Most of her front was relatively clean, but she already could feel the mud caking against the back of her knees.

On the trek back to the Jeep, she counted two children, three couples and two retirees who heartily laughed or offered a chuckle with a compassionate word for her predicament. Lenny remained silent, but each time they crossed the creek over one of the makeshift bridges, Lenny took her hand so she wouldn't fall again. Eventually they came to a place where the trail ran parallel to the calm creek and a beaten path cut through the foliage down to the water.

"I know we need to get out of here, but I can't stand this anymore," she growled.

She threw off the daypack and trotted into the icy water. She gasped, but the sensation of the mud sloughing off her body was like shedding a second skin. As the mud disappeared so did her anger at Lenny. She scooped water onto her calves and knees, knowing she was probably minutes away from being drenched in a rainstorm. *What the hell?* She immersed herself completely. Her head lolled back and the gray-black sky offered a striking picture through the trees.

Lenny stood on the shore, watching intently. When their eyes met, she quickly looked away, pretending to study a plant on the trail.

We're having a moment here. I'm going to make the most of it.

She stood and emerged from the creek, well aware that her thin cotton T-shirt clung to her breasts and that her nipples, aching from the cold, were standing at attention.

She was most amused when Lenny remained as motionless as a statue until she'd grabbed her daypack and started back down the trail. "C'mon, Lenny," she called.

When they got to the parking lot, Lenny pulled out a black garbage bag and covered the passenger seat before Sloane climbed in. They headed back to town, the silence growing between them. She longed for a hot shower, and she was frustrated that she hadn't closed the deal. She felt as if she'd been played, but really there was no way for Lenny to be certain the log would roll away.

"I can't believe you did that!" she blurted. "Was that payback because I want to buy your store?"

"Maybe," she admitted. "I guess it was me exerting *my* power."

She looked out the window and bit her cheek. It was all she could do to keep from yelling at her. She was mad. She was hurt. She was completely flummoxed.

Lenny started humming "Precious Time." She glanced over at her as an invitation to join in, which she did. Her anger disappeared again.

"What if I'd somehow managed to stay on it?"

Lenny stopped humming and shrugged. "Then I guess I would've lost."

"Would you have really given me the shop or was that just a ploy?"

She shook her head. "No, I keep my promises. Did you ever see Van in New York at the Beacon with John Lee Hooker?"

"Uh, no, I only saw that video."

"I'll bet that was amazing, don't you think?" she asked excitedly.

When she looked at Sloane for affirmation she was carefree. There was such purity in her intentions, no hidden agendas and no games. She was beautiful. *I want to see that expression again. I want to kiss her.*

She was dumbfounded. Lenny had taken a huge risk with her future and Pru's legacy—but she'd won.

I'm the one covered in mud. I lost. I never lose.

"Why did you do it? Why take the chance?"

Lenny grinned. "Why not?"

CHAPTER TEN

Lenny gazed at the San Juans from the chaise lounge on her deck. Twilight painted the mountains shades of blues and greens prettier than most landscapes she'd seen in museums. She turned to the empty chaise next to her—Pru's spot—and sighed. Her spirits lifted when Rocket jumped onto the cushion and curled into a brown ball. He was always so close to Pru and having him nearby was a perfect antidote for the loneliness that overcame her periodically.

According to the calendar, Pru had been gone a year almost to the day. Yet time froze for Lenny, who could still remember the smallest details of Pru's service—the overpowering perfume Sue had worn, Carlotta's quiet crying in the pew behind her and the unexplainable and completely inappropriate thought that she was grateful Seth had been spared from attending. She guessed his grief coupled with her own might've been too much.

She'd agonized over whether to call him. She wasn't even sure if his cell number was still the same since they had not spoken for so long. She'd stopped trying to reach him after they moved to Colorado, but as Pru withered away, she had pulled out her cell at least once a day, determined to make amends and give him the opportunity to come say a proper goodbye. Once, she'd punched half the number before disconnecting, fearing his reaction. Losing Pru forever was inevitable, but she still thought someday she'd reunite with him. For now he was a kite high in the sky, and hope was the sliver of thread that kept him tethered to her. If he had refused to come to the service, her hope would have died and he'd have been as dead as Pru.

She realized she sounded melodramatic. Of course he wasn't dead. She should be grateful, but that was difficult when she counted the birthdays he'd missed, the holidays that passed without acknowledgment and the void of constant communication that would have kept them anchored in each other's life.

Now he was no more than an acquaintance, and she knew nothing of his likes and dislikes, his experiences or his daily routine. He was a man now, and she'd lost that time of awakening into adulthood. What adventures had he taken? What career had he chosen? Did he still have a girlfriend? Maybe he'd finally learned to like vegetables.

Rocket nudged her hand with his nose and she offered a sad smile. He knew her moods. "You're the best boy," she cooed the way Pru used to do. He shook his head and she was certain he understood.

She thought of the strange encounter with Regina. It was odd that a total stranger would help her save the store, but Regina probably felt sorry for her. From her expression, Lenny guessed Regina knew about loss. She had come into the shop with the critical eye of a marketing executive, but hearing of Pru's death had seemed to strike her at a visceral level, so much so that she had struggled to recover. Usually when she explained Pru was gone, customers breezed through their sympathies and moved on quickly to haggle over a price or ask about the restaurants in town. Regina had seemed to receive the news like she'd just picked up a bowling ball.

And there was Sloane. She laughed out loud, thinking about her covered in mud. She'd almost reached into her pocket for her cell while she struggled out of the bog. A picture of the Wilderness Campaign CEO flat on her butt would've been a great post on Facebook—or possible leverage if she wouldn't back down from her quest to own Pru's store. She was dangerously clever—and interesting.

When she'd picked her up at Kate's Place, gone were the fancy pressed clothes, exchanged for cargo shorts and a white T-shirt. She looked like she belonged in western Colorado.

She couldn't believe that Sloane had made a pass at her! She was certain the overture was motivated by the business deal. She was a lonely widow, vulnerable to a beautiful woman like Sloane, who had amazing lips.

There was the near-kiss, but there was also the moment when she'd reached for her in the bog. She'd seen her eyes. They'd turned crystal blue from her rage. Lenny had nearly gasped, as they were exactly the same shade of blue as Pru's. The highlight of the afternoon, though, was the moment she emerged from the creek. Lenny closed her eyes. She'd never erase the image of Sloane coming toward her. Completely wet was the same as completely naked—well, almost. Her stomach folded like a sandwich.

How odd that both Sloane and Regina had appeared on the same day, one vowing to help her stabilize the business and the other desiring to destroy it.

Rocket jumped off the chaise and bounded to the door, his tail wagging frantically. He looked back at her in anticipation. He wanted his walk. Before she rose, she glanced at the lounger next to her, expecting to see a memory of Pru smiling at her. Her breath caught. For the first time in a year, all she saw was an empty seat.

Is that a good or bad sign?

They wandered back through the house toward the mudroom, but instead of following him into the kitchen, she headed down the hallway into the spare bedroom. In a second he was at her side offering a low whine, wondering why she wasn't following the ritual.

She lifted the pewter frame and stared at the two photos side by side. It was hard to believe the grinning seven-year-old boy holding an Easter egg on the left was the same serious young man on the right, wearing his red graduation robe and mortarboard. Gone was the carefree goofiness of youth replaced by the typical teenage hatred of being photographed. At least he hadn't been scowling.

Pru had given her the framed pictures for her thirty-sixth birthday, which came a month after his high school graduation. At the time they'd struggled to find room on their overcrowded shelves, which were already filled with family photos. After their falling out, she removed every picture except this one.

She gazed into his eyes, and for the thousandth time since he'd left, she imagined what he might be doing right at that moment. She didn't know if he was still in South Carolina or if he'd moved. Maybe he went back to Arizona? Maybe he was in school in Alaska? Was he still an advocate for those in need? What community service groups did he support? She remembered the time he'd opened a lemonade stand on the corner to help a Little League teammate pay for his jersey because his family couldn't afford it. In the end, Lenny and Pru had bought most of the lemonade, but the three dollars and fifty cents he had raised was the most important contribution.

Anything was possible now. She pictured him grocery shopping, carrying his cloth bags, for he was always reminding them to take the reusable grocery bags when they shopped. She could see him buying a bag of pears, his favorite fruit.

She sighed. They'd tried for so long, sending him cards and phoning but he'd never responded. Finally, Pru had told her they needed to move on with their lives. "If Seth wants to be with us," she'd said, "he'll catch up."

Rocket whined again, reminding her that the sun was setting. She returned the frame to the shelf and followed the dancing dog into the mudroom. He stood still long enough for her to clip the leather leash to his collar and they headed to the road. It wound up the hill, passing expensive homes with expansive views. Pru had always been somewhat envious of her wealthy neighbors whose homes were much larger. Lenny periodically reminded her they were lucky to afford a place in the Cathedral Hill subdivision, which had been built on the side of a mountain that faced the San Juans. Almost all of the owners were retired or semi-retired and didn't mind the dusty and bumpy two-mile drive down Route 48C, an unpaved road that led to the highway and into Pinedale. They were weary of city life and didn't want to live in the middle of the action anymore.

Lenny and Rocket spiraled up the asphalt drive until they reached a plateau. To her left was the trailhead and to her right were a cul-de-sac and a heavy metal gate. On the other side was a private road that wended its way through a grove of aspens and ended at Carlotta Ochoa's place, an architect's dream of glass and cedar beams that sprung from the mountain as if it were an appendage. She had been inside only once for a homeowner's association meeting. As the president, Carlotta had invited everyone over at the last minute one night when a pipe burst at their usual meeting place, the town library.

She unclipped Rocket's leash and he bounded up the trail ahead of her. She knew he wouldn't go far, but the freedom of being off the leash was one of his true pleasures. She trudged behind, reminding herself the walk was his greatest joy and kept her in shape. Those were the two reasons she continued the ritual after Pru's death despite the sadness that always pierced her heart when they reached the overlook and stared into the valley separating Cathedral Hills from the San Juans.

He barked and she picked up her pace. He'd rounded a corner and was out of sight. She hoped he hadn't found a skunk. She groaned when she saw Carlotta and her boxer, Bailey, ahead on the trail. Rocket and Bailey were sniffing each other while Carlotta watched, amused.

She glanced at Lenny and flashed a toothy smile. A headband secured her dark black mane behind her ears. She looked ready to grab a nine iron and hit the links in her white Polo shirt and crisp walking shorts. She had been married to the CEO of Dollar Mart, a man thirty years her senior, until his death ten years before. Lenny had heard she was the daughter of his Mexican housekeeper and had grown up in his Houston mansion. When his wife died, she'd swooped in to provide companionship. She was exotic and the subject of much gossip amidst the Pinedale citizens.

When she wasn't running her collectibles shop, her restaurant or her bar, she was a golf junkie who spent at least two afternoons a week at the nearby Hidden Hills Golf Resort. Pru had loved golf too, and they had played together more than a few times. Once Lenny had feigned jealousy, and Pru had become outraged by the joke—too outraged—and Lenny was reminded of Shakespeare's point about ladies protesting too much. She'd never made an issue of it, confident her relationship with Pru was solid, but she was still unsure if Carlotta and Pru had had an affair.

Carlotta was a constant thorn in her side. As a member of the town council, she constantly called about issues or to complain about the monthly agenda. She also frequently spoke about the high unemployment rate at the meetings, and Lenny knew half of the town was in her corner. She was determined to change Pinedale by owning as much of it as possible—including Pru's Curious Curios.

"Hi there," Carlotta said.

"So, did you go up to the ridge?"

"Uh-huh. The sunset was beautiful."

"It was," she agreed. "That's why we're a little later than usual. I wanted to see the whole thing from the balcony."

"I was wondering where you were. You usually beat us."

She nodded. She and Rocket constantly ran into them on the trail, and most of the time she was forced to stop and chat, which she hated. She hated small talk in general. Pru was the one who had always engaged strangers in conversations, whether they were sitting at the movies or waiting in the check-in line at the airport. Once on their way to San Francisco, Pru had learned the couple behind them was also going there, and much to her chagrin, she'd arranged to meet up with them and tour Fisherman's Wharf together. Lenny had to admit the day had been fun and they had kept in touch until Pru's death. Their condolence card suggested she visit them, but she knew she never would.

"My sources tell me an out-of-towner arrived today. I checked her out. Have you met Sloane McHenry yet?" Carlotta asked.

"Uh, yes," she said, turning back. "We spoke today." She neglected to mention that they had taken a hike and physical contact had been involved.

"Then you know what she wants. We need to stick together on this, Lenny. We can't let her get a store in here. A Happy Burger is bad enough, but we can't allow the big chains to invade our town. It'll just be a slippery slope and they'll dominate us. Do you agree?"

"I'm not in favor of any kind of monopoly," she replied.

She was taken aback but only for a moment. "If you're implying that I own too many of the businesses, I think my employees would disagree with you."

She shook her head, regretting the comment. She didn't want to fight. She just wanted to walk her dog. "I just think there's room for everyone."

"Well, of course." She smiled and changed the subject. "Are you going to Dreama's show on Sunday?"

Dreama Patton was a local performance artist whose shows attracted a crowd from as far away as New Mexico. Lenny suspected the high attendance was due to the likelihood something would explode or a fight would break out amongst the patrons who were offended by the presentation. There was also the possibility Dreama would be nude for most of the evening as she had been during her last show, appropriately titled *Epidermis*.

"I wasn't sure. What's this one called?"

"*Harvest*."

"Sounds innocent enough," Lenny said.

"But you never know with Dreama."

"That's true. Maybe we'll be asked to plant vegetables."

"Or maybe," Carlotta said, "we *are* the harvest and she'll want us to strip as a sign of renewal."

They glanced at each other and burst out laughing. "You know, I'm worried you're right."

Carlotta said something in response, but she wasn't sure she'd heard it correctly, caught on the tail of their laughter. She was going to ask her to repeat it, but the smoky look in her eyes befuddled Lenny. Carlotta had shifted the mood to a place that made her uncomfortable.

"Well, we should get going," she said. She headed up the trail and patted her leg for Rocket to follow.

"Enjoy the view."

She felt Carlotta's eyes on her back as they pushed on. Recalling the conversation about Dreama and the audience getting naked, she was almost positive that when she'd said, "I'm worried you're right," Carlotta had replied, "I hope so."

If that was the case, then the woman who was a constant thorn in her side had been the second person that day to make a pass at her.

CHAPTER ELEVEN

The dining room of the Chatsworth Hotel was located on the second floor. As Regina climbed its magnificent grand staircase, she admired the mansard roof, a series of pitched dormer windows that framed the glittering stars against the black backdrop. White balconies wrapped around the second and third stories like ribbons on presents. A guest who stepped outside her room could see most of the hotel's interior and all of the comings and goings in the lobby below. It was intimate and friendly. She climbed to the landing and stood in front of the grandfather clock, where she imagined more than a few brides had been photographed. *This is a great spot for a wedding.*

She followed the murmur of voices to the dining room. Soft lighting brushed against the polished rosewood and rich maroon wallpaper. Couples sat inches apart, exchanging kisses and whispers, cloaked in the secrecy of the romantic atmosphere. Suddenly she felt a pang of loneliness for Seth, but she was ready to have it out with Sloane.

After she'd left Pru's shop, she'd gone back to the inn and burned a few hours on her Wi-Fi connection to do her own research. She'd combed through public records and used various search engines to create a biography of Lenny and Pru. They owned Pru's Curious Curios and the property upon which the shop sat. The coffeehouse-bookstore and an ice cream store were owned by a woman named Sue, who rented the space. Also, they owned a home outside of Pinedale with several acres of surrounding forest. Google had provided her some lovely photos of the tan and avocado clapboard home that sat on the side of a peak. She knew they'd paid nearly a million dollars for the land and the three-thousand-square-foot home, which was full of angles, its backside completely glass.

There were very few hits on the Internet for Pru's Curious Curios, and no website existed, which disturbed her. She'd sifted through several reviews, all of which were positive, but they seemed to have done very little to publicize their store.

From the local paper, *The Watch*, she'd learned Lenny was the town mayor and was very involved in the community, helping to build the neighborhood animal shelter, marching in the Fourth of July parade and serving as chairwoman of the Pinedale Democrats.

She found Sloane at a table in a corner of the room, away from the rest of the patrons. She dropped into a chair and didn't bother to pick up the menu in front of her.

"Why didn't you tell me Pru was dead?" she asked.

Sloane looked up hesitantly from her menu. "I didn't think you would agree to come."

"I didn't *agree* to come. I haven't agreed with any of this, but you're right. If you'd told me the whole story, if you'd explained that your plan was to snatch away Pru's legacy from Lenny—"

"Hey—" Sloane protested, but she would hear none of it.

"Don't make excuses, and don't tell me this is just business."

"But it is."

She couldn't believe what she was hearing. She knew Sloane was ambitious and at times could be ruthless, but she'd taught her there was a time to exercise compassion and a failure to do so often came with a heavy PR price.

"No, this is my potential *family*." When Sloane showed no emotion, she added, "And it's not like I've got an extensive number of people who fall into that category."

She knew she'd hit a nerve when Sloane slumped in her seat. "That was a low blow."

"Not if it's true." She refused to back down. In the same situation, Sloane wouldn't. "You know I appreciate everything you and Aunt Mimi have done for me, but my future is with Seth. He needs his mother, and now that Pru is gone, she needs *him*."

"Are you sure of that?" she asked, waving off an approaching waiter.

"Yes, I'm completely sure of it. She may not know it, or she may be wishing he'd call her and reach out. I'm going to find out where she stands and then I'm going to reunite them."

They stared at each other intently. She knew Sloane was judging her sincerity and commitment. She was resolute and nothing would change her mind.

Sloane looked away and shook her head. When she met her gaze again, it was as her second aunt and not her boss. "Honey, I understand your passion, but it may not be what's best. When you get older, you realize some things should be left alone and other things must come to pass only in time. They can't be forced."

"Does that apply to business?"

"It does," she admitted.

"So what if I told you there was someone else interested in Pru's store?"

Her head shot up from the menu. "What?"

"I guess your research didn't uncover Carlotta Ochoa, the widow of the Dollar Mart CEO? Apparently she owns half the town, and according to Lenny, she'd love to buy Pru's property."

Sloane grabbed her cell phone from her bag, and Regina knew she was calling the R and D team. From the look on her face, they would be lucky to keep their jobs. Sloane left a short, terse voice mail that was nearly unintelligible and dropped the phone back in her bag.

Sensing a lull in their argument, the attentive waiter swooped in and persuaded them to order the fish special and flew away just as quickly to get them each a rum and Coke.

Sloane drummed the table, and Regina knew she was adjusting her strategy. She *hated* surprises. Competition added layers of complexity, making the deal more time consuming. They would stay in Colorado longer, and it would be more expensive—and it wasn't a sure thing as she'd thought. Regina made a note to call the travel agent and to cancel her Friday meetings.

Sloane's hand froze in mid-drum. "How did you find out about Carlotta?"

"Lenny told me today when I stopped by the store."

"Why would she tell you that? How would that information come up in casual conversation?"

"We were just talking about the store, and I mentioned I was in marketing."

She raised an eyebrow and crossed her arms. "And?"

Her willpower slowly deflated. She could never stand up to Sloane for very long. "And I offered to help her make improvements," she said quietly.

"You what?" She leaned over the table and Regina thought she might strangle her. "You offered to *help her*? This is unbelievable!"

A few nearby diners glanced in their direction, and she shot them a withering look. She leaned back in her chair and closed her eyes. "I really need a cigarette."

Regina cringed inwardly. Sloane rarely smoked. She'd given it up twenty years ago except for those high-stress days that occurred once or twice a month. Regina would find her down by the building's delivery door with the head of maintenance, a butch dyke who had a thing for her. *Why is it that every lesbian falls for her?*

Their dinner arrived and they set aside work conversation after Sloane compared her salmon dinner to one she'd had years ago in Toronto. Soon they were talking like aunt and niece, caught in a rambling conversation where topics changed after only a few sentences and laughter served as the punctuation. Tears streamed down her face as Sloane recounted her fall off the log and the look on Lenny's face when she emerged from the creek.

"I must have looked wet and wild," she mused. "Lenny seemed to be enjoying the view immensely."

"Oh, really?" Regina teased. "Did *you* enjoy it?"

"Hardly," she scoffed. "That woman is nothing but a large child." She leaned over the table and whispered, "After what I endured today, I am more determined than ever."

"Well, what if I manage to re-engineer Pru's Curious Curios? Lenny won't want to sell to you."

A sly smile crossed her face. "We'll see who the better businesswoman is." She raised her highball glass. "Here's to friendly competition."

They left the hotel separately and met up on a residential side street. Both were slightly tipsy from the three rum and Cokes they'd each consumed and walking was a bit of a challenge. Sloane's phone rang from the bowels of her purse, and the entire contents spilled to the ground in her quest to answer the call.

Regina scooped everything back into the bag while Sloane spoke to Reece from R and D. She grunted a few times and hung up. "We need to make a stop before we go back to the lodge," she announced.

"Where?"

Her question was more of a whine. All she wanted was to sink into the pristine bathtub at the lodge and wait for Seth to call. She didn't know the exact statistics on this issue, but she knew there had to be a correlation between soaking in a bathtub and stress reduction.

"We're going to a bar," Sloane replied, pointing east.

"At least it can't be far," she mumbled as they toddled down the street.

Charlie's was one block over on High Street. Country music seeped onto the sidewalk, and people mingled outside, smoking. They parted the ancient saloon doors and entered the 1850s. Regina marveled at the massive oak bar that stretched the entire length of the room. Rows of liquor lined the art deco back bar, three Doric columns dividing it into sections, each one ornately lit like a small stage for the array of colorful bottles. It was the most reverent display of alcohol she had ever seen. She glanced at the metal ceiling, a hypnotic swirling pattern. She couldn't imagine how the craftspeople had created it.

A line of pub tables and stools hugged the opposite wall, leaving a sliver of a walkway between. She dropped onto the first open stool and Sloane ambled through the crowd toward a vacant spot a few stools away.

Regina pulled out her phone and texted, *Why are we here?*

Sloane only glanced at her phone, too busy scanning the room, surveying the situation and looking for leverage. Laughter exploded from one of the tables, and her gaze settled on an attractive woman whose dark hair was pulled back with a clip. She wore a gauze blouse cinched over her flowing black skirt by a large leather belt. She was talking and joking with a straight couple seated at a nearby pub table. The man pointed to her red cowboy boots and she held one up for his inspection.

That's her, Sloane texted back.

Who?

Carlotta Ochoa. Owns this place, widow of Dollar Mart CEO. Woman who wants to buy Pru's place.

You mean ONE of the women who want to buy Pru's place.

Sloane scowled at the reply and returned to her surveillance. Carlotta looked very much the owner, making a point of checking on every table and group of customers. All seemed pleased to meet her, and she dipped into conversations effortlessly. Her voice was unique, and it carried over the hum of the crowd and the noise of the bar. She heard Carlotta say the word birthday in regard to one of the customers, and soon there were cheers from those nearby and a round of drinks appeared in front of the birthday patron.

They each ordered a beer and people-watched. A pool table and a jukebox sat in the back by the bathrooms, and a few couples were slow dancing in a tight circle to an old Patsy Cline tune. By the time they were halfway through their beers, Carlotta had mingled her way over to Sloane. Regina strained to hear the conversation over the jukebox.

"Well, hello, stranger. Are you having a good time here at Charlie's?"

Regina rolled her eyes and gulped her beer. It happened every time they traveled together for business or pleasure. Any lesbian or bisexual, in Carlotta's case, within a ten-mile radius found Sloane and usually slept with her. Regina *always* went back to the hotel alone. It seemed tonight would be no exception.

"This is a fabulous place," Sloane said. She caressed the marble bar top and added, "The craftsmanship is outstanding."

"It's all handmade," Carlotta said, pointing to the crown molding on the back bar. She seemed oblivious to Sloane's subtext and shared all of the beautiful features and history in such a way that suggested she was frequently asked the same questions.

Sloane listened attentively and asked several other questions while Regina scrolled through her messages and sent a text to Seth. She missed him horribly and hated that she wouldn't be home by Friday. She couldn't believe he was so far away and she was so close to his mother.

After five minutes of conversation, when Carlotta didn't stroll away to greet another set of customers, Regina knew Sloane had hooked her.

"I'd love a private tour," Sloane said. "Could that be arranged?"

"Perhaps. When are you available?"

"I'm here for another few days or I could wait until after closing."

"That's three hours from now."

"I'm fine," Sloane said. "I'll get some work done. I'll be here." She tapped her phone's screen and turned away. Carlotta seemed surprised and hesitated to step away.

What are you doing? Regina texted. *Why are you attempting to seduce her?*

She turned and offered Regina a look of triumph before she began texting furiously. *Because we're going to win. You help Lenny and I'll get close to Carlotta. We'll control the situation from both ends and stay one step ahead of everyone.*

Don't you think Carlotta is wise to your game? What if she's just playing you? She's got to know who you are by now.

Probably, but it'll be fun. Pillow talk is powerful, but it's what you do with the information that counts.

Regina sighed and prepared to pay her tab and leave. *You're certainly sure of yourself...*

Sloane drained her drink and cast a long look at Carlotta, who was leaning over the pool table, showing off her fine derriere. When she finally met Regina's stare, she wore a wicked grin. She mouthed, "Yes, I am."

CHAPTER TWELVE

Rocket always knew when Lenny was really depressed because mornings started much later. Sometimes when Pru was alive they got up a *lot* later, and Rocket couldn't understand the strange sounds that came from the bed. If they were awake, why weren't they getting up and feeding him? He'd known better, though, than to stand up and bark from his little bed by the window. The one time he'd interrupted them, he'd been shooed out to the hallway and forced to wait next to the closed door until the sounds stopped.

Now that Pru was gone, Lenny didn't sleep in as much, and when she climbed out of bed and mumbled his name, he followed her to the kitchen and waited by the food bowl. She crossed the tile, first left, then right and then left again. Cabinet doors opened and closed until the coffeemaker started gurgling. After the refrigerator blew a cold breath on his face, he knew it was his turn. His tail wagged and drool dripped from his jowls. Breakfast time had arrived!

He savored each bite until his reflection stared back at him from the empty bowl. It was over and time to go outside. He waited by the door until Lenny noticed him and let him out, following behind carrying her coffee and iPad. He darted across the yard, sniffing every inch and reclaiming his territory anywhere a raccoon or other animal had visited the night before.

He loved spending time in his yard while the scents were still fresh, each one unique and challenging his nose. Humans had no idea what they were missing! Their noses were so stupid— and so far from the ground. Maybe that was the problem. If they could enjoy the morning outdoors the way he did, they'd never go back inside.

Too soon it was time to get into the Jeep and head to Kate's Place. He waited for Lenny until she reappeared with her cup of coffee and headed to the shop. Sometimes when she'd had a bad night there wasn't a drive, but that was okay. She still let him run over to the park and sniff around before the shop opened.

There weren't many people in the park yet. He circled the perimeter and glanced toward the bench where his friend John would be, but he wasn't there—at least not on the bench. He lay on the ground, clutching his burrito. Something *smelled* wrong. Underneath the sweet odors of sausage, onion and egg was a sick stench. He automatically backed away and ran toward the shop to get Lenny. He darted past Pugzie, ignoring the deep hisses from the cat, and through the connecting doorway into Pru's shop.

He found her in the office in front of the safe pulling out the cash box. She peered over the swinging door when he started to whine.

"What's the matter, boy? I know you got fed and you went to the park." She stood up and set the cash drawer on the desk. "I'm not up for a drive today, Rocket."

Of course he knew that. He went back into the store, barked and turned in circles. She needed to go with him. John was in trouble.

She emerged from the office. "Rocket? What's wrong with you?"

He went to the front door and barked again. She stared at him, but she didn't follow. He paced the floor. How could he tell Lenny? He could hear Pugzie hissing in the store next door—and he got an idea.

"Rocket, I've got to open the store. C'mon, boy. Quit screwing around."

There was no more time. He ran into the coffee shop and jumped on Pugzie's throne. He'd never been this close to her. She smelled like fish. She flashed her talons and he nipped her paw. She yelped in horror and was on him in a second. He heard Sue screaming for Lenny. Now was his chance!

He flew out the dog door, knocking Pugzie off his back. She chased him, screeching and meowing across the street. He could hear Lenny and Sue yelling at them, following behind. No doubt they were both shocked to see Pugzie off her throne. He wasn't sure she'd ever been outside.

He ran through the park to John, circling around the bench, Pugzie right behind. She didn't care or couldn't smell the badness coming from John. She launched herself at Rocket, who pivoted left. When she landed, she somersaulted twice and landed in a puddle made by the morning sprinklers. Now she was *wet*. She crawled out of the puddle and began cleaning herself, the chase forgotten.

"Oh my God!" Lenny exclaimed, seeing John on the ground.

The women dropped to their knees, and Sue felt for a pulse. "He's still alive."

Lenny tapped on her phone to get help. Whoever she was talking to asked several questions and told them to lift John's head from the ground. Several minutes later, Rocket's ears perked up at the wail of the fire engine coming around the corner.

Soon Lenny and Sue were next to him, watching the two firefighters at work. The clean smell from their silvery instruments and plastic suitcases covered John's sick stench, and Rocket felt better. Maybe he would be okay.

They took him away on a moving bed and one of the firefighters came to talk to Lenny and Sue. "Did you ladies find him?"

"No," Lenny said. "I think my dog found him and came and got us."

The firefighter looked at him and nodded. His tail wagged in return. "Well, I can't know for sure, but I think John had a heart attack. If he'd been left out here much longer, he would've died. Mayor Barclay, your dog is a hero."

All three humans smiled at him and he wagged harder. He'd done something good.

"Give me a smile, Rocket!" A man holding a camera snapped several pictures. "This is going in the paper," he said to Lenny. "What a great story!"

The fire engine drove out of the park and a crowd of people who'd gathered on the sidewalk started to clap. He realized the only smell left was that of the breakfast burrito lying on the ground. He sniffed it and looked up at Lenny.

"Go on," she said. "You've earned it."

Product

Consumers must find value in what is offered. It must improve quality of life or provide a new avenue of possibilities.

CHAPTER THIRTEEN

Sloane flung off the covers and padded toward the coffeemaker. She had to hand it to Regina. The woman excelled at researching and did a great job finding charming accommodations when they traveled. It was Regina who had introduced her to Riya and the Carnation B&B.

She hadn't expected to spend the night at the lodge, believing that after Carlotta closed Charlie's they would engage in verbal foreplay during the ridiculous tour of the tiny bar, which would lead to an invitation to her house—and her bed. While she had learned many interesting facts about Pinedale during the tour, they'd had sex on Carlotta's desk and she had been shown the door after that.

The tour had concluded in an impressive wine cellar underneath Charlie's. The old brick room naturally cooled itself and was solidly constructed. After patiently listening to the history of the cellar, which in a past life had been a hiding place for outlaws, and growing cold from the underground location, she made her move, pulling Carlotta against her as the story concluded. They had stayed locked in the embrace for some time, the heat of passion warding off the chill. She'd pressed her against a wall to make her intentions known, but Carlotta suddenly broke the kiss.

"Not here. It's too cold."

They'd fled back upstairs to the comforts of her office. Once the door was locked, she had instantly stripped and leaned against her desk, spreading her legs wide enough to whet Sloane's appetite.

Her gaze had settled on Carlotta's plump breasts, which were far too perky for a woman her age. Yet, her plastic surgeon was a master because she saw not a trace of a nip or a tuck. She undressed and slid between her legs, burrowing her face between her breasts. She tenderly sucked on each nipple while Carlotta moaned in pleasure.

"Take me," she'd whispered, wrapping her legs around Sloane's waist.

Sloane lowered her on the desk and slid her tongue southward until it settled on her glistening clit. As her pleasure intensified, she gyrated her hips, sending file folders and office supplies crashing to the floor.

Sloane paid no attention to the chaos around her. Carlotta held her head firmly against her center. She was wonderfully trapped, enjoying the smells and tastes of a new woman. Carlotta came with a guttural cry and attempted to push her away, but she would have none of it. Only after she'd coaxed two more orgasms from her did she raise her head and stare at her spent body.

"Well, fuck *me*," she murmured.

"I think I did," Sloane replied. She retrieved a pack of cigarettes from her jacket and lit one for each of them.

Carlotta took a long drag and held up the burning ember. "I haven't had one of these in fifteen years. Gave 'em up for Harry. He hated smoking."

"And you still wanted to marry him?"

She sat up and shrugged. "I wanted a *life*. He was there."

"So he wasn't your true love?"

She flashed a cynical grin. "No such thing, right?"

"Right," Sloane agreed. "Did he know you liked women?"

She shook her head and said, "I'm not a lesbian. I'm not anything, I guess. I'm about opportunities."

She took Sloane's cigarette from her hand and stubbed it out on the corner of the desk. Once again she wrapped her legs around Sloane's thighs so she couldn't move. She tucked her hair behind her ear. There was nothing hurried in her efforts. She seemed to have all night as she inhaled on her cig and dragged her index finger from Sloane's collarbone to her breast. She circled her areole, and Sloane quivered. She was wet and hot, but Carlotta did nothing to satisfy her. She just smoked and touched her—endlessly.

When Sloane reached for her, she pulled away. "No, not yet. Leave your hands by your sides."

She stroked her abdomen and Sloane closed her eyes. Her entire body was ready to be taken. Her nipples ached, and she knew that despite her best efforts and experience, when Carlotta touched her, she would come. She was certain of it.

Carlotta stubbed out her own cigarette and hopped off the desk, pushing her back against the closed door. She dropped to her knees and massaged Sloane's thighs.

In a breathy voice she said, "I know who you are, and I know why you're here."

It wasn't the comment she expected, and she was helpless to craft a lie. Everything she was feeling was rolled up into an impending orgasm. She sat on the edge of ecstasy and could only whisper, "Who do you think I am?"

"The competition," she purred, her lips dangerously close to Sloane's center. "We want the same thing I believe, yes?"

"I doubt that," she managed to say, but the comment lacked conviction. She was defenseless, naked and sexed up.

"Oh, yes, we do," she whispered into her center. "Admit it and I'll eat you up."

Her gaze slid up Sloane's body, pulling her lips away from the core of her need.

"Yes," she hissed. "Now fuck me."

She'd come twice and then it was over. Carlotta redressed in a flash.

"Sorry I don't have time to bathe in the afterglow," Carlotta said sarcastically as she lit another cigarette. "But you don't look like a cuddler."

"I'm not."

While she'd dressed, she'd felt Carlotta's eyes all over her.

"Maybe we can do this again sometime. I believe adversaries can be lovers. It makes the sex hotter."

She nodded, her clit still throbbing as Carlotta led her to the front door without another word and locked it behind her.

Staring in the mirror, she wondered if she was losing her touch. The sex had been satisfactory but not exceptional. They'd gone through the motions, fed each other's libidos, and she'd been dismissed, something that had never happened. She was usually the one who ended the liaison, whether it was an hour after the sex or the next morning. *But those women aren't powerful CEOs. Carlotta's a different breed. She's like me.* She hung her head. For some reason the comparison stung. *Why is that bothering me?*

She dressed and headed down Harrison Road, noticing a crowd and a fire truck near the park. Her pace quickened when she spotted Lenny in the center of the commotion, speaking with a police officer near the ambulance. She was pointing and shaking her head, as if she couldn't believe what had occurred. Two paramedics guided a stretcher toward the ambulance, its passenger a man with an enormous gut.

Poor slob. He needs to get some exercise. He *would certainly benefit from a visit to Wilderness Campaign.*

She leaned against a tree and surveyed the interactions of the townspeople. It was as if they'd formed a queue and each one wanted to hug Lenny and pet Rocket behind the ears. The little dog was in his glory, sitting at attention and wagging his tail for each member of the receiving line.

She smiled, remembering the only pet she'd ever owned—a purebred Yorkie named Cookie. Her father had given it to her for Christmas, along with a stern lecture about his expectations of Cookie's care. Only eight, she quickly forgot the six-point list he'd taped to her bedroom door. She came home from school one day and he was gone. When her father came through the front door that evening, she was waiting for him, tears in her eyes. He explained she'd broken the agreement, so he'd given the dog to the neighbors. Perhaps seeing Cookie periodically would remind her of responsibility.

And it had taught her something, just not what her father expected. She spent the rest of her childhood peering out her second-story bedroom window any time she heard Cookie's bark. She'd gaze into the neighbors' backyard, watching them play with *her* dog. When her father once again offered a pet for a birthday gift, she'd refused, for she'd learned that love was something that could be manipulated, and she would never give him the chance to control her again.

The crowd dispersed and Lenny and Rocket made their way across the street again. She followed, eager to see the inside of Pru's store. She climbed the wraparound porch steps, loving the ample space for customers to sit outside. She'd used the same concept at many of her stores. The porch allowed customers to form an orderly line that originated at the gun counter, snaked through the store and headed out the door. It happened every time a Democrat got elected or gun control legislation was considered. All the gun enthusiasts thought it was the end of the Second Amendment and flooded the stores. The NRA was great for her profit margin.

She decided to visit all three shops, ending with Pru's Curious Curios. She didn't want Lenny to see her until she'd had a chance to survey the other two businesses. She headed into Two Scoops Ice Cream Confectioners, which occupied only a few hundred square feet. A doorway connected the ice cream store to the coffee shop, and she remembered the same woman owned both businesses. A picture window afforded her a view of the interior of the coffee house and of a large Persian cat perched on a futon busily cleaning flecks of mud from her coat. A sign pinned to the wall above her said her name was Pugzie and she did *not* like to be touched. Her equally disagreeable expression conveyed the sign's truth. She stared through the window at Pugzie and Pugzie stared back.

A tall, thin woman ventured from the back room and smiled. What Sloane noticed was her green-spotted hair bow. It reminded her of Minnie Mouse. She wasn't young and looked utterly ridiculous, as did the bobbed haircut encircled by the bow. She was thirty-eight going on nine.

"Hi, there! Did you see what happened in the park?"

Her face was full of concern and worry. She obviously needed to rehash the morning's events with someone.

"No, I missed most of it. What happened?"

"John's the owner of the True Grit Bar and Grille, a really great guy. He just doesn't know how to stay away from the deep fried food, you know? Firemen think he had a heart attack. Well, maybe not a heart attack. It might have just been palpitations, but it looked like a heart attack to me, but I'm no doctor. Rocket, that's Lenny's dog, probably saved his life. He came running in and Pugzie chased him. I guess she's sort of a hero too."

She refrained from rolling her eyes and waited for a break in the woman's eternal run-on sentence.

"What kind of ice cream do you have?" she asked when she paused.

"All kinds," she said automatically, shifting into customer service mode. "Would you like a sample?"

When she glanced into the freezers, expecting the usual vanilla, chocolate, and strawberry, she was surprised to see Colorado Melt and Fenway Fudge Ripple.

"Are these your own creations?"

"Yup. All of them are family recipes, *secret* family recipes, I should add. Those Ben and Jerry guys came around a few years ago, but Pugzie sniffed 'em out."

She glanced through the window at the cat, whose gaze remained locked on her. "How would your cat recognize someone from Ben and Jerry's?"

"Pugzie knows ice cream. She can smell it. First time during the work hours she'd ever jumped out of her chair and come into the ice cream store. I knew something was off."

"I see." She scanned the other flavors, noting Boston Baked Bean Bedazzle, Cranberry 'n Raisin, and Dionysus Delite, a lemon-looking Greek yogurt. She pointed at Paul McCartney Pistachio. "I'd like to try that."

"Excellent choice," she said, as if Sloane had just ordered a fine bottle of wine.

Instead of handing her a tiny plastic tasting spoon, she filled what looked like a large thimble with the green ice cream and handed it to her with a small silver paddle.

She gets points for creativity and presentation. This woman knows how to sell.

The ice cream was decadently good. She realized three other sets of customers had joined her in the cute shop, which was decorated in eclectic chic. No two pieces of furniture were from the same era. A child had already claimed the chair shaped like a giant hand, circa 1970, and the pair of Victorian wingback chairs looked comfortable. She slid onto one and watched the woman serve the other customers, wondering how much business Pru's Curious Curios garnered from the ice cream shop.

This place is gold, a model of the Seven Ps in action—the complete package. Of course, if this were ever part of a Wilderness Campaign I'd have to change the name of the ice creams to fit the theme of the store. Something like River Rafting Rocky Road or Trail Mix Mash. Definitely no cat.

More and more people trickled in and out of the store. Most of them were tourists who knew where to stop, and she remembered her R and D department had commented on the popularity of the ice cream store.

She finished her sample and crossed into the coffee shop, feeling Pugzie's sharp gaze upon her as she passed. The coffee shop doubled as a bookstore and was roughly twice as large as Two Scoops. She paid for a latte and strolled through the adjoining sitting room where customers sat perusing books from the shelves that filled most of the central space. Couches and French café tables accommodated couples or larger groups. She pictured the space filled with the customary Wilderness Café wooden benches and dinette sets. It would be cramped but not impossible.

She wandered back outside and crossed the parking lot, noting the forty-two slots that bordered Harrison Road. It wasn't enough parking but it was a start. She gazed toward the small house that sat behind the building. It was a shack, and she imagined for the right price, whoever owned it would gladly vacate and a suitable back parking lot could be built.

She climbed the front steps again and went into Pru's. An obnoxious bell tinkled above her and only ceased when the door closed again. She inched up and down the crowded aisles, shaking her head.

This isn't a store. It's a hoarder's house. How in the hell did Pru ever make a business out of this? She was too smart. This must be Lenny's doing.

Lenny was at the back of the store talking with a man who was holding a chipmunk in a small cage.

"I think I have to draw the line at animals, Bill. They certainly aren't a curious curio."

"C'mon, Lenny. Wynonna needs a good home. I'm leaving tomorrow, and I can't take her with me. Please?"

She shook her head but held out her hand. "I can't believe I'm doing this. I'm only keeping her for a day, Bill. If nobody takes her, I'm letting her go. So, you should probably check back tonight."

He grinned. "Thanks, Lenny. You're the best," he called as he hurried out, free of his problem.

She doubted he would be back to claim Wynonna. She was Lenny's problem now.

Lenny noticed Sloane and shrugged. "What could I do?"

"You could've said no. Don't you need some kind of a permit to sell animals?"

"Oh, I'm not selling her," she said quickly. "She's up for adoption. Bill got so friendly with her that she just started living in his cabin. He named her Wynonna because he loves Wynonna Judd. He's moving to Denver to take care of his dad."

"Well, as noble as that is, Wynonna shouldn't be your problem."

Lenny cocked her head. "Why not?"

"Because she doesn't belong to you. You have your own concerns."

"You mean all the people attempting to take away my business?"

She sighed. The conversation was ridiculous, and Lenny would never see her as anything but an adversary, which she supposed was the truth. She looked around at the piles of junk. There were probably four more chipmunks living in the merchandise that she didn't even know about. "Where did you get all of this stuff?"

"People bring it in. Some of it Pru found. She used to love to go to garage and estate sales. It was our Saturday morning thing."

Sloane held up a small jewelry case. A sign that read "Make an Offer" was taped to the top. Inside were several pieces of cheap costume jewelry that would have been perfect for a cocktail party in 1976 but would never make the twenty-first century scene. A glint of green caught her eye and she dug beneath the cheap stuff.

"So how did you become mayor?"

"I missed a meeting."

She looked up from the emerald broach she was fingering, one that she thought might actually be real. "I don't follow."

"Around here, things tend to happen by default. I was one of the town council members, but I'd been absent from my duties after Pru died. When I finally showed up two months later, they'd appointed me interim mayor."

"What happened to the previous mayor?"

"He'd died the year before."

"The town went an entire *year* without a mayor? Is that legal?"

She headed to the front of the store with Wynonna. "I don't know, but nobody seemed to care. Maddie, the clerk, runs things. The other members kinda bullied me into running for office."

"Don't take this the wrong way, but I'm having trouble picturing you campaigning."

Lenny grinned. "You're right. I made a poster on the laser printer and stuck it up outside the café. That was the extent of my campaign."

They both laughed and she asked, "So what's your vision for this town, Lenny, seriously? There's no economic growth. This place is on the edge. That has to mean something to you."

She considered the statement before she said, "I want to be a good mayor, but I'm not a visionary. I'm not the one to ask." When she looked up she was embarrassed. "I'm not much of a planner."

"I don't understand that at all," Sloane said.

"I'm not surprised. You probably wouldn't have become a CEO if you didn't know what came next."

"Not just next, but what happens four steps *after* next."

She faced her. "So, what's next for Pinedale, Sloane? You're the astute businesswoman. Tell me what you predict."

She may not have been an adept mayor, but Sloane could tell she cared very much about the welfare of the town. *And I love looking into her eyes. I can see into her heart.* She set her hand on top of Lenny's and gave it a squeeze.

"I don't predict good things, Lenny. Your town needs a shot of *something*. If it's not a Wilderness Campaign, it will probably be whatever your friend Carlotta has in store for you."

She sighed, a look of resignation on her face. "How do you know about Carlotta?"

"I know about everyone in this town. It's my business to know. This town needs to plan for its future. Industry is critical to survival. Without it towns die. Most don't have a choice. Their geography works against them and there's no way to create a revitalization plan. Luckily, that's not Pinedale. Your geography works in your favor." She pointed to the highway and said, "As long as that road leads to Telluride, you will be an artery of commerce." Lenny was listening intently, and she leaned over the counter until she was only inches away from her gorgeous eyes. "I want to be a part of that. I want to help."

She sensed Lenny was equally aware of their nearness. She counted to three, and when Lenny didn't shy away, she kissed her softly. She didn't bother to close her eyes, certain that Lenny's would grow to the size of saucers, which they did.

When she pulled back, she saw her mortified expression. "Sorry it was so horrible for you," she said sarcastically.

"No, it was very nice, but just…" She raked a hand through her hair and grabbed Wynonna's cage, moving it from one side of the counter to the other. She plucked a marker from a cup and made a sign that read "Please Adopt Me." Without looking up she added, "I haven't kissed anyone except Pru in more than twenty years."

Keeping the counter between them, Sloane said, "I'm sorry if I overstepped, again. After yesterday, I just wanted to follow up."

Her eyes shot up from the sign. "Please don't do that again," she pleaded. "We both know the only thing you want is a store in this town. I understand why you're here, and, truthfully, I imagine if you're patient enough, you'll get what you want. I'm sure you know all about my business troubles and what I owe in taxes, so eventually, I'll lose the store. You don't need to make a pass at me."

There wasn't a trace of resentment, sorrow or anger in her voice. It was as if she'd already accepted her fate.

Why won't she fight for it? Doesn't she care about Pru's dream? How can she not have one iota of business sense? Where's her rage? Why doesn't she haul off and slug me?

"By the way, I heard about you and Carlotta," Lenny added. This time, the judgment in her tone was clear. "I hope you got what you wanted. I know you want to win."

Sloane wanted to argue with her. She wanted to explain the truth but then realized she didn't know what the truth *was*. She did know, though, that as a businesswoman, she answered to her board and her shareholders. It was all about the profit margin. The facts once again righted her conscience, which had teetered dangerously toward sympathy and pity for Lenny. She gazed into her pale blue eyes and saw vulnerability, which only motivated her more. "Oh, I'll win. I always do," she said icily.

It wasn't until she was safely outside on the marvelous wraparound porch that she grabbed the railing and felt her shoulders sag.

CHAPTER FOURTEEN

By afternoon Lenny was in a foul mood. The morning had been crazy with John's heart attack, and Sloane's visit had ruined her day. Her mind zigzagged between the sensation of her kiss and her final pronouncement that she'd win. The kiss stayed with her and the softness of Sloane's full lips, which were so different from Pru's in every way. Whereas Pru's were thin, Sloane's were thick like Lenny's—and covered in lipstick. She'd forgotten how much she enjoyed the slick reminder that she was kissing a *woman* while their lips were pressed together. She'd loved Pru, but her lips weren't her best feature.

Every time she relived the moment, though, she remembered that Sloane's gorgeous lips also had covered Carlotta's body with kisses yesterday. If Jimmie, the waitress from Kate's Place, was to be believed, that is. Returning from her second job in Ouray in the wee hours of the morning, she'd seen Sloane slipping out of Charlie's long after it was closed. Jimmie claimed she was still adjusting her bra strap and Carlotta was in the doorway looking far too pleased with herself. It was quite a tale from someone who was just driving by, but Jimmie's gossip had an uncanny track record for accuracy.

Regina arrived to assess the damage Lenny had done to Pru's dream, and from Regina's constant frowns, she'd guessed it was significant. She'd counted the people who walked through the front door (eight) as compared to those who drifted through the connecting door between Pru's and the coffee shop (twenty-four). She'd always known Sue's shops were popular, but she hadn't realized how little business Pru's generated on its own. She couldn't believe it had always been this way, certain there had been a time when the front bell had rung incessantly.

She was barely paying attention as Regina made notes on a diagram of the store. While she tried to frame all of her comments in a positive light, there was nothing good to say. Everything needed to be changed, or rather all of the good things Pru had done needed to be reinstituted.

As Regina discussed the importance of grouping like items together, she remembered the stack of books on Pru's nightstand. She'd pored over titles such as *Own Your Own Business*, *Small Business Ownership in a Competitive World* and *The Seven Ps*. Everything Regina mentioned now was something Pru had considered and executed until she'd died.

She hadn't read any of the books, and what she remembered from her three business classes was eclipsed in her despair over losing Pru. It had taken her two months to reopen the store after the funeral, and the following two months were a never-ending cascade of memories. Pru's heart had been in the store, and while she'd intended to keep it running as Pru would have wanted, every decision was agony. She could hear her voice reminding her to refocus the lighting over the merchandise or reorganize the table displays so everything was visible. The only way to get her voice out of her head had been to ignore all of her good business sense.

"Lighting is really critical," Regina said as she moved quickly from the main room to the second room, which featured a beautiful bay window. "In here you have a distinct advantage.

The eastern exposure is perfect during business hours so we want to accentuate the merchandise in its path. This part of the shop would be perfect for all of the jewelry and clothing you feature. Lenny, are you listening?"

Her head jerked up and she nodded. She remembered hanging a sign that said *Vintage Apparel*. Where was it now? She scanned a nearby wall and noticed an oversized door. She slid it to the right and revealed the sign.

Regina grinned. "I guess Pru had the same idea."

"Pru had lots of good ideas," she said. "I don't want you to get the impression she wasn't a good businesswoman. She was. I'm the one who let it fall apart."

Regina put a hand on her shoulder, a look of sympathy on her face. "I'm sure she knew what she was doing, and we can put it all back together if we work as a team."

The sincerity in her voice gave Lenny hope. Maybe it was possible to escape a takeover from Carlotta or Sloane.

"Now, we really need to talk about all of these *things*. Every store should have a focus. This is Pru's Curious Curios, and while I'm curious about why a lot of this stuff is here, I'm not really interested in buying much of it." As if to make her point, she held up a metal exit sign. "Now, I know there are stores who specialize in the resale of commercial items, but is that what you want to do here?"

"That came from The Prospector's Diner," she explained. "It was a restaurant that closed. Artie, the owner, was able to sell a lot of his furniture to a restaurant guy, but he had a bunch of stuff left. I told him I'd help him out."

Regina narrowed her gaze. "I see." She scanned a tabletop covered by cardboard boxes. Each one was filled to the brim with items Lenny had not sorted. Regina cleared the table except for one box. She unpacked it and lined up five items: a doll without a head, a fire truck without a wheel, a book with a broken spine, a half-melted candle and a used toilet seat.

"Do you see anything here that you could sell?"

She scratched her head. "Not really. When Nellie Sharpe asked if she could do consignment, I probably should have checked through her things, but she was pretty desperate. She brought in some stuff that sold immediately so she made her mortgage payment."

Regina cocked her head as if she wanted to ask a question and then changed her mind. She wandered slowly around the cluttered tables, sifting through various boxes and picking over entire shelves, her clipboard abandoned. She popped up and down, searching the items on the floor, the sounds of reorganization floating through the room. Lenny watched, her gaze constantly returning to the array of worthless trinkets from the Sharpes. She'd just wanted to help them.

Regina carried several items back to the table and lined them up next to the Sharpes' junk. Displayed were a swimming medal, a beautiful rhinestone broach, a funky electric clock from the sixties and a leather-bound copy of Shakespeare's works. None of the merchandise looked familiar except the works of Shakespeare. She clearly remembered the day Pru had found it during one of her estate sale jaunts about a month before she died. She'd been giddy when she returned since she'd only paid ten dollars for the beautiful book. Lenny could still see the look on her face as she babbled for twenty minutes about the quality of the leather and its excellent condition.

She recalled that Pru had displayed the book on an ornate wooden stand. It hadn't sold before she died, and a few months later the town mortician bought the stand to display urns at his funeral parlor. She hadn't seen the book since then, and she imagined it had been nudged to a corner as she acquired more stuff.

"I think these are quality items. I'm guessing Pru found these?"

She shrugged. "Probably. I don't remember any of our neighbors bringing in those things."

Regina exhaled and faced her. "Lenny, your store isn't gone."

"It's not?"

"No, it's buried. The quality merchandise is here, but it's being smothered by everything else." She reached into a box and pulled out a shriveled, half-eaten apple by its stem.

"We can probably throw that out," she said.

Regina shook her head. "Do you ever say no? I hope I'm not hurting your feelings," she added quickly.

She sighed. She knew she was right. "No, you're not hurting my feelings. This is all good to know."

Regina reclaimed her clipboard, flipped to a new page and wrote furiously. She was a woman on a mission.

"Why are you helping me? I mean, it's very nice of you, but you don't even know me."

Color rose in Regina's cheeks as if she were embarrassed. She quickly turned away and scribbled some more notes. "I'm a believer in small businesses. In fact, I've thought about opening my own."

She sensed she was being told a secret, for Regina barely whispered the idea. "Well, that's great. What would you sell?"

She hugged the clipboard against her chest, a look of excitement on her face. "I wouldn't really sell anything, but I'd provide a service. I'd like to open a pet-grooming place, maybe even have a self-serve area. I'd also like to start an animal rescue for exotic animals."

"That's really ambitious. I bet the pet-grooming place would take off."

"I think so, too. You'd be amazed what people will spend on their pets. It's one of those industries that's recession-proof."

"You don't have to convince me," she chuckled. "I've known women who feed their dogs better food than they feed themselves."

"Exactly," she replied. "I guess I'm somewhat guilty of it myself. My dogs are like my babies."

Gone was the stiff business demeanor, replaced with a genuine passion. "How many dogs do you own?"

"Five."

Her eyes widened. "Five?"

She threw her head back and laughed. "Everyone has the same reaction. They're all rescues that wandered into my life. I'll show you some pictures." She pulled her phone from her back pocket and tapped on the screen. "This is Tillie, Rico and Zuma and Archie and Rover."

"Rover? You really have a dog named Rover?"

"Yeah, my boyfriend named him."

"I thought I was the only person who had a dog named Rover. Actually, my son named him Rover because he was always jumping the fence and roving through the neighborhood. Does your dog do that?"

"Um, sometimes," she said. She frowned and quickly put her phone away. The moment was gone and the professional business demeanor resurfaced. "I need to go but give me the rest of the day, and I'll come up with a plan of action."

She bolted out the door, leaving Lenny to wonder what she'd said wrong.

CHAPTER FIFTEEN

Regina eased up on the gas when she realized the Jetta was doing seventy. She didn't know the exact statistical probability of a state trooper patrolling the highways between two tourist towns, but she guessed it was high. There were plenty of soft shoulders and tree stands along Highway 550 that could provide great cover for a speed trap.

She chastised herself for not paying attention to her speed. No doubt Steven Wade Pearlman's same lack of attention had made her an orphan.

She couldn't remember much about her parents' death. She'd been too young and in shock. Her strongest vision was their departure that night to visit a sick uncle in a rural part of Montana. She'd been left with the neighbor. It was only for a night, her mother had assured her. She'd watched through the front room window as they'd left in the old Datsun. The rain was pouring outside, but they'd both waved as they got into the little car for what would be their final journey. They hadn't realized that one-fourth of all crashes occurred during inclement weather.

The neighbor had awakened her early the next morning. She'd immediately known something was wrong. Standing in the bedroom doorway had been a state trooper. She couldn't remember what was said, and much of the next few weeks—the funeral, the packing of the house, the move to Boston with Aunt Mimi—became random images lost in her fight to remember her parents waving goodbye on that night.

She swallowed hard and glanced at the mountains for strength. She'd decided to drive to Ouray for the rest of the day as a way to escape Sloane. She didn't want to see her any time soon as she was incredibly angry for many reasons. She hated lying to Lenny. She hated that Carlotta and Sloane were trying to destroy Pru's dream, but most of all, she hated that Sloane was right—a Wilderness Campaign could solve Pinedale's economic problems. Lenny couldn't save the town *and* keep Pru's Curious Curios afloat. At this point, she wasn't doing either very well.

She'd never been to Ouray, population nine hundred and fifty. The town was less than a square mile, but during the winter and summer it bustled with tourists. Nicknamed the Switzerland of America, Ouray sat against the head of a mountain and was buttressed on three sides by sheer rock walls that cupped the ancient buildings and homes.

Seth would absolutely love this place. She'd read about the trails that hovered above the town, providing a bird's-eye view of the entire community.

Her phone rang. *He must be reading my mind.* It was nearly seven in Boston, and she wondered what he had planned for the evening.

"Hi, honey," she said cheerily.

"You sound happy," he joked. "That must be some conference, or you're just happy to be away from me."

"Never," she said. She bit her lip. *I can't even tell him about this place. I hate lying to him, too. Somehow that's Sloane's fault as well.*

"So, how's it going? Are you learning everything you can about the best tent flaps or the newest developments in hiking boots?"

She rolled her eyes. He was teasing her because he knew her one secret: she really didn't like traveling. "Don't make fun, Seth. It isn't that kind of conference."

"Oh, sorry. I get all your little jaunts confused."

That part was true. She traveled extensively for many reasons, and she'd given up explaining the purpose of every trip. In the beginning when they were still developing trust, she'd made sure to review her itinerary with him, including the reason for the trip and the biographies of her companions. She wanted to make sure he knew why she was leaving and with whom she was spending her off-hours with so he wouldn't be jealous.

After three trips she realized he was only feigning interest, and by then she'd learned he didn't have a jealous bone in his body—unlike her.

It had been a struggle to accept all of the women in his life, neighbors, co-workers and friends who wanted his help and enjoyed a platonic relationship with him. Many were married or had boyfriends (and girlfriends), but that hadn't automatically quelled her jealous nature, which sprung from her natural competitiveness.

What *had* extinguished the wrath she experienced every time he left to help a female friend was his promise to walk out. She would trust him or it was over. She accepted his ultimatum since it was the right thing to do, and he'd never given her a reason to doubt him.

"Babe, why does the TripTracker say your phone is in Ouray, Colorado?"

She was so shocked by the question she nearly rear-ended the car ahead of her. "Um, I have no idea. Is that what it says?" She pulled over, her heart beating wildly. She'd completely forgotten he'd bought the app before her first trip and programmed her phone so he could find her.

"Maybe there's some kind of glitch. I didn't even know you still had that app."

"Of course I do," he said lovingly. "I always check it while you're away, but not every minute, just once or twice while you're gone. It helps me feel closer to you."

She couldn't help but smile. *God, I love him, and he loves me.* "I don't understand why it says that, honey. I'm in Colorado, so maybe there's something weird going on with the satellites…or something. I don't know."

"Weird," he concluded, and she could tell he'd already let it go. Unlike her, he wasn't one to hang onto a mystery for very long. He just accepted things for what they were.

"Is there a reason you called me? I mean, I love to chat with you, but I thought you were in the middle of a project."

"Yeah, I need to know if you want the swing on the west side or the east side of the porch. If I put it on the west side, you could have a lovely view of Mrs. Arnold's roses, but if it sits on the east, you can watch the Franklin kids play when they're outside. I *know* how much you adore them."

It was true. She loved those kids. She loved *all* kids and animals. He knew if they stayed together, they would eventually have a brood.

"East side. Did you really need to ask?"

He laughed softly. "Nope. I just wanted to hear your voice again."

"Okay. I love you."

"I love you too."

She stared at her phone after he'd hung up. A knot curled up in her stomach when she thought of being caught in this tremendous lie. *He's going to be furious when he finds out I've met his mother. He might actually break up with me. And would I blame him?* She wiped some tears away and for a moment contemplated an escape from Colorado. She could be back on a plane by nightfall. Sloane would understand and she might actually prefer her exodus from this project.

But she couldn't. She thought of him sitting on the porch steps in the middle of the night, and she remembered the shoebox of mementos.

He needed Lenny and she needed him. During both of the encounters with Lenny she'd seen glimpses of him in Lenny's easygoing nature, her soft laugh and helpful demeanor. Mother and son were so much alike.

"I can make it happen," she decided.

She got out of the car, yearning to stretch her legs. A vacant store sat in front of her parking space. It was appealing, with a large picture window and a glass door ensconced in ornate molding. She peered inside. The types of abandoned fixtures and cabinets suggested it had been some sort of café or restaurant, and the thick sheen of dust on the countertops told her it had been this way for a while.

After scouting a few hundred locations for Sloane, she'd become an expert at assessing the remains of bankrupted businesses. It always made her sad to think that half of all small businesses failed in the first five years, destroying someone's hopes and dreams in the process. She sighed, remembering that as a VP for a large chain, she *was* one of the destroyers, a bad guy who could offer products at a lower price.

She walked south down Main Street, marveling at the old buildings that now housed twenty-first century merchandise and services. Each business was unique, and while it was apparent Main Street survived on the tourist industry, interspersed were services and goods needed by the locals, such as a hardware store and post office.

Everyone she passed smiled and acknowledged her, nothing like Boston where people avoided each other on the sidewalk. She loved her little house because of the neighbors, who helped and supported each other. It was a true community tucked away in a teeming city, a smaller version of Ouray.

She stopped along the school fence and watched the children at recess. A group of boys had organized a kickball game on the diamond, while a group of girls played four square on a cement court. The enormous stone cliffs surrounded them like protective parents. She closed her eyes and listened to the cries of glee and laughter. *What would it be like to raise a child here?*

She found herself standing in front of the Beaumont Hotel, a historic landmark. She knew if she continued east on Fifth Street she'd pass the Carnation Bed and Breakfast, which was owned by Riya, Sloane's most consistent lover. All the other women came and went except for Riya. She'd once asked Sloane to explain their relationship, but she'd sputtered an unintelligible answer, and Regina realized she couldn't explain it herself.

Along the way she noticed posters in the windows and tacked to electric poles announcing a jazz festival on Friday night to be held in the park. She loved jazz music, and since Sloane was an amateur musician, she imagined she would want to come as well. The idea of hearing it outdoors in such a beautiful location was tremendously enticing. She knew they would still be in Pinedale by the end of the week since it seemed Sloane's charm wasn't working on Lenny.

She found the hardware store and reviewed her list, all the while feeling caught in the middle between them. She desperately wanted Lenny to forge a relationship with Seth, *needed* that to happen, but her loyalty was to Sloane, a woman who had essentially saved her life after her parents died.

While Aunt Mimi had done the best she could, she was only twenty-five, and she had no idea what to do with an inconsolable twelve-year-old. It had been Sloane, Aunt Mimi's best friend, who'd ensured she went to a good school and not the failing neighborhood school down the street. It was Sloane who'd helped her make a plan for college and spent many weekends chauffeuring her to activities or taking her and Aunt Mimi camping. She had always been there for her.

Why does it seem like we're on opposite sides now?

"Miss, are you all right?"

She blinked away tears and nodded at the hardware store clerk who'd come outside to rearrange a display.

"I'm fine, thank you. I just got something in my eye."

She studied her list once more and went inside the store. She'd do what she could to help Lenny even if it was fruitless. She knew Sloane was a force, and if Carlotta was anything like Sloane, then Pru's Curious Curios was doomed.

CHAPTER SIXTEEN

Lenny's least favorite days of the month were the first and third Wednesdays when she had to preside over the bi-weekly town meetings. The only consolation was that most of them ended in less than an hour because the only people who bothered to show up were the five council members, three unfortunate spouses, Lenny and Maddie, the town clerk.

As was her tradition, she spent Wednesday afternoon with Maddie, reviewing the various matters on the agenda that Maddie had created. Even though Lenny was the mouthpiece of Pinedale, everyone knew Maddie was really keeping Pinedale afloat. She was just too shy to be mayor.

As she, Maddie and Rocket entered the Pinedale Library, which served as the town hall, she was surprised to see a few dozen Pinedale residents setting up additional chairs in the audience. Normally Paul Getts, the Pinedale librarian, placed four chairs facing the long table and the Pinedale City Council. A large audience meant trouble was brewing, and she should have known about it before tonight. Sloane was handing out chairs. She'd changed into a proper charcoal gray suit and red blouse adorned with a bolo tie, chic business Western. She saw her and offered a slow smile. *She looks fabulous.*

She set her stack of papers at the head of the table and directed Rocket to his usual place, which was under the table at her feet. She snaked through the crowd, offering hellos and nods until she reached Sloane.

"I'm surprised you're here," she said cheerily. "These meetings are usually rather boring."

"Here you go," Sloane said to C.J. Dooley, handing him a chair. He tipped his hat at her and nodded at Lenny. Picking up a chair for herself, Sloane said, "I wanted to watch you work, and besides, there could be some fireworks." Lenny's face fell, and she blinked in surprise. "You didn't know?"

"Know what?"

She abandoned the chair and steered her into the children's section behind a tall bookcase. "You really need to turn on your cell phone, Lenny. I've tried to call you three times today."

She shrugged. She hated technology, which she viewed as a leash around her neck. "Why were you trying to reach me?"

"I wanted to talk about our kiss," Sloane teased.

She could feel the heat in her face and she knew she was beet red. "Sloane—"

"I'm kidding. Well, I'm sort of kidding." She stroked Lenny's cheek, and Lenny stepped away.

"Sloane, c'mon…"

She crossed her arms. "Fine. I overheard some talk at Kate's Place this afternoon. Nobody was very specific about the topic, but Carlotta's behind whatever's going on. Her name was mentioned a few times."

She shook her head, perplexed. "There's nothing remotely interesting on the agenda. I can't imagine what she's plotting." She peeked out at the growing crowd. "I should probably get back there."

She touched her arm. "Look, I *do* want to apologize for my behavior yesterday. I shouldn't have kissed you without your permission, and I shouldn't have said what I did about winning. I just got angry. Do you accept my apology?"

"Yes, of course," she said. Staring at her pillow lips and feeling as if she needed to say more, she added, "I, I, well...," but she lost her thought when Sloane dragged her tongue across her lower lip. *Her mouth is absolutely incredible.*

As if she could read her mind, Sloane cupped her chin, preparing for another kiss. They gazed at each other, lost in another world behind the bookcase.

Please, please, yes. Yes!

"I want to kiss you again, Lenny, make no mistake about that, but I won't unless you ask me to."

"What about Carlotta? Are you seeing her?"

Sloane looked embarrassed, a fact that pleased Lenny immensely. *At least she's sorry that it happened.* When she looked up, her blue eyes blazed into Lenny's. "There is nothing between me and Carlotta. It was a moment of weakness, a mistake. I would never want to hurt you or give you the wrong impression."

She stepped away and slid her hands into her pockets. "Now, Madame Mayor, I think it's almost time for your meeting to start. Keep your eye on Carlotta."

She disappeared and Lenny fell against the wall, her knees buckling. Her heart was racing, and she was rather certain she was having a hot flash.

Or, for the first time in a very long time, I'm completely aroused. Why does she affect me like this? I was never this way with Pru. I loved Pru. I don't even like her very much. She's using me to get the store. Maybe I don't care at this point. I just need to feel something.

She took a deep breath and emerged from the children's section looking as mayoral as she could muster. Four of the five members of the council, including Carlotta, were hovering over their assigned chairs behind the long table. Joe Bass, a local welder, chatted with Donny Beck, the owner of God's Rods. Dreama, the performance artist, gestured feverishly with her arms as she talked to Carlotta. Absent was John Snyder, the owner of the True Grit Bar and Grille. He would remain in the hospital for a few more days. She frowned. She missed her friend, who was the voice of reason and a town leader. She could have used an ally against whatever Carlotta had planned.

She took her place at the head of the table and banged the gavel once to call the meeting to order. The council members took their seats while she scanned the audience, realizing that over three dozen people were present, nearly a town record. The last time so many people had showed up was when they had added a stop sign on Harrison. She recognized many of them as supporters of Carlotta who were vehemently opposed to carpetbaggers like Sloane opening businesses in Pinedale. From Lenny's perspective, Carlotta's monopoly on industry was equally if not more damaging to the economy, but she had endeared herself to many in the community with free alcohol, restaurant discounts and some key charity sponsorships.

She noticed Regina in the back, sitting in a chair away from the group. Sloane had settled in the middle of the fourth row between the Herrold and Kowalski families. She winked at Lenny, whose heart started thumping wildly again. She cleared her throat and led them through the customary Pledge of Allegiance and reading of the minutes.

"I'd like to make a motion to move the public comment portion of the meeting to the end," Carlotta stated when she asked them to accept the agenda. Carlotta motioned to the audience and said, "With so many of our citizens present, I think it would be a better use of time to attend to our slated business and ensure enough time is allotted to hear their concerns."

Lenny pressed her lips together to hide a scowl. They had strategically placed public comment time at the beginning of the meeting *to limit* comments and especially follow-up remarks by the council. Everyone wanted to get home at a reasonable hour and there was always a tendency for people, especially Dreama, to drone on with every issue. If Carlotta wanted to rearrange the agenda, something was on it that she had missed.

"I'll second that motion," Donny said.

She called for the vote, and since no one could see a reason not to honor Carlotta's request, public comment was moved to the end.

"I have one other motion," she stated. "I'd like to move the tax grace period approval from the consent agenda and add it to the regular agenda."

Her ears perked up and she glanced at Sloane, who offered a wary look. "May I ask why?"

She looked away. "I believe the reason will become clear later."

"I'll second the motion," Donny said.

She put it to a vote, and when it passed unanimously, she felt a conspiracy coming together. The four of them stole glances at each other, as if they just had gotten away with something.

They proceeded through the agenda quickly. There was no discussion about renewing the contract with the Ouray recycling company or purchasing a new diving board for the town pool, and the entire council was in favor of instituting an annual pancake breakfast to support the volunteer firemen.

"I'm sure Carl and the rest of the crew will be grateful for the extra funds," she noted.

The only remaining item for a vote was the tax grace period that Carlotta had commandeered from the consent agenda.

She tapped her finger on the table, which sounded incredibly loud in the silent library. After a long pause she said, "I'm going to ask that we reverse Maddie's budget update and the tax grace period discussion. It would make more sense to me that we know where we stand financially before we discuss abandoning the grace period." She stared at Carlotta and added, "That is what this is about, isn't it? Otherwise, why would it need to be pulled from the consent agenda?"

"I don't believe the agenda should be reordered, Mayor Barclay," Carlotta replied.

"Your opinion is noted, but don't the rest of you think that before we discuss abandoning a policy we've had in place for many years, we need to know where we stand?" She looked out at the audience, many of whom were nodding, and her gaze found Sloane's approving smirk.

Donny, Dreama and Joe glanced at each other and nodded. Carlotta's audible sigh pleased her greatly.

Maddie's report carried the same theme as the last month's and the one before that. The town was slowly recovering from the economic recession, but unemployment was still too high and small businesses were still struggling. "That's why," she made a point of saying, "the grace period for tax collections is so important. It will allow some of our struggling businesses to stay afloat a little longer. That's the end of my report."

She flipped her notebook shut and folded her hands in front of her. Lenny gazed at Carlotta, who leaned forward and faced Maddie.

"I respect your opinion, Maddie, and I'm all about small businesses, as everyone knows, but in the last ten years haven't *all* of those businesses eventually gone bankrupt?"

She glanced at Lenny. They both knew—and Carlotta knew—that there were currently three businesses on the list, including Pru's Curious Curios.

"Yes, historically the grace period has kept them open for a few months more, but eventually all of them have closed. However, that doesn't mean it will always turn out that way," she added quickly. "We have a responsibility to our citizenry—"

"Thank you for answering my question, Maddie," Carlotta said smugly. She turned to Lenny. "I have nothing further, Mayor, so unless anyone else has anything to add, I think we're ready to vote on the grace period."

She blinked and her gaze was drawn to Sloane, whose expression was surprisingly compassionate. If the grace period were eliminated, her building would be a prime target for takeover. Sloane and Carlotta could fight over it. *I don't get it. She should be grinning with glee.*

"Excuse me! Can I say something before the vote?"

She looked toward the back of the library. Regina was advancing to the front of the room.

"I know I'm out of order and that public comment is after this vote, but I believe I have some vital information that members of the council don't know."

A hum ebbed through the audience, and Carlotta automatically stood. "This woman is out of order," she announced. "She needs to wait until public comment."

The audience grew boisterous, dividing itself between the Carlotta followers and those who now believed she was hiding something from them. Lenny started to speak and found she wouldn't be heard over her noisy neighbors. Rocket started to bark but went silent when she pointed at him. *At least the dog listens to me.*

She glanced at Sloane's empty chair. She searched the crowd and found she'd moved against the wall. She was staring at Regina, her arms crossed. Regina was staring back, and it was clear they were having a nonverbal conversation with raised eyebrows and widened eyes.

They know each other.

She banged her gavel over and over until it was the only noise in the room. "Finally." She looked at Joe, Donny and Dreama. "We've never had a lot of rules at these meetings because we're more concerned about the truth and helping people than we are about procedures. I'm fine with letting Regina speak if you guys are." When Carlotta started to talk, she pointed a finger at her. "I'm not talking to you."

"I'm more than curious," Joe said.

Dreama's eyes narrowed to slits. "I'm sensing there is a story to be told here."

Donny shrugged. He was the most loyal to Carlotta, but he was clearly outnumbered. "Whatever."

"Go ahead, Regina. I think we're all interested in what you have to say." She directed her last comment to Sloane, who seemed visibly upset.

Regina took a breath and composed herself. She scanned the audience, making eye contact with as many townspeople as she could. "You don't know me, but my name is Regina Dewar, and I am the vice president of new accounts for the Wilderness Campaign Corporation. I'm sure many of you are familiar with our stores, and I'm here, with my boss, because we'd like to build a new store here in Pinedale."

The crowd gasped and broke into chatter.

"Who's your boss?" someone asked over the noise.

"I am," Sloane said, moving toward Regina. "My name is Sloane McHenry, and I'm the CEO of Wilderness Campaign."

The crowd roared, many jumping to their feet. Lenny banged the gavel, worried she might have a riot on her hands. Some circled around Sloane and Regina, pointing their fingers and vocalizing their hatred of chain stores. She dropped the gavel in defeat and looked at her council. Joe and Donny were arguing with Carlotta while Dreama had climbed onto the table and assumed the lotus position. Maddie seemed oblivious to the mayhem, scrolling through her Facebook newsfeed.

Paul, the librarian, squeezed through the crowd and leaned over the table. "Should I go get the gun I keep at the circulation desk?"

Her jaw dropped. "You keep a *gun* at the circulation desk? Is it loaded?"

He looked at her incredulously. "Of course it's loaded. People can be downright hostile about their overdue fines. Should I go get it? I could fire a shot into the air."

His excitement about the possibility frightened her more than the angry crowd. She scanned the faces of her neighbors. They were shouting and pointing, but the group huddled around Regina and Sloane were listening as they tried to explain their point. *I bet they'll be here until midnight.*

Carlotta, however, wasn't faring as well with Donny and Joe, who wouldn't listen to anything she said.

"Please let me get my gun," Paul whined.

She shook her head and stood up. "No, Paul, no gun." She gathered her notes and snapped her fingers. "C'mon, Rocket, let's go home."

CHAPTER SEVENTEEN

"You can give them to me or I'll just drive to Montrose and find an old guy who thinks his prescription pad is an extension of his hand," Sloane said.

Dr. Young, the square-jawed resident, remained unflappable and scribbled on the chart. "You can certainly try that, Ms. McHenry, but I doubt you'll be successful. I see absolutely nothing wrong with you except a nasty addiction to painkillers. My recommendation is that when you get home, you find some treatment." He closed the folder and headed for the door. "The good news is that I won't charge you for the visit. Have a nice day."

He disappeared and she slunk against the sink. She needed to bounce back and clear her head. Vicodin and Red Bull was the automatic cure. *What an arrogant asshole! I'm not addicted to anything!*

She'd waited until she was nearly out of vikes before she'd placed a call to Dr. Greenfield's office. The good doc would quickly fax a script to the Ouray pharmacy and she could put her life back on track. What she'd forgotten was his planned vacation to a remote jungle in South America. He was miles from a fax machine.

She could go to Montrose, but she had no idea if she'd find a Colorado version of Dr. Greenfield or another uptight resident whose goal was to dispense as few medications as possible. She thought of Dr. Young's spiky-haired receptionist. *There* was a possibility.

She strolled back to the lobby and struck up a conversation with Dionne, who seemed quite receptive to her flirting. She asked for the restroom and Dionne pointed to a door on the other side of the lobby. She slipped beyond the bathroom and explored the back rooms until she found Dr. Young's private office. She tossed aside several files on his desk in her search for a prescription pad.

"Get out now, or I'm calling the cops."

Dionne leaned against the doorjamb, a hand on her hip. There was nothing Sloane could say, and any attempt at lying would be ridiculous. She held up her hands and walked out, refusing to look back at Dionne. She walked swiftly to the Range Rover and locked herself inside.

I could have gone to jail. That would've made the news. My shareholders would crucify me.

She dropped her head against the steering wheel and closed her eyes. Everything was a mess. After she and Regina had managed to exit the town council meeting around midnight, they'd fought all the way back to the inn. Granted, Regina's announcement was a stroke of genius and stopped the tax grace period vote, but she'd severely tampered with Sloane's master plan.

Sloane had fired her, and Regina had packed her bags and disappeared. She knew she needed to disappear as well until she could talk to Lenny again, so she'd left a few hundreds on the bed to cover the bill and stolen away to Ouray and the security of Riya's bed.

Then Riya had kicked her out. She'd known Sloane was thinking of someone else, and that was true. She couldn't stop thinking of Lenny, her gorgeous eyes, her free spirit and how upset and hurt she must be that they had played her.

Up until the moment the meeting had exploded, she had been so impressed with Lenny's skill as a leader. She stood up to Carlotta, and it had been artful the way she'd strategically rearranged the agenda, ensuring Maddie's report preceded the tax vote that never occurred.

She's clearly not the idiot I thought she was. She's so much more…

She'd tried to call Lenny, but she wouldn't answer. She pictured herself hopping on the log, absolutely jubilant at the idea of taking Pru's dream. *Why did Lenny make that bet? Did she already know she'd win? Maybe I'm not the first person who's fallen off the log.*

She leaned back in the Rover's bucket seat, which really wasn't much different from Seat A in Row Three on her doomed airplane flight. Even though many months had passed, the memories were clear. The plane bumping through the sky. The man across from her barfing in the airbag. Chris holding her hand.

Chris. I should've kept in touch with her.

She drove out of Ouray, up the steep road toward the Million Dollar Highway. She pulled off at a trailhead and grabbed her water bottle. If she couldn't get high in the traditional way, she'd do it literally, climbing up the San Juans. She poured everything out of her mind and filled it with nothing but the smell of the trees, the sound of her boots crunching on the trail and the warmth of the sun against her cheeks. Only when she reached a divide in the trail that looked out over Ouray did she stop and gaze toward Pinedale, home of the next Wilderness Campaign store. She smiled. Despite a few hiccups, her plan was progressing nicely.

CHAPTER EIGHTEEN

Regina and Lenny stared at the mountain of junk. It was four thirty in the afternoon, which meant that for nearly nine hours they had separated viable merchandise from the detritus Lenny had amassed because she couldn't say no to her neighbors. Regina estimated the pile was approximately seven feet high at the center with a fifteen-foot circumference.

"What on earth will I do with this stuff?" Lenny asked. "If we don't get rid of it, I'll get a citation. That's probably not good if the mayor gets cited for neighborhood blight."

She had a point. Their original plan had been to organize the outgoing merchandise by degree of worthlessness. She had collected some items, such as the commercial-grade exit sign, that were in fine shape but not appropriate for Pru's shop. Those could be sold on Craigslist or donated to charity. They also thought some of the slightly broken items could be repaired. How hard could it be to reattach a wheel to a wagon?

But after an hour of trekking through the back door it had become apparent that most of the stuff belonged in the third category: trash. No one would want to re-sew three hundred sequins to the front of an evening gown or find a matching leg to save an over-stuffed ottoman. The third pile quickly overtook the first two, and without articulating a decision, it became understood that if an object went outside, its next stop would be the landfill.

"How far is the dump?"

"About an hour. How many trips do you think this will take if I borrow Donny's pickup?"

"Too many," she replied. "You'll need to call someone with a really big truck."

Lenny plucked a broken picture frame from the pile and studied it. She shook her head and tossed the frame back onto the heap and sighed. "I can't believe I let this happen. None of this stuff is Pru's. I *allowed* all of this to be brought into the store, and because of me, her dream might die."

"That's not going to happen, Lenny. We won't let it."

Although the store was a complete disaster and totally disorganized, Regina was confident every item that remained could and *would* sell once they gave the place a complete makeover. She could already see the new and improved Pru's Curious Curios in her head. It would put the Schoolhouse Emporium to shame.

They headed back inside. She glanced into Lenny's tiny office. That would be the second project, reconfiguring *how* Pru's Curious Curios did business. Persuading Lenny to adopt twenty-first century marketing strategies, such as online shopping, might be a challenge, but she would help her every step of the way. Since Sloane had fired her, her schedule had certainly opened up, and once she told Seth about his mother, she was sure he would want to help as well. *There's just that one little detail about telling him...*

"How about we get an early supper?" Lenny suggested. "I wanted to stop by and see John at the True Grit."

"Sounds great," she said, pleased that Lenny wanted to spend time with her outside of the project. For a fleeting moment, she pictured Lenny helping her pick out her wedding dress.

They walked across Harrison, Rocket at their heels. Her gaze darted left and right, looking for Sloane. She doubted she'd packed up and left, despite the debacle at the town meeting. If anything, she loved a good fight and a worthy adversary like Carlotta Ochoa.

"Do you like Sue's B and B?" Lenny asked.

After abruptly leaving the Pinedale Lodge and a very confused Kirby, she'd called Lenny, who had suggested Sue's. In addition to running the ice cream store and owning the coffee house, Sue rented out the top two floors of a spacious Victorian a few blocks away.

"It's great. Thanks so much for telling me about it."

They arrived at the True Grit and John immediately enfolded both of them in a bear hug. "It's great to be alive!" he exclaimed. "Look at the new menu additions." He pointed to a chalkboard that listed five vegetarian and vegan dishes under the heading *For the Heart.* "We're making some changes."

He showed them to a booth and brought Rocket a bowl of water. She imagined John had decided the health code about animals in eating establishments didn't apply to a dog that saved the owner's life.

After they'd ordered, Lenny rested her arms on the table and leaned toward her. "I think we need to talk about the subject we're avoiding. I'd like to know why you didn't tell me that you worked for Sloane."

She looked away, ashamed. "I'm sorry I kept that from you. Sloane isn't just my boss. She helped raise me after my parents died." She glanced up at Lenny's sad eyes. "They were killed in a highway accident when I was twelve. I went to live in Boston with my Aunt Mimi. Sloane was her best friend, and Aunt Mimi wasn't really ready to have kids. She was practically a kid herself."

"How did she know Sloane?"

She rolled her eyes. "You can guess."

"Oh, I see. They were lovers."

"No, not lovers, not really. It was a one-time thing, and then they became friends. Definitely odd for Sloane, but it happened. They had so much in common that the friendship stuck. They're still friends to this day."

Lenny was looking at her thoughtfully. "I'm sorry about your parents, but Sloane and your aunt must be very proud of you. You've done quite well for yourself, and it's obvious to me that you know how to market a business."

"Thanks," she said sheepishly. "I learned from the best, and speaking of business, there's something that's been bothering me since the town meeting."

"What's that?"

"I guess I didn't realize how much of a force and an influence Carlotta is in Pinedale."

Lenny snorted and nearly spit up her beer. "Force is an understatement. She has more clout than anyone else. People either side with her, stay out of her way or just try to stay off her radar. That's my choice."

"Hard to do when you're the mayor."

"You're right there," Lenny conceded. "Fortunately, I see a lot less of her than I did when Pru was alive." When she looked puzzled, Lenny added, "They were friends, or rather, acquaintances who liked golf."

She couldn't hide her surprise. "Oh, I had no idea."

"It wasn't a big deal. They just spent a lot of time together."

The tone of her voice and her expression significantly changed. There was more to the story, but Regina didn't want to pry. Yet it added to her initial concern. Their meals arrived and they shared more stories about hiking and dogs, but Regina kept thinking about Sloane.

She couldn't understand how Sloane didn't know about Carlotta and her desire to buy Pru's Curious Curios before they arrived in Pinedale. It didn't make sense. Sloane always knew *everything* before she launched a takeover, and if Pru had had a strong personal relationship with Carlotta—perhaps an affair, from what Lenny implied—then the Research and Development department at Wilderness Campaign should have uncovered it.

"So, what's the deal with Sloane?" Lenny asked suddenly. "She runs hot and cold. One minute she's declaring she'll take my shop and the next she's kissing me."

Her eyes widened. "She kissed you?" When Lenny nodded, she said, "Have you..." She couldn't even finish her sentence.

She looked startled. "No, I'm not ready for that." After a long pause she added, "Well, I don't think I am."

Her face morphed into a grin. "She does have quite the effect, doesn't she?"

"She does indeed." Lenny couldn't meet her gaze.

"You asked why she runs hot and cold, and I think it's because she doesn't know what to do with people, at least not in a personal context. She's a great businesswoman. The fact that she can run a major corporation and keep her entirely male board of directors happy is a feat in and of itself, but the truth is, she has no real friends, and she's never had a girlfriend."

Lenny's coffee mug froze in midair. "You're kidding."

She shook her head. "No, she's never had a partner or lived with anyone."

"Why?"

"I can't say for sure because we've never really talked about it, but I think her relationship with her parents, especially her father, has something to do with it. I've heard her make lots of comments about her childhood, and she's never said anything positive. There wasn't a lot of love in her family, and she was raised in an incredibly strict and rigid household. Her parents never showed affection and they never once told her they loved her."

"Not once?"

"No. It sounded like a house completely devoid of feeling."

Lenny looked distraught. "That's horrible."

"It is," she agreed, "especially since I think Sloane has so much love to give. She raised me, and she certainly didn't have to do that." Lenny didn't respond. From the look on her face, she guessed she was deep in thought. "You know," she said slowly, "she's different around you. You...hold her attention."

"Really?" Lenny chuckled.

"Yes. She doesn't dismiss you like she does everyone else, even me sometimes."

"Well, it's not like we haven't fought. Did she tell you about how I tricked her into falling off the log?"

She laughed and nodded. "You see, that's what I mean. If anyone else had done that to her it would have been an act of war. She would've felt horribly betrayed and never forgotten it. Forgiveness is not in her vocabulary." She leaned across the table, suddenly amazed by her own epiphany. "Why are you so different?"

She shrugged and slid out of the booth. "I have no idea."

They headed back across the street and took a detour through the park so Rocket could do his business.

"Will you look at that?" Lenny said. "The one time we close and a tourist *wants* to shop."

She had been watching Rocket chase his tail. She gazed across the park and saw a tall man peering into the window, despite the large sign that announced the store was closed for a week. He wore shorts and a T-shirt. There was something oddly familiar about his backward baseball cap. As they crossed the street, he stood up straight and turned around. They saw him at the same time. Seth had arrived in Pinedale.

Price

The worth of a product or service must be competitive and carefully calculated to maximize profit. Consumers will ask, "What is this really costing me?"

CHAPTER NINETEEN

Lenny couldn't comprehend what was happening. No emotion registered at first at the sight of her son—the boy she'd given birth to. Then every emotion clamored at the door of her heart simultaneously and she was overwhelmed. She couldn't move.

It was Regina who ran to him. She attempted to embrace him, and he stepped back, holding his hands up defensively. She continued to speak, but his words rolled over hers. Then she started to cry. Their voices increased, the tone sharper. He was pointing at her, and Lenny could see the veins in his neck. He seemed to tower over her, his voice bellowing.

They definitely know each other. What the hell?

"Stop it!" she ordered. He abruptly shut his mouth and both of them faced her. She didn't understand where the commanding voice had come from, but now they looked at her as if she needed to *do* something about this situation.

She trudged up the porch steps and stood between them. "I don't know what is going on, but we are in public in a little town. Unless you want everyone and her Aunt Hildy to know your business, I suggest we go inside."

She opened the door but waited until both of them grudgingly crossed the threshold. The only one who seemed delighted to return to the shop was Rocket, who bounded past all of them and headed straight for the cookie jar. She dropped a treat into his mouth, noticing that Seth had sulked into a corner against an empty bookcase while Regina paced nervously on the other side of the room.

She debated what to do. Mediation was not her strength. *That's one reason I'm a rotten mayor. I hate dealing with everyone's problems.* She plopped onto the stool behind the cash register.

"Would one of you like to tell me what's going on? How do you know each other?"

"We're practically engaged," Regina said.

"We're dating," Seth corrected.

Regina looked crushed. "That's all this is to you?" she cried. "Dating? We're *dating*?" She said the word as if it were evil, and that told Lenny everything she needed to know.

He swallowed hard and dug his hands into his pockets. She noticed the set of his jaw and his broad shoulders. He was a *man*. The boy was completely gone.

"Okay, so it's more than dating. We're serious about each other, but anybody who was practically engaged, to use your words, wouldn't traipse off across the country in secret."

"I came here on business—"

"Yeah, right! You came here to see my mother." He whirled and faced Lenny. "Did you invite her up here? Is this your doing?"

She opened her mouth to explain, but Regina immediately defended her. "She doesn't know anything about us! Sloane has a business deal here. It happened to be in the same town where your mother lived."

He laughed and threw up his hands. "Right. Like I'm going to believe anything involving Sloane would be purely coincidental. Who do you think called me?"

Regina gasped. "She called you?"

"Yes! And then it made sense why your GPS tracker said you were in western Colorado. You lied to me. You should have told me you were coming here to see her."

"I came here on business," she insisted, "but you can believe whatever you want. In fact, you can *do* whatever you want. I don't care!"

She ran out of the store, the screen door slamming behind her. Lenny slowly turned to face her son. The situation seemed completely surreal. She adopted a fake smile and said, "Hi, son, it's good to see you again."

His gaze dropped to the floor and he shuffled his feet. The air conditioner came on, and the squeaky wheeze of the old compressor became the only sound in the store.

"Hi, Mom," he managed, looking horribly embarrassed.

She sighed. "Okay, I don't know what to say. I'll admit I've thought about this moment a lot in the last few years. I even wrote a script once, but I didn't expect this today, so I'm not prepared. Pru was always the one who could think on the spot."

He looked up quizzically. "What do you mean *was?*"

She was momentarily tongue-tied. *Of course he picks up on the past tense verb.* It was difficult to say the words. "Pru's gone, honey. She died a year ago."

In an instant the man disappeared and tears pooled in his eyes, just as they had when he was a boy. He'd rarely cried, as he'd learned she didn't know what to with that reaction. The closest he came to crying was his eyes welling up with a broken expression on his face. She realized he wasn't sad as much as he was *hurt*.

"I'm sorry I didn't call. I wanted to. I thought about it every day when she was so sick, but I didn't realize until just this moment how big a mistake I made in not calling you."

"Of course you should have called me!"

He dropped onto an old couch, and she moved next to him, to embrace him, but he turned away. Instead of accepting his rejection, she rubbed his back until he finally fell against her and sobbed. She let him cry, amazed that her heart wasn't breaking again. Instead she was almost euphoric in the moment. He was back.

He composed himself and asked, "How did she die?"

"She had cancer, honey. She went peacefully. We called hospice, and she didn't feel anything. I held her hand the whole time." She watched him closely as he absorbed the information for the first time, remembering how hard those early weeks had been after she was gone. Suddenly a lump formed in her throat. She rose abruptly and walked across the room. *I can't fall apart. It's not my turn. It's* his *turn.*

"And that was a year ago?"

She closed her eyes. She imagined he would berate her for waiting so long to tell him. "Yes, a year next Tuesday."

He rose from the couch and she sensed his approach. When she turned, he was facing her, his arms crossed. "Did she want you to call me, or did she tell you *not* to call me?"

She shook her head. "She didn't say, son. It all happened very quickly. She denied she was sick for a long time. *I* denied she was sick for a long time. I should've insisted she go to the doctor—"

He snorted. "Fat chance. Pru never went to the doctor. I remember how hard it was to get her to go to the dentist for a cleaning." He cocked his head to the side. "Why was she like that?"

"She hated bad news. She believed the mind could overcome any ailment, and in some cases she was right." Her gaze dropped to the floor. "But you can't wish away cancer."

The word hung in the air with the incessant drone of the air conditioner. She had no idea what else to say or what to do. So much time had passed.

"I really am sorry I didn't call you," she said again. "That was a mistake. It's just..." She searched for the right words, the ones that would make everything she was feeling go away immediately. There were none. "We'd grown so far apart," she finally said.

"You should've kept trying. That was *your* job!" he shouted. "You're the *mom*!"

They stared at each other, and she realized he had a point. She *was* the mom. She would always be older and wiser. Most anything he would enjoy or endure she had already experienced. His footsteps would follow hers, and he would arrive at every destination long after she had been there and moved on. She would always be *the parent*.

"You're right. I should've made more of an effort, but I did try, over and over again. I sent you inspirational cards, funny emails, voice mails, but I got nothing in return. You're not a child, Seth. Some of this is on you." His expression shifted, and at that moment she pictured Pru waving her arms, signaling her to back off a little.

"I know," he admitted.

"So, I'm guessing you dumped the religious girlfriend you were with the last time we spoke?"

He snorted. "Yeah, you were right."

She cupped her hand over her ear dramatically. "I was what?"

"You were *right*!" he yelled.

She crossed the room to an old record player Regina had unearthed. Conveniently an appropriate forty-five sat on the turntable. She dropped the needle and cranked up the volume. The *Hallelujah Chorus* filled the room.

She looked up and they burst into laughter at the same time. Whenever it was just the two of them, face-to-face with no interruptions, they connected.

She turned off the record player and their eyes met. "I have so many questions. When did you move to Boston? How did you meet Regina? How are you supporting yourself? What did you think of the new *Star Trek* movies? But right now, the only question I want to ask is, why didn't you ever call me back? Why didn't you bother to answer one of my emails?" She took a breath and added, "Is it because you were ashamed of us?"

Recognition flooded his face. She'd seen that same expression when he'd comprehended subtraction and on the day he realized what happened to all of the dogs and cats no one adopted. He finally understood how his absence had affected her. *This is one of the moments every parent waits for.*

"I was never ashamed of you. So many things have happened over the last six years. For a while Dad and I weren't talking."

She couldn't hide her surprise. "But you're talking now?"

"Yeah, we made up." He realized what he'd just said. "It isn't the same, Mom."

"Why not?"

He shrugged and looked away. "It just isn't."

"I need an answer, Seth. How can you ignore us for six years and not make an effort? Why don't I get the same courtesy as your father?"

"Because he doesn't really matter!" he screamed.

In the silence she realized the air conditioner had finally quit, and the only sound was her man-son shuffling his feet.

He took a breath and said more calmly, "I'm not sure you'll understand. What I have with Dad is superficial. It will never be important, and that means everything is at the surface with him. Yes, it's easier to make up with him after a fight, but I've never really cared what he thought, and until Regina came along, I didn't really have anyone to share the good things with."

"You could've called—"

"It's just that for so long you made me feel guilty, like I owed you."

"You *do* owe me," she snorted. "I gave you life. You can never repay me that, and I can't repay my mother either. It's how it goes. Is that why you didn't call?"

"Not the whole reason. There was the girlfriend thing," he said dismissively, "and then I was embarrassed. So much time had gone by, like four years. I figured you probably hated me by then, or at the least you were disappointed in me. I haven't even told Regina much about you. Just that we'd drifted apart. I figured *she'd* hate me if she found out it was my fault that we weren't speaking. Her mother died, and mine's alive and I wasn't even talking to her." He hung his head. "I didn't know where to begin."

She took his face between her hands. "You start with what's most important. 'I love you' and 'I'm sorry.' And I do and I am."

Tears streamed down his face, and for the first time, she wasn't the least bit uncomfortable.

"I love you too, Mom. And I'm sorry."

She pulled him against her and said, "I'll make you a deal. I'll try a little harder not to remind you that you owe me, and you try a little harder to remember that you *do*."

Rocket jumped and landed in Lenny's lap. He gave them each a lick on the cheek and they both laughed. Lenny scratched his ears. *Great timing, boy.*

"Tell me about Regina," she said.

At the sound of her name his whole body relaxed and a goofy smile covered his face—until he remembered he was angry with her. "She's my supposed girlfriend," he hissed. "She told me she was going to a convention in Denver. She lied to me. She should have told me she was coming here."

A thought occurred to her. "If you haven't talked about me, then how would she know I was here?"

He shrugged. "I don't know. I *do* know that there's nothing coincidental about her and Sloane being here. There are no coincidences, accidents or unknowns in Sloane McHenry's life. I've known her long enough to understand that—and Regina's just like her. Everything planned and it's always based on what the data says."

She ambled over behind the counter and pulled two Cokes from a little fridge. He joined her on a stool and accepted the sweaty bottle. "Then I guess whatever data she has on you must be pretty good."

"I think it's because of what happened to her parents. They were killed in a car wreck. Did she tell you that?"

"Uh-huh, and she mentioned Sloane helped raise her. The woman can't be all bad," she added.

"You don't know her like I do," he disagreed. "She thinks I'm a loser."

She frowned and sat up straight. "What do you mean?"

"I'm not good enough for Regina. I've never gone to college—"

"You haven't?"

He groaned. "Mom, not now. We can rehash the last six years in a future conversation."

"Fine."

"I tend bar and I spend a lot of time helping people and working for nonprofits. I really like working with animals. Regina likes them too, so we have a lot of dogs." He looked up, his blue eyes matching hers. "Sound like someone you know?"

She chuckled. "Like mother, like son." They drank in silence and she finally asked, "Do you love her? Is this serious?"

His face told the story before he said the words. "Yeah. We live together, and I want to be with her forever."

She smiled and tousled his hair. It was too long, but she wasn't going to tell him that. She would work to be a better mother, one who supported his decisions and didn't nag. "You said we'd talk about the last six years in a future conversation. So, this isn't it, then? You're not going to disappear on me again?"

"No." He gazed at her thoughtfully, and she realized she was very much going to like having her adult son in her life.

"Well, if you're going to love Regina forever, I think forever starts today. You should probably go find her."

"You're right," he said, finishing his Coke and standing up. His gaze traveled around the store. "Sloane wants to buy this place?"

"Apparently."

He smirked. "Why?"

CHAPTER TWENTY

Sloane had lost track of the number of nasty texts Regina had sent her in the last day, but she expected it. She'd known when she called Seth and explained that Regina was here visiting his mother, he would gladly accept her offer of a plane ticket to Montrose. She also knew that he would tell Regina how he'd found out and who had told him.

She was a little surprised, however, at how quickly he'd forgiven Regina and patched up his relationship with his mother. Apparently he'd joined them in renovating Pru's Curious Curios, and they were now a team of three, determined to save the shop from a takeover by her or Carlotta, which is why she sat parked across the street from the Schoolhouse Emporium.

She could see why the shop lured customers away from Pru's Curious Curios. Carlotta's flagship business was the original Pinedale School in its previous life, a large building with several rooms and many windows. The front was the most attractive, complete with bell tower and steps that led up to a wide porch.

Although it was only ten thirty, the parking lot was already half-full, the cars there bearing license plates from many surrounding states. She watched the comings-and-goings for another five minutes before she headed for the entrance. Her phone dinged again, but she ignored it. She doubted Regina had anything new to say.

She was immediately impressed by the entry, which overlooked the massive store. The first view customers had would excite them and make them eager to visit every nook and cranny. A handcrafted wooden railing separated them from the interior and required them to stroll either to the left or the right and funnel through one of the established aisles. Creating traffic patterns was a clever trick she used in all of her stores that guaranteed buyers would be exposed to a majority of the merchandise during their visit.

She scanned the room for Carlotta, but there was no sign of her. She eased down one of the long aisles, surveying the layout of the store and its features. Many interior walls had been removed to create the wide-open space that was the heart of the store, and a loft perched against an opposite wall with floor-to-ceiling bookshelves. Several customers sat on couches perusing the books, and one man used the sliding ladder to reach a hardbound volume from a top shelf.

She ascended the spiral staircase and admired the old bookcases with their ornate crown molding. Unlike in many second-hand stores, the books were shelved alphabetically, and a brass plate affixed to the front of each bookcase announced the subject matter to be found. She was impressed. Carlotta had been attentive to detail.

She couldn't help but peruse the nonfiction titles. She loved books about business, leadership or management, and she devoured every new title she could find. Although many of the shelves were filled with biographies or self-help books, she found some familiar titles on the bottom shelf, including one slightly worn copy of *The Seven Ps of Business: How to Ensure Your Success*. Of course she had this book and had read it many times, but the cover was different. She thumbed through the first few pages and found the copyright date. Her eyes widened when she realized it was a first edition. *What a find!*

The book was in good condition, considering the fact that it was decades old. She checked the inside cover for a price and was shocked to see the name of the previous owner written in flowing blue ink: Prudence Cavender. She had Pru's copy. Why would Lenny give this up? Did she give away all of Pru's books?

She descended the spiral staircase with the book and saw Carlotta emerge from a side door with a young woman. Sloane advanced in her direction until she caught her gaze. Carlotta quickly excused her employee and confronted her.

"I'm surprised you're still here," she said. Although her tone was friendly, Sloane felt the sharp edge. "I thought the town was quite clear at the meeting. We have no interest in your store. You should just pack up and find another location. What about Telluride?"

"I'm not sure the town sees the big picture yet."

Carlotta raised an eyebrow. "Which is?"

An older couple offered their apologies as they bumped into her. "Can we find a quiet place to talk?"

"Just talk?"

The memory of them splayed across her desk, hot and wet, contradicted the innocent tone in her voice. "I'm not sure," she replied. "Let's see how the negotiations progress."

Another employee approached and Carlotta held up her hand, instantly silencing the young man. "I need another hour here. I'll meet you at my place. Do you know where that is?"

"Of course."

* * *

She drove slowly up the Cathedral Hills access road, checking the numbers along the way. She knew Carlotta's place sat near the top, a position of prominence and affluence, but somewhere in the middle was Lenny's house. She glanced at her iPad, which held the entire file of the Pinedale transaction, the *only* complete file that existed.

Not surprising, Lenny's metal-art mailbox was in the shape of a doghouse and on the side it said, *Rocket's Pad*. A stand of trees blocked the view of the house, but she edged past the driveway and caught a glimpse of tan-and-avocado-colored siding. It wasn't a mansion by any means, but the photos she'd acquired from various sources indicated the design was cozy and luxurious. There was certainly enough room for Regina and Seth, who she imagined were staying there.

She reached the end of the road and stopped at the massive gate. She pressed the intercom and the gate whirred open without acknowledgment. The driveway wended closer to the side of the mountain for another quarter of a mile, and she realized she was actually facing east. She imagined several balconies afforded Carlotta a view of a gorgeous sunrise every morning.

Barking echoed through the house until the face of a boxer pressed against the decorative glass panel next to the enormous steel door. Carlotta's voice followed, and when she swung the door open, she wore only a slinky purple teddy that barely contained her enormous chest. A wicked grin covered her face.

"Not fair," Sloane said, her eyes feasting on the sensuous curves of Carlotta's legs and buttocks. "You have home court advantage. I didn't bring anything sexy."

"You're sexy enough," she said, grabbing her hand and leading her into an extraordinary great room, the southern wall of which was completely glass and offered a perfect view of the San Juans. The decorating had been professionally done in matching peach tones.

Carlotta led her around the house for a three-minute tour that culminated in the bedroom. She dropped her hand and crawled onto the bed. She was determined to put on a show, it seemed—a very persuasive show. She licked her middle finger and slid it under the lacy edge of the teddy. Her lips parted and she emitted little gasps of pleasure that rolled toward an orgasm.

Sloane thought of what she'd told Lenny—Carlotta was a one-time distraction. She wasn't interested in her. *But I want her to think I am.* She'd freed her left breast from the teddy's bodice, and the strap hung loosely around her bicep while she teased her areola until it was pointing at Sloane.

Sloane grabbed her ankles and slid her the length of the bed. She replaced Carlotta's hand with her own, expertly fondling her clit with her thumb while her fingers stroked her slick wetness. Carlotta wrapped her arms around Sloane's neck and pulled her closer.

"Deeper, harder," she cried in a ragged breath, pumping her hips up and down to match the rhythm of her fingers.

"I know what you want too," Sloane cooed.

Rough sex was her specialty, and more than a few women had come back begging for more. The harder she pumped the more noise Carlotta made until she was practically screaming. Eventually her body stilled and she lay spent on the bed while Sloane washed her hands.

When she returned, Carlotta patted the pillow beside her. "We need to make it even," she said.

The last thing she wanted was to grunt and moan in front of this woman. Wearing her electric PR smile, she sat primly on the edge of the bed and took her hand. She kissed each knuckle and murmured, "Now isn't a good time. It seems you jump-started my monthly visitor the other night."

Her face registered horror at the thought of blood all over her expensive peach sheets and she nodded her understanding. Sloane breathed an internal sigh of relief that she believed the lie.

"I have a question for you, if you don't mind?"

Carlotta looked at her shrewdly. "You think you can trip me up just because you made me come?"

"I doubt I could trip you up," she said.

"You're right. You couldn't. What do you want to know?"

"Why do you want Lenny's store? You already have a fabulous collectibles store, why another? Why would you want to create competition against yourself?"

Carlotta tensed and the sexual energy fizzled away. "It wouldn't be in competition with Schoolhouse Emporium. I have other plans for that shop."

She raised an eyebrow, very curious. "Such as?"

She shrugged. "Who knows? I do know that Lenny is entirely incapable of running a business. I'd be doing the town a favor."

"What about Lenny? That's all she has left of Pru." Carlotta looked away and smoothed the bedspread. *There's something going on here.* "I want to know why you're so set on taking this store away from Lenny."

Carlotta leaned closer until they were practically kissing. "What if I told you I wanted to buy the shop and keep it as Pru's Curious Curios? What if I told you I wanted to buy it to ensure that Lenny didn't ruin Pru's dream? What if I told you I wanted to be Lenny's partner?"

A thought occurred to her. "Business or pleasure?"

Carlotta blushed and flicked her eyelashes. "Both." She met Sloane's hard stare with an almost girlish expression. "I think Lenny's fascinating. She just needs a little more time to get over Pru."

"And then she'll be ready for you?" Sloane asked skeptically. "Do you really think she's going to hook up with the woman who's trying to destroy her?"

"I'm not going to destroy her. I'm going to help her," she argued. "It will be the best thing that could happen. She has no idea what she's doing. I could create more jobs and revenue for the town, and in the process..." Sloane imagined she was picturing her and Lenny doing it on her desk. "All I need to do is convince those other idiots on the town council."

Sloane shook her head in disbelief. "You really think you're something special, don't you, like some sort of town savior? Really, I think all you care about is yourself."

"That's not true at all. I care deeply for Pinedale, but it just so happens that my interests are the most important in Pinedale."

"What's good for you is good for Pinedale?" Sloane summarized.

"Something like that."

"Here's something to think about. You might be able to create a handful of jobs, but I could create more," Sloane said. She watched Carlotta's reaction closely as she processed the situation.

"You want it too," she concluded. "You want to take over Pru's shop."

"Actually I want the whole building. Wilderness Campaigns are very large, and I'd need to take over the ice cream shop and the coffee bar."

Carlotta shook her head. "I should've seen this coming." She stared at Sloane and scrambled from the bed. "You need to go."

She led her to the front door. With her hand on the knob, Sloane turned to her and said, "She'll never want you. You're not good enough for her."

The door slammed behind her and she grinned. "If we weren't enemies before, we are now," Sloane said.

CHAPTER TWENTY-ONE

Seth waved goodbye as he pulled the large truck onto Harrison and headed for the county dump with the last load of junk. Regina and Lenny went back into the shop, which was still a dismal mess.

"Now, the real work starts," Regina said, opening her iPad and pulling up a design. "This is the floor plan I've created and I want your approval."

Lenny waved her off and headed for the mini-fridge for drinks. "I'm sure whatever you have planned will be great. I think I've proven that I'm rather worthless when it comes to managing a store. I'm good with whatever you decide."

"Then at least let me show you," she pressed. She took a cold Coke from Lenny and propped up the screen. "The west wall is reserved for books and knickknacks, and the east wall will be for the greeting cards. The second room is for vintage clothing and the bay window will be filled with jewelry stands. That way the midday light will play off the beautiful colors of the earrings and necklaces Pru acquired." She flashed a wide smile. "Lenny, it's going to be marvelous. I can't believe how much wonderful stuff is in here."

She meant what she said. The shop had turned out to be an archaeological dig. What had began as a mundane task of carting trash outside had become an ongoing surprise party as they unearthed treasures that had been relegated to corners of the shop or buried under the neighbors' junk. Now it was just a matter of properly displaying everything.

"You really don't have to give me all the details," Lenny said. "I totally trust you and Seth. Are you two okay?"

She knew she was blushing. They were more than okay. "We're good. He forgave me for lying to him, and we had a really good talk about the past."

"He and I had a good talk as well. I hope it continues. We have a lot to catch up on."

"I know," she said with certainty. "We talked about that, too. He understands how important family is to me, and since I think we're going to be family…"

Her words trailed off into a smile. He had all but proposed the night before, and while she knew a more formal proposal was in the works, it was clear marriage was what they both wanted.

Lenny struggled to contain her emotions. "I can't think of anything that would make me happier. You're an amazing woman, Regina. Have you told Sloane?"

She shook her head. "We haven't spoken since the morning after the town meeting when she fired me, and I don't plan to speak to her anytime soon."

"I'm not one to dispense too much advice, but I think you need to practice what you preach."

"What do you mean?"

"You came here to reunite me and Seth because family was so important, but Sloane *is* your family, honey. I know she isn't perfect, but she and your aunt are it. She deserves the same consideration and care. As an adult, sometimes the child has to take care of the parent. Don't forget she's the reason all of this happened. If she hadn't wanted to open a Wilderness Campaign in tiny Pinedale, we never would've met, Seth and I would still be estranged and Carlotta would probably be fitting my front window for curtains." She patted her arm and stood to go. "Now, it's time for me to go check in with Maddie. I'll leave you to start the resurrection of Pru's. I'll call you later and maybe we can all go to the concert together."

She looked up from her iPad, puzzled. "Concert? What concert?"

"The jazz concert at Fellin Park in Ouray."

She remembered the concert poster she'd seen on the storefront window. "Oh, yeah."

"We can't miss that. Seth didn't mention it to you? I guess he got distracted." She winked and disappeared out the front door before Regina turned beet red.

She gazed at the clutter that surrounded her and decided the easiest strategy was to get each object near its final location. She went to a corner and picked up a Louisville Slugger bat that was at least forty years old and a cast-iron skillet.

"One thing at a time," she murmured as she walked through the store, moving merchandise and redistributing items to their new home.

She replayed her confrontation with Seth at Lenny's house and how well it had ended. The truth was that neither of them liked to fight since they both respected each other so much. He'd understood and they had made up quickly, or rather, not so quickly, which is why he'd been distracted and forgotten to tell her about the concert.

She smiled as she positioned an old hat stand in a corner. No matter. The concert would be fun. She wondered if Sloane would be there. She loved jazz as much as Seth, and Regina imagined that she was staying with Riya at the Carnation B and B. Where else would she go?

She couldn't picture her making her own arrangements—ever. She rarely planned anything, always counting on her team to support her. She didn't like being alone and always took others with her to meetings, conventions or scouting trips. The fact that she'd been by herself during the plane crash was almost impossible to believe.

So it would be completely out of character for her to find her own hotel accommodations, but the more Regina thought about it, the more she realized the entire trip was odd. Sloane had deliberately withheld information from her. That was a first. She constantly used her as a sounding board whenever she was putting together a deal. She had never kept her so completely out of the loop before. Perhaps, though, since Regina had a personal stake in what happened to the optimal location, she'd wanted to spare her from the conflict of interest.

She set down a stack of books and surveyed her progress. After only thirty minutes, she'd cleared out one third of the second room. Of course, nothing was really organized, but the store was compact and it was easy to shift everything around. She suddenly realized Pru's Curious Curios was…smallish. It wasn't tiny, but it wasn't anything like an empty big box store, which was the customary building Wilderness Campaign acquired when they were looking for a new store location. Even with the coffee shop and the ice cream store added, the square footage was still short.

"What are you thinking, Sloane?" she said out loud.

She went to her iPad and pulled up the file on Pinedale as well as the acquisition requirements laid out by the executive team at Wilderness Campaign. For the first time she analyzed the deal from a purely financial perspective, comparing square footage, town size, geography and other criteria necessary for consideration. Pinedale barely qualified, and Pru's Curious Curios should have been eliminated as a potential site after the initial first pass of locations.

She looked through the file and realized none of the customary protocols had been followed. Sloane had put this deal together herself, leaving everyone on the team out of the decision-making process. None of it made sense. It was questionable if a store in Pinedale could be profitable at *any* location, but there was no possible way it could remain solvent at Pru's. The square footage was thirty percent shy of the suggested amount, which would require cutting corners and translate to lost profits.

"Why didn't I see this before?" she muttered.

Because I was too focused on my personal life, worried that Lenny would hate me and Seth would find out I was here.

She hadn't asked any of the important questions and had let Sloane make all of the decisions, ones that would cost Wilderness Campaign serious money. She wondered how Sloane would answer to the board of directors when the Pinedale store started to tank. The chain had a history of staying in the black every quarter. This store would be the only one with a negative output. It certainly didn't meet the Seven Ps.

She went to the front door and faced the disheveled mess of Pru's Curious Curios. She closed her eyes, determined that when she opened them she would do so as Regina Dewar, vice president of new accounts for Wilderness Campaign, LLC, trusted associate of the CEO.

She blinked. What she saw made her stomach turn. She imagined every dollar that would be spent to renovate the interior, the electrical and the plumbing. Spreadsheets flashed in her mind, and she readily assigned dollar amounts to each of the expenses. The total cost was astounding—and unnecessary.

She picked up her iPad and scrolled through the pages on Pinedale. Pru's Curious Curios was *not* the optimal location. Was there one?

* * *

Fellin Park was overflowing with people. Regina realized that even when the entire town showed up, there were still parking spaces for the visitors.

As if reading her mind, Seth offered, "This certainly isn't Boston."

He'd insisted on driving, and Lenny had insisted on sitting in the backseat with Rocket, despite Regina's protest that it was her car and she should sit in the front.

"We're fine back here," she said. "You kids enjoy the view."

Lenny was like a different person. They chatted all the way from the house to the park about various topics. She wanted to know all about their dogs, Seth's charity work and Regina's favorite foods. Never once did she feel left out, and she was grateful Lenny wasn't the kind of person who wanted to bridge the six-year gap in an evening. It had been awkward a few times as both mother and son struggled to find the next sentence, but she was optimistic, and both seemed inclined to reach back into the past in measured doses. They would be fine.

The concert had already started by the time they toted their chairs, blankets and cooler to an open space on the lawn. Some people had started dancing in an area near the stage and wonderful smells were wafting from several food trucks lined up near the base of the mountain.

They settled in and Lenny looked around. "Do you think Sloane will be here?"

She shrugged. "I don't know. She may have gone back to Boston, for all I know."

"Oh," Lenny said, and she saw the look of disappointment.

"Then again, it's not like her to run away from a fight, and she's a big jazz fan too. We should probably keep an eye out for her."

Lenny scanned the crowd, looking toward the other side of the park. "You know, I think I'll take Rocket over to the dog area for a little while. Did you want anything to eat? I could stop at one of the trucks on the way back."

Seth's face lit up at the offer of food. "Yeah, how about a hot dog? I thought I saw a sign for those. Or maybe some sliders? I think there's some Mexican burritos too." He looked at both of them, and they started to laugh. "What?"

Lenny patted his shoulder as she stood to go. "I'm glad to see your appetite hasn't changed."

She and Rocket disappeared through the crowd while he watched them go. "Are you okay?" she asked.

When he gazed into her eyes, he wore a broad smile. "I'm great."

He kissed her and took her in his arms. She closed her eyes, immersing herself in the music. A light breeze danced across her face, and she knew in that moment she was completely at ease. The statistics about gunmen in large crowds or the chance of catching food poisoning from a mobile eatery would not dissuade her from having a wonderful time. She was safe. She was home.

CHAPTER TWENTY-TWO

Rocket bounded across the play area, a bloodhound on his heels. He skittered into a turn and zoomed through a cement tube in the play area, knowing the bigger dog couldn't get through the obstacle as easily. When the other dog didn't emerge, he rushed back to the opening and saw him standing in the tube sniffing the side. That was always the problem with hound dogs. They were so easily distracted and sniffed *everything*. He gave a short bark, gaining the hound's attention. The chase was on again!

They circled the perimeter several times. The dog park was so much fun, and for the first time in a long time, Lenny was happy. He could smell her happiness, and he was certain it had something to do with the man named Seth who smelled like her. Rocket could tell he loved dogs, and as long as he kept sneaking him treats, they would be buds!

He rounded another corner and noticed the hound was gone. He stopped and looked around for another playmate. Who would chase him? Certainly not the uppity poodle that sat next to her owner on a bench. *She* wouldn't follow him through the tube. The Australian shepherd only wanted to chase his ball, so he was out. He heard a high-pitched yip and swung his head to the side. A Chihuahua sprang up and down with each bark. He cocked his head to the side. *Really? You?*

He let the Chihuahua chase him for a lap, but by the second turn the little dog had dropped onto the grass, panting. *Typical.* He looked for Lenny and saw her at the fence talking to the lady who'd gone hiking with them in the mountains.

He studied her, a low growl in his throat. She smelled different, and when she was around Lenny, *Lenny* smelled different. For some reason, it reminded him of Pru. He couldn't decide if she was good or not, but he would keep an eye on her. If she hurt Lenny, she'd answer to him.

CHAPTER TWENTY-THREE

"Hi."

"Hi."

"I know you probably don't want to see me, but I was hoping you'd give me a chance to explain why I didn't tell you about Regina and her relationship with Seth. It's difficult when your personal life and business cross. Things become very complex."

"You called him to come out here, didn't you?"

"Yes, I felt that the situation needed a catalytic change—"

Lenny kissed her. It was a bold kiss that claimed her lips, and just as quickly as it began, it ended.

She caught her breath and said, "What was that for?"

"You brought Seth home. I'm sure you're hoping to gain some sort of leverage from it, but I don't really care right now. He's here and we're talking for the first time in six years. So, thank you."

"You're welcome. For the record, I don't need any more *leverage* with you. You see what needs to be done. You know what this community needs."

She gave a short laugh. "You expect me to believe you brought him back here just to be altruistic?"

"Ooooh, big word," Sloane teased. When Lenny scowled playfully, she added, "I did it for Regina as well. I would do anything for her."

"You need to go talk to her. The two of you need to make up."

She called Rocket and clipped on his leash. Sloane followed them back to their spot on the lawn, noticing Seth and Regina were wrapped together as one.

"Look who I found."

When Regina saw Sloane, she sat up and pointed at her. "We need to talk."

"And we will," she said, "but not right now." She took Rocket's leash and gave it to Seth. "Right now, I want to dance."

She took Lenny's hand and pulled her to the dance area, ignoring Regina's protests. "Round Midnight" started to play, and they glided across the grass. She was surprised how easily Lenny followed her lead.

"You're a good dancer," she whispered in her ear.

"Pru and I took lessons for a while, but then we quit."

"Why?"

"She didn't have a lot of rhythm, so she didn't think she was very good."

"I don't think I'm very good either, but that's not what it's about."

"So, what's it about?" Lenny asked, her lips grazing Sloane's cheek.

"It's the world's best excuse to get close to someone. You touch, you move together rhythmically. It's sex's cousin."

"Your metaphor is quite interesting."

She didn't reply. She didn't want to talk anymore. She just wanted to enjoy *feeling* Lenny. That's what she hadn't told her. What she loved most about dancing was the connection— fingers clasped together and the innocent touch of a hand on a back or shoulder. Her mind ran wild as she imagined Lenny grinding against her, grabbing her shoulders for support while she massaged her lower back and buttocks until they came violently.

"I want you."

Lenny stopped dancing and stared at her. Her cornflower blue eyes were nearly opaque in the moonlight. "I don't know. I don't know if I'm ready."

She started dancing again, forcing Lenny to follow. "I don't think anybody's ever ready. Let's just get out of here and see what happens."

She shook her head. "No, I think it's too soon."

"I can't believe I'm getting pushback from the woman who lives life in the moment."

"This is different."

"You're right. It is different. This is exactly the kind of thing you *should* do in the moment. Forsaking your college degree, quitting your job, letting your son slip out of your life, *not* things for the moment. But this is."

Lenny's expression turned stony and she stomped away.

Why did I say that? She followed her toward the street. "Where are you going? Are you just going to leave Seth and Regina here?"

"I'll walk back."

"To Pinedale? It's ten miles."

"Then I'll hitch."

"Don't you think that's a little unsafe?"

"You big city types are all the same," she scoffed. "Everyone you meet is a potential murderer or rapist."

"Well, it happens," she said, stepping alongside her. "Look, I'm sorry. Can we stop walking? We're going in the opposite direction from my car."

"And that's the first thing that enters your mind," Lenny snorted. "How inconvenienced you'll be. It's always about what's best for you!"

She grabbed Lenny's arm and spun her around. "What happened to, 'Thank you for reuniting me with my son'? I thought you were grateful."

"I am grateful, but we both know you're just playing the situation. If helping Seth and me had cost you more time or more energy, you wouldn't have bothered. We both know the price was right, and now I owe you. Believe me, I'm aware of that and that eventually you'll expect me to pay up."

She bit her lip and stormed back up the street to the Range Rover. She leaned back in the seat unable to decide what to do. *What is happening to me? I am not an emotional person.* Lenny's words stung. She was offended and hurt. She was also horny. In an hour she could be in Telluride and hooked up with a buxom honey. It was a plan.

She flew back up Main Street, ignoring the too-slow speed limit. Up ahead in the dwindling twilight, Lenny hiked past the gas station, her hands in her pockets, her head down.

"Shit," she whispered.

She gunned the engine and spun the vehicle to a stop a few feet in front of Lenny. She climbed out of the enormous SUV and faced her. She was irate—with Lenny, with herself, with her libido.

"Get in the car." Lenny crossed her arms and raised an eyebrow. "Get in the car, *please.* I want to talk to you, but I refuse to have a conversation underneath a Conoco sign."

Lenny gazed up. "I don't know. There's a certain ambience in the glow."

She moved close enough to touch her, but she refrained. "Here's what's on the table. I take you to the quaint, secluded little cottage I rented that smells like an old lady wearing lavender air freshener. On our way back through town, I will hold your hand and possibly stroke your left thigh since I think you have incredible legs. When we arrive at said cottage, I will light some candles, pour us each a drink, and lead you into the bedroom, not to have sex," she quickly added, "but to be in the appropriate location should our heavy petting lead to other opportunities. So, I only have one question: does any of what I have just described sound remotely appealing to you? Because if it doesn't, I will gladly give you a chaste car ride back to

Pinedale and we can swap cute dog anecdotes, even though the Maltese I mentioned previously is completely fictitious." When Lenny opened her mouth to comment, she raised her hand and added, "That's an explanation for another time. After I drop you off, I will head to Telluride where a discreet escort service will provide me with some company for the evening. So, back to my question. Do you want to come home with me? Yes or no."

"You'd really go get a prostitute in Telluride?"

"I'd need to forget you. Forget our dance. Forget that you kissed me. *You* kissed me, remember?"

"I do."

"Answer my question."

"Take me to the smelly cottage."

* * *

The house Sloane had rented was up the hill off Main Street. "Did you tell Seth and Regina where you went?"

"No," Lenny said, slipping her phone into her bag. "I just said not to wait around for me."

She laughed. "They'll know what you're doing."

"I'm not sure *I* know what I'm doing."

Sloane kissed her persuasively. Many women had told her she was a great kisser, but it seemed to matter more with Lenny. She'd figure out why later.

When Lenny broke away, she said, "Let's go inside."

Lenny stopped and inhaled as they crossed the threshold. "I smell it. You're right. It's antiseptic and lavender, not a great combination."

Sloane grabbed two glasses and a bottle of bourbon and led Lenny to the bedroom. She poured the drinks while Lenny perched on the edge of the bed, her hands folded in her lap, her back ramrod straight.

She looks like she's sitting in an ER waiting room. Remember, she hasn't been seduced in nearly twenty years. I need to go slow. Foreplay really exists even if it's not in my usual vocabulary.

The first drink was mostly talking and little affection, although she never let go of her hand and used every opportunity to nuzzle her neck or plant a sweet kiss on her lips. By the time they'd poured a second drink, Lenny was loosening up, and dialogue gave way to affection. Their lips had found something better to do.

"So tell me about this fictitious dog. Why did you lie?" Lenny asked.

She lifted her head from the folds of Lenny's open shirt. "It wasn't really a lie." She saw the look on her face, and sighed. "Okay, it was a *lie*, but I only told it so you'd feel more comfortable around me. Do you remember how tense you were on the drive out to Blaine Basin?"

Lenny nodded, downed the rest of her drink and fell back on the bed. Sloane cuddled against her and stroked her cheek. "We don't have to talk about it."

"No, I want to tell you." She took Sloane's hand and held it against her chest. "That trail was the last hike Pru and I ever took together. I'd been trying for three months to get up enough nerve to hike it without her and I couldn't do it." She grinned and said, "Then you came along."

"I wasn't the one who suggested that hike," Sloane reminded her. "That was *your* idea. You dragged me up on that mountain, and then you tricked me into falling into a bog!" She feigned anger and Lenny laughed heartily. "I am the CEO of a very important company! You completely humiliated me!" Lenny's shoulders lifted and her head rolled back she was laughing so hard.

I've never seen her like this. She must be reliving the moment. This is what she looks like when she's joyous.

Lenny glanced at her and laughed harder. She joined in, not minding at all that she was the butt of the joke. They only stopped when they couldn't breathe, both of them wearing goofy expressions on their faces.

"This is *not* what I had in mind when I brought you here," she said.

Lenny arched an eyebrow. "So, would you rather be trolling Telluride?"

"No, I'm glad we're here together."

They leaned forward at exactly the same moment for a kiss, a certain sign it was something they each wanted. She savored it, even though she thought it was probably one of the last they would share.

"You're not ready, are you?" she asked, already knowing the answer.

Lenny shook her head, and Sloane saw tears in her eyes. "I want to be," she said. "When I got in your car, I thought I could give you what you wanted."

Sloane kissed her forehead and pulled her tighter. "You are."

"No, I'm not, but nice try."

Sloane chuckled. "Okay, I admit that I'd like to get you naked and hear you moan, but I understand. I really do."

Lenny snuggled into her chest and they stretched out on the bed. "Hold me. Put your arms around me and hold me. I want to fall asleep in your arms."

Lenny's words echoed in loneliness. Sloane realized that as much as she wanted to make love to her, it was more important to extinguish the pain in her heart, and if cuddling were the answer, then so be it. She kissed her hair, wrapped her arms around her middle and curled a leg around her calf.

"Thank you," Lenny whispered.

"My pleasure," she replied. And it really was.

CHAPTER TWENTY-FOUR

Lenny awoke refreshed. Her eyelids fluttered open, and everything was strange—an unusual bed, a blanket tossed over her, the smell of rain. *Sloane.*

What would Pru think of me right now? She imagined she was somewhere clapping vigorously, just as she did whenever she watched a fabulous solo at the symphony. Pru had always been the first to jump up and shout, "Bravo!" Lenny laughed, picturing Pru giving her a standing ovation for her first night with another woman. Of course, they'd only *slept* together, but it was a step. She realized how much she missed the safety and security she felt from the curve of another body against her own.

She'd only woken up once—when she felt Sloane's hand caressing her buttocks. She remained still, pretending to be asleep and enjoying the light touch. She'd imagined Sloane's fingers trailing down her ass, exploring between her legs. The thought had made her tingle, and she'd almost grabbed her hand—almost. Then fear had overtaken her and she'd remained immobile, secretly hoping Sloane would take advantage of her, which she didn't. Eventually her hand had gone still and they'd fallen back to sleep, Lenny regretting she'd been too chicken to act.

But she wasn't afraid now. She thought again of Sloane touching her—and began touching herself. She was already wet. She heard Sloane on the phone, and the sound of her voice aroused her even more. She couldn't make out the words, but the cadence of her speech fed her imagination. She knew what Sloane would say to her, how she would make her come.

I don't want to lose this moment.

She stripped off her clothes and padded through the cottage. The French doors were open and Sloane was pacing the length of the patio talking on her cell. She was arguing with someone, but she was trying to modulate her voice, probably because she thought Lenny was still asleep.

"Look, I'll get it for a song. The woman who owns it is in distress. She's a mental case still pining over her lost partner. The cost of the renovation will be covered by the deal I'm going to make. It's the right move, Steve. Trust me."

Lenny bit her lip. She shouldn't be listening. Eavesdropping was unrefined and distasteful.

"They're a bunch of hicks. We'll incentivize the deal, but we'll get what we want. I've got everything under control. Believe me."

She couldn't listen to another word. She redressed and disappeared out the front door. She headed down the road to Main Street, numb. *How could I be so foolish?*

She'd find a coffee shop and call Seth to come pick her up. As luck would have it, Dreama's colorful van was parked in front of the New Age shop that sold incense. Everyone knew her ride because it was covered in a mural of a lake. She crossed the street just as Dreama came out.

"Hi, Lenny! What are you doing in Ouray so early?"

"Uh, well, I stayed with a friend last night after the concert. Are you going back through Pinedale?"

"Yes, I'm in a hurry, though." She motioned to the back of the van and Lenny noticed several cages full of butterflies. "They're for my show tomorrow night. You *are* coming to see *The Harvest*, aren't you?"

"I wouldn't miss it. Could you give me a lift?"

"Of course!"

Dreama spilled all of the details about *The Harvest* on the ten-mile ride back to Lenny's place, so much so that Lenny thought she could skip the performance. When Dreama dropped her off, she couldn't bring herself to go inside. She studied the house Pru had insisted they buy. *Pru's house*. It had always been Pru's dream, all of it. Periodically she resented Pru for dying and saddling her with the shop, the huge house, the debt and the job of mayor.

That would have never happened if you hadn't died, Pru. Why the hell didn't you take care of yourself?

She needed to shake her anger before she went inside and faced Regina and Seth. She trudged up the familiar path toward the top of the hill, sorry that Rocket wasn't beside her to enjoy the walk. She'd make it up to him later.

Seth, Regina and Rocket—the three not on her shit list. She was angry with Pru, she hated Sloane, but she was furious with herself for not seeing Sloane for what she really was: an unscrupulous, conniving, greedy bitch with absolutely no compassion for anyone else. She'd toyed with her emotional state. Lenny was ashamed to think the first person she'd turned to since Pru's death was a shallow narcissist.

What she couldn't understand was how Sloane could be so horrible to Regina. She'd manipulated her in unspeakable ways. Seth was right. She shook her head and sighed. He understood people in ways she did not. She'd have to go back and tell them what she'd overheard and what a miserable human being Sloane really was.

She should convene the town council for an emergency session to vote on the Wilderness Campaign store. Now that she and Carlotta were on the same side, she had no doubt the council would show up with an hour's notice, ready to vote no. Afterward Maddie could draft the official letter to Sloane McHenry, CEO of Wilderness Campaign.

Then again, I might enjoy writing that letter myself, just the mental case mayor letting the big shot corporate executive know that her plan to invade our little hick town had failed miserably.

She grinned, picturing Sloane reading the terse and succinct note. Maybe she'd write it on a napkin from Kate's Place. That would be what hicks would do.

She reached the top of the trail. Carlotta's driveway was in sight. She trotted over to the intercom and pressed the button that sat next to the enormous gate.

"Ochoa residence," a voice said. "May I help you?"

"This is Lenny Barclay. I need to speak with Carlotta if she's home."

"One moment, please."

While she waited, Lenny gazed at the valley and tiny Pinedale in the distance, the community she'd vowed to support and guide. She'd never really taken her job as mayor very seriously. Perhaps it was time to change her attitude.

"Please come in," the voice squawked, and the enormous gate rolled open.

It took another two minutes to walk the distance to the front of the mansion. Carlotta stood in the doorway wearing her standard golf attire. She'd looked exactly the same all those times she'd stopped by to pick up Pru for a round of golf. *Pru had always looked so happy on Saturday mornings as she laced up her shoes and grabbed her bag. Did they really just golf?*

"Lenny, what a pleasant surprise. What are you doing here?"

"Did you have an affair with Pru?"

"Why...why would you think that?" she sputtered.

"I always wondered and there was talk."

She'd never seen Carlotta speechless. "I...uh—"

"I'm not mad, Carlotta, at least not at you. Lately, you're the one person that I *get*. I understand you. You are exactly who you present yourself to be, and I respect that. So you can tell me, and I won't slap you across the face."

Carlotta nodded slightly, and she felt her world collapse.

"Come inside. We're not going to talk about this at the front door."

She led her to a luxurious couch in the TV room and headed to the wet bar. "I know it's early, but I think you need this," she said, handing her a highball of whiskey. "It was the shortest affair in history, just twice in the same week," she continued. "You'd gone on that rappelling trip with the hiking club, the one Pru wanted you to skip?"

She remembered it well. Pru had insisted she was too old to be rappelling off the side of a mountain with people half her age. She'd gone to spite her and come back with a broken ankle. Apparently Pru had dealt with her anger in a different way.

"She was so upset that it ruined our golf game. We came back here and made mint juleps. One thing led to another. Afterward, I don't think she was sure how she felt. She was devoted to you, but here's a newsflash, Lenny: you're not that easy to live with. That's what I learned during all those weekends of golfing with your partner. I never would have told you this if you hadn't shown up this morning, but Pru golfed as a way to survive you. It was her way of achieving balance."

"Did she say that?"

"She didn't have to. She said everything else. I was like her therapist, listening to her complaints, her concerns about your relationship and her unfulfilled needs." She took a sip and added, "I know most of your secrets, Lenny."

The alcohol was muddling the swirl of emotions she felt. She'd never really worried that Pru had cheated on her. It had been just a little annoying thought, and while it never had gone away, there was so much happiness between them, and in those moments she'd been certain it wasn't true.

She knows my secrets. What the hell does that mean? Does she know all of my fears? How I worry about being a bad mother to Seth? How I feel like a failure for never finishing college? How I told Pru I wasn't good enough for her? Did Pru really tell her those things? Was I the subject of their pillow talk?

An image of Pru riding Carlotta filled her brain and wouldn't disappear. Pru was a good lover but not adventurous. Lenny had forgiven her that point, telling herself that Pru's fine qualities compensated for her disinterest in trying new positions or incorporating sex toys into their bedroom life. *What if Carlotta got her to do things I couldn't?*

She poured a third drink, determined to push the image away. "If you fulfilled her unfulfilled needs, why did it end so fast?"

Carlotta stared at her glass. "Because she was too good to cheat. After our second tryst, she knew she couldn't continue, even though we were having a great time in bed. You see, I *am* an amazing lover." Lenny gave her a sharp look and she grinned. "It's true."

She couldn't parlay or offer witticisms. She took another sip and put the glass aside. If she drank any more she might be sick. *Why did I ask? Why did I come here?*

Carlotta moved against her and whispered in her ear. "You know, the ironic part is that I've always had it bad for you. Pru was my golfing buddy, but you were the one I wanted. You were the rebel, always living on the edge. I'll bet you like to have a lot of fun in bed."

She kissed her earlobe and nibbled her neck. Lenny knew she should stop it, but maybe this was why she'd pressed the intercom button in the first place. *I want Pru to suffer the way I'm suffering.*

When Carlotta climbed on top of her, she was already half naked, her perfectly augmented breasts teasing Lenny mercilessly. Lenny cupped them and sucked on each nipple tenderly. Carlotta cooed and ground her pelvis into Lenny's thigh. They found a rhythm, and Lenny smiled at Carlotta, sitting on the edge of ecstasy—until she came hard. Her body trembled and she crumpled against Lenny's shoulder.

"Hmm. Just what I wanted this morning."

She unbuttoned Lenny's shirt and looked up, asking permission. Lenny closed her eyes and lolled her head against the couch. For a fleeting moment she pictured herself naked at Sloane's cottage, filled with the anticipation of what the morning might bring.

Carlotta's teeth nipped at each breast as she slid off the couch between her legs. When she tugged at Lenny's waistband, her only response was to lift her hips so Carlotta could peel off her shorts and underwear.

She turned to the side and stared into a mirror across the room—at two half-naked, middle-aged women having sex on a couch.

I'm not really here. I'm not that woman in the mirror.

With her thighs spread open and a woman she despised about to go down on her, a thought occurred to her: she was giving Carlotta what she wouldn't give Sloane.

Process

Calculating how goods or services will be provided to the customer is often the key decision to a venture's success.

CHAPTER TWENTY-FIVE

Regina checked her watch again. It was nearly noon and there was still no sign of Lenny. She wasn't answering her cell and they'd given up waiting for her at the house and decided to head into town and continue working on the store. She imagined Lenny and Sloane might still be curled up in bed, which wasn't a horrible thought, but she knew Sloane's track record with women. Lenny was almost certainly going to get hurt. She needed to talk to both of them as soon as possible.

She added some more detail to her floor plan sketch, thinking it would be great to include platforms for flashy merchandise. Customers enjoyed visiting different levels of a shop. It made them feel as if they were on an adventure. Seth leaned over her shoulder and wrapped his arms around her waist.

"Are you sure we want to do this much planning, Reg? What if Carlotta or Sloane manage to pull it away from Mom?"

"They won't," she said assuredly. "Pru's Curious Curios is going to be around for a long time."

"Can you put a statistic to that?"

"One hundred percent sure," she said, and she was. *I know what you're up to, Sloane.*

"If you say so, then I believe it."

He kissed her once more and resumed his handy work, leaving her to create the vision of what would be. She knew he was a jack-of-all-trades and there wasn't anything he couldn't fix or build. It was one of the benefits of never picking a career. He'd worked for so many tradesmen that he'd perfected the "Do-it-Yourself" motto. She watched him guide the circular saw through a two-by-four and smiled. They would have Pru's back in business in a month.

The doorbell jingled and Lenny appeared. Her hair was wet from a shower, and she wore a smug grin. Rocket ran to her, and she bent down to scratch his ears and give him a treat.

"Well, where have you been?" she teased.

"Many places." She surveyed their progress and said, "This is going to be what Pru wanted. Carlotta won't be able to take us over, if she still wants to."

Regina looked surprised. "What does that mean?"

"It's been a productive morning. Carlotta and I have developed an...*understanding*. And Sloane is out."

"Out?"

She crossed her arms in a defiant pose. Seth appeared from the other room and gave her a hug. "You both need to hear this. Sloane McHenry is a conniving bitch who has no regard for this town, for me, and I'm sorry to add, no regard for you either, Regina."

She was stunned. "What? I thought the two of you—"

"No, that didn't happen. Almost, but no." Lenny threw a glance at Seth. "Sorry, son, but your mother's human."

He shrugged and said, "Mom, it's no big deal. I don't want you to be alone."

"Wait, wait," she interrupted. "Why is Wilderness Campaign out? How did that happen?"

Lenny took a breath and moved to a stool as if she were about to tell a long story. "I overheard her this morning on the phone when I got up. She was obviously talking to someone about Pinedale, about *me* and about how easy it was to buy up the shop from a bunch of *hicks*."

Seth threw up his hands. "I knew it! I knew she was just using you, Mom."

Regina shook her head. "Lenny, no, you've misunderstood—"

"No, I heard her quite clearly."

Seth came to the defense of his mother. "Reg, I know she's like your aunt, but c'mon."

Everything was spinning out of control, but she needed the rest of the story. "Put that aside for a moment. You said it was an eventful morning. What else happened? Did you confront her?"

Lenny looked away, embarrassed. "No, I just left. I was too mad. I got a ride back to town and took a walk. I wound up at Carlotta's and we…talked. We called an emergency meeting of the town council, and we voted Wilderness Campaign out. There won't be a store here, Regina. I'm sorry if that hurts you professionally, but we're not doing it."

"Good for you, Mom," Seth said.

She closed her eyes and processed. From Lenny's body language and tone, she knew there was something she wasn't telling her, something about Carlotta. She didn't recognize how dangerous Carlotta was to her personal livelihood, of this Regina was certain. The point was that they had secured the votes to drive out Wilderness Campaign. She had to find Sloane.

"Honey, are you okay?" Seth asked, rubbing her back. "I know this is a lot to take in."

"I have to go. I'll be back."

She headed out the door, ignoring their parting questions. She climbed into the Jetta and sent Sloane a text. *You're about to lose Schoolhouse Emporium.*

She turned onto the highway and her phone chimed with Sloane's response—the address where she was staying in Ouray.

* * *

Sloane was putting the last of her suitcases into the Range Rover when she pulled up. "Where are you going?"

Sloane slammed the back door shut and said nothing. Regina followed her into the cottage and watched her down two vikes with a swig of Red Bull.

"You didn't answer my question. Where are you going?"

"Home."

"I know what you did. I figured it out."

"Good for you." She dropped the empty can into the trash, grabbed her purse and headed out the door with Regina close behind.

"You're walking away from the deal."

"Yup."

"How's that going to look in the monthlies, Sloane? What will the board say when they see all the entries for travel, my time, R and D's time, *your* time and there's no return." She stepped in front of her and prevented her from opening the driver's door. "How will you explain the loss?"

Finally she looked up. There was something wrong with her eyes. They were red. *Had she been crying?*

"I'll think of something. As for your job, do you want to come back to work for me or not?"

"I don't know. I want to talk about what you did."

"I don't. Now, please get out of the way."

"No, I won't. You totally played me that night at the hotel. You acted so surprised about Carlotta, calling R and D and pretending to be upset, convincing me that you wanted Pru's place." She shook her head in disbelief. "I want to talk about what this deal is really all about. I got so caught up in the personal side of this trip that I didn't look closely at the numbers." She rolled her eyes. "I can't believe I ignored the figures. *Me.* I can't believe that I didn't see it."

"We see what we want to see."

"That's true, and right now no one but me knows the truth. Lenny and Seth think you're a conniving bitch, and Carlotta thinks she has the upper hand, which, after this morning, I believe she does."

"What happened?" she asked apprehensively.

"Apparently Lenny heard you talking on the phone this morning. I'm guessing you were talking to someone on the board?"

"I was debriefing Steve."

Steve was the board chairman and an arrogant chauvinist who constantly questioned Sloane's ability to run the company. "You called the town a bunch of hicks, offended Lenny who overheard you, and she ran straight to Carlotta."

Her eyes widened. "She went to Carlotta?"

"Yes, and I'm not sure what happened between them."

Her face darkened and she looked away. "I can guess. So they're together now."

"Well, they're aligned, and they called an emergency meeting of the town council and voted down the Wilderness Campaign deal."

She shrugged. "So what."

"Why didn't you tell me the truth? Why didn't you tell me you were secretly after Schoolhouse Emporium? Why all the subterfuge?"

She didn't answer right away, and when she finally looked at Regina, it was with a tenderness Regina had never seen. "You probably won't believe me, sweetie, but for the first time, this wasn't about the deal. This was about you."

"Me?"

"Your happiness. I couldn't understand it, but I saw how much you loved Seth, so I wanted you to be happy."

"Even though you don't approve of him?"

She winced at the truth. "That was before I met his mother. Lenny isn't like anyone I've ever known. I saw in her what you see in Seth, and I wanted to help. I know you're at your best when you have a cause to champion. So I gave you one. I knew if we were in competition, you'd do everything you could to win, and you did." She offered a sad smile. "I never wanted to purchase Pru's, you know that. When I realized there was an optimal location in Pinedale, though, I saw the chance to get a store and help you. Once I met that snake Carlotta, then I *really* wanted you to win." She sighed. "But I guess it's all for naught. Damn it."

Regina couldn't believe what she was hearing. Sloane wasn't altruistic—unless things were different.

"Does this have anything to do with the plane crash?"

She shrugged and kicked the driveway gravel. "Maybe. I guess. I made a promise as that plane was going down that I would be better to you. I guess that's most important at the end of the day. We may have lost the store, but you got your family."

She stepped past Regina and opened the SUV's door. "I need to get back to Boston. I can spend the plane ride thinking of excuses for Steve."

"What about Lenny? You need to talk to her."

"Why? She hates me, and maybe that's a good thing," she added with a little laugh.

She wasn't buying any of it. Sloane was nervous. She was fidgety and she was hardly looking at her. "You're scared."

"I am not," she scoffed. "That doesn't even make sense."

"You said that when you met Lenny you understood what I saw in Seth. You're attracted to the same qualities in Lenny."

"You're twisting my words. Just because I understand what you see in Seth *doesn't* mean I want Lenny."

"So you're fine with her hooking up with Carlotta."

She frowned and looked away. "What she does with Carlotta is her business."

"And you're not jealous."

"Why would I be jealous? I have no reason to be jealous. She can do whatever she wants and so can I. Last night we wanted each other, or at least I wanted her and she just wanted to cuddle. But if twelve hours later she wants to be a slut and run to another bed, doing God knows what, probably because it's been so long since she's gotten any at all, then that is her business!" she shouted.

"A slut?"

"Isn't that what you call a woman who traipses from bed to bed?"

"Does that make you a slut?"

Her face turned crimson and she hissed, "Yes, I am a slut and I don't give a shit. If you decide you still want your job, send me a text." She yanked the door closed and sped out of the driveway. Gravel flew everywhere, and when the cloud of dust disappeared, she was gone.

CHAPTER TWENTY-SIX

Sloane decided the Montrose Airport was a joke. The guy who checked her bags grabbed his vest and fluorescent batons and headed out to the tarmac to help direct the plane. The voice over the loudspeaker was not computerized but a live person who forgot to mute her microphone when placing her coffee order with a co-worker. The entire airport learned she favored triple mocha cappuccinos.

The thought of a five-hour drive back to Denver was totally unappealing. Originally, she'd flown in to Denver and checked on two other Wilderness Campaign locations, but now she just wanted out of Colorado. So after haggling with the rental car company and paying an extra fee for abandoning the Range Rover in a different city, she found herself sitting in the tiny dining area nursing a beer and waiting for her flight to Portland. She wasn't thrilled about going to Portland since it was in the opposite direction from Boston; however, her travel agent had already found a connecting flight for her, and she'd be back in her own bed by nightfall.

She rummaged through her bag and found two vikes from the stash her assistant had FedExed her. *Thank god for overnight delivery.* She washed them down with the beer and powered up her laptop. She needed to work. She would spend the next several hours crafting a memo to the board explaining the ill-fated attempt at opening a Wilderness Campaign in western Colorado and what went wrong—the unbending town council, the presence of small-town drama and politics and the most incompetent mayor she'd ever met. Yes, she could place much of the blame at Lenny's feet. She'd attach her ridiculous résumé to the memo and that would be enough. They would definitely understand.

In just a few hours Lenny would be out of her life for good. Of course, Regina might be gone as well. Her gaze wandered away from the laptop screen and settled on the distant Rockies. She'd always loved the mountains, and Regina was a kindred spirit. How many hikes had they taken together? Throughout her teenage years they'd always found a week in the summer to traipse through a forest, climb a mountain or raft down a river. When was the last time they'd shared a meal over a campfire? She tried to count backward but lost track. After college, Regina had become a businesswoman and finally a girlfriend to Seth. Sloane had consoled herself with a bevy of honeys who were good hiking companions and lovers. She could see their smiling faces illuminated by a multitude of campfires.

It was proof that Lenny was wrong. She could live in the moment. She'd had *many* moments with a variety of women of every race, creed and religion imaginable. It had been a lot of fun.

It was hard to believe she'd been curled up with Lenny less than twenty-four hours before. She'd been completely surprised by her own willingness to give up control. Instead of seducing her, which she was certain she could have done if she'd really tried, she'd held her in her arms all night. Of course, she'd caressed and fondled her a little while she snored lightly, but that was nothing.

The cappuccino-loving woman announced the flight to Portland was boarding. She packed up her laptop, realizing she'd never opened a single document. She found her seat on the small plane, sandwiched between a teenager wearing headphones and an elderly woman who was already pulling out her knitting. Warning bells went off in her head. She could tell the lady was a talker, and she would need to keep busy the entire time if she didn't want to find herself looking at every family picture the woman had managed to save on her "new-fangled" iPhone that she barely knew how to operate.

She avoided eye contact as she dropped into her seat and immediately withdrew the folder on Pinedale. She knew it by heart, but until the plane reached ten thousand feet and she could once again bury herself in technology, she'd read it once more. Perhaps there were a few other nuggets she could share with the board. She imagined Steve would be the only one to give her significant grief, and he'd probably renew his request to remove her as CEO. She hated giving him any ammunition, and in retrospect, she wished she'd never launched her plan, despite the positive outcome for Regina and Seth.

That damn plane crash.

If the plane had never crashed, she never would have sought out Alexandra, the two-hundred-and-fifty-dollar-an-hour therapist who told her she needed to listen to her conscience. Up until the crash she had convinced herself she didn't have one. The therapist convinced her otherwise, and she'd looked for an opportunity to greatly improve Regina's life.

And what an inconvenience this has been!

It wasn't until summer and her trek to Colorado that the Pinedale opportunity emerged. The Schoolhouse Emporium was an amazing building and a decent choice for a Wilderness Campaign store. The R and D team had done a full study of the town, and it had been true serendipity to learn that Lenny Barclay, Seth's mother, was the owner of a rival business. She knew all about Regina's constant worries regarding Seth and his mother and her belief that if he and Lenny were not reunited, her marriage to Seth was doomed—at least statistically. Countless times she had watched Regina stare at the greeting card she'd pilfered from Seth's shoebox of memories. She loved her statistics, but she loved him more. Sloane had easily manipulated the situation, and now they were together. Yet she and Regina were apart.

Maybe that's the cost. You'll just have to live with it.

And then there was Lenny.

She felt a tap on her shoulder. "Excuse me, dear. I've dropped my needle on top of your bag. Could you retrieve it for me?"

Without a glance, she reached for the needle and held it up for the woman.

"Thank you, dear. This damn arthritis is a bitch. I don't even know what the hell I'm knitting anymore."

Despite the woman's colorful vocabulary, she refused to be drawn into the conversation. She merely nodded and pretended to read. When the flight attendant directed everyone to put away all electronics, she felt another tap on her shoulder.

"Excuse me, dear. Can you sit back for a second?"

She leaned back just as a knitting needle passed her face and poked the teenaged girl on the other side of her in the arm.

She jumped and pulled the headphones off. "Ouch, Grandma! You didn't have to do that."

"You need to pay attention to the announcements or they'll throw you off the plane, or worse, they'll make you ride with the luggage."

The girl's eyes widened. "They wouldn't do that, would they?"

She looked at Sloane, who shrugged and said, "You never know. I heard of a guy who got in trouble and had to clean up all the barf bags."

The girl made a face. "That's gross."

Sloane looked at the grandma and said, "Would you like to sit next to your granddaughter?"

She shook her head. "Not particularly. We bought these seats apart for a reason. I'm sorry you're caught in the middle, but frankly, dear, after the time I've had with that wild child, I'm not that sorry."

"I can hear you," the girl growled.

"Well, there's a first," Grandma replied. "Besides, you're supposed to be reading. Remember, that was our deal. You put off your summer reading and promised me you'd do it on the plane ride home. Well, that's now, missy. Get to it."

Sloane took a breath. The vikes were starting to work, but she guessed she'd need at least two bourbons if she were going to get through the plane ride without saying something incredibly rude.

Why should I care? I don't know these people. I did my good deed. Carlotta can have her!

The girl muttered something under her breath and shoved the headphones into her backpack. She pulled out three paperbacks: *Gulliver's Travels, Othello* and *Effectively Using the Seven Ps in Any Business Venture.* She instantly set aside the literary classics and picked up the business book.

The last title got Sloane's attention. "What grade are you in?" she asked.

"Eighth."

"You're reading about the Seven Ps in eighth grade?"

"She's gifted," Grandma said proudly.

"Stop saying that," the girl said flatly without looking up from the book.

"Well, you are," Grandma affirmed. She turned to Sloane and added, "She started reading novels when she was five, and by the time she was in sixth grade, she'd decided she wanted to own a business. She invented this wonderful candy…" Grandma leaned forward. "What did you call it, Allie?"

"Combusto," Allie said in a bored voice.

"Yes, that was it. It was this fizzy stuff that melted in your mouth. It wasn't that it tasted so great, but the kids loved the feel of it. You see, Allie's parents are chemists so she knows all about combustion. Her real name is Allele."

"Allele?" She glanced at Allie, who remained glued to her book. "So are you still making Combusto?"

"No."

She rolled her eyes. *Teenagers.* "Why not?"

"Too much overhead and too time consuming."

"So did a teacher assign the Seven Ps?"

"No, it was my choice. Free reading."

"So, out of anything you could read, you picked a book about the Seven Ps."

"Yeah. I've already read it."

"Allie, you weren't supposed to pick a book you've already read," her grandmother chided.

Her long dishwater-blond hair hung loosely over her shoulders and was in desperate need of a brushing. Several buttons were pinned to her jean jacket with sentiments favoring free thought or self-expression. A few contained some inappropriate language. *I guess Grandma hasn't noticed those.*

"Do you have a business now?" she asked. When Allie's gaze shifted slowly from the page, she said, "I'm asking because I own a company, and I'm always looking for investments."

"What company do you own?" Grandma asked.

"I'm the CEO of Wilderness Campaign. Have you heard of it?"

"Isn't it the big camping store with all of the taxidermy animals in it?" Allie asked in a disgusted tone.

"Yes, it is, and those animals bring in a lot of revenue. Parents bring their children in to look at the animals, and they inevitably buy something."

"It's a draw," Allie said.

She smiled. "Exactly."

Allie narrowed her eyes. "That's what I need...a draw."

"What are you trying to sell?"

"Uh, I'm not going to tell you. You might steal my idea."

She laughed. "I assure you, I won't."

"You never know. It's happened before."

"Well, I'll tell you," Grandma interjected. "She's designed a backpack lock so kids can keep their stuff safe when they're at school. Apparently this generation has no scruples and steals from each other constantly."

Allie gasped and dropped her book on her lap. "Grandma, don't say any more. We don't know her."

Sloane reached inside her purse and handed a business card to each of them. "Sloane McHenry. I am who I say I am. Do you have any pictures of your lock or perhaps a prototype?"

Allie wore a look of suspicion that reminded Sloane of the first time she'd met Regina. She'd been so hurt by the death of her parents. Trust had not come easily. She could see Allie was the same way.

She fixed her gaze solidly on her and said, "This flight is approximately two hours long. During a normal day I rarely agree to meet with salespeople and listen to their pitches, and on those occasions when I do, they're lucky if I don't toss them out after five minutes." She gestured at the plane and said, "You, however, have me as a captive audience, and I have offered to listen to you. I can think of at least fifty salespeople who would sell their own children for the seat you're sitting in right now. Either start talking or I'm getting back to work."

Perhaps it was a sign, but at that very moment the captain informed the passengers they could use their electronics. Allie pulled out her cell phone, pulled up her photo gallery and started her pitch.

CHAPTER TWENTY-SEVEN

Lenny swerved to avoid a pothole deep enough to break an axle. Dreama had placed cones by most of the hazards on the dirt road that led from the highway to her farm, but the summer rainstorms had mercilessly slashed the earth, leaving deep, corrugated ruts.

"This road is terrible," Seth commented from the backseat, Rocket at his side. "I'm glad you're driving, Mom."

"It's worse than usual," Lenny agreed. "Wait until we have to come back in the dark."

He had offered to drive, but she insisted she be the one to chauffeur them to Dreama's show, *The Harvest*. She remembered the first time she and Pru had gone to the studio. The road had been nearly impassable, and they'd come upon some of their neighbors whose little car had gotten stuck in a mud bog. After that everyone told Dreama she had to do something about the road or no one would come to her shows.

The road forked at an enormous sign that spelled out DreamaWorks in twisted sheet metal, and she veered left.

"So, what is this place, Mom? Are you taking us to some sort of compound? Are we joining a cult?"

"Oh, honey," Regina said. "I've met her. She's just an eccentric artist."

"That's a good way to describe her," Lenny agreed. "She came to Pinedale nearly thirty years ago after she suffered a mental breakdown."

"A breakdown? What happened?" Regina asked.

"She worked at one of the big companies on Wall Street. She had a corner office and was described as a wunderkind. She was a millionaire at thirty. This was during the junk bond era."

"Oh," Seth said. "I think I can guess where this is going."

She nodded. "At some point she realized how many people her company was defrauding, had a breakdown and then walked away just before the whole thing came tumbling down."

"That was smart," Regina said.

She pulled onto the shoulder behind a Lexus. "She is smart. She took her money and got out. She came here to pursue her two passions, metal work and drama. She turned this farm into an artists' colony, and people with different talents come here to work. Some stay for a week, some for a month and a few came and never left. She's created a self-sustaining community."

Regina glanced at the row of cars that stretched to the farm's entrance. Several groups of people traipsed along the road headed for the show. "This is a very impressive turnout."

A series of life-size animal figures made of dark wood greeted them. Two bears faced each other, their front paws touching to form an entry arch.

"Dreama has many followers. People fly in from the East Coast to see her shows."

"Are they really that good?" Seth asked.

She chuckled. "I can't say. It's always entertaining, that's for sure, but that could be because of the homemade wine she serves."

"She makes wine too?" Regina asked.

"Uh-huh, and it's potent. After two glasses you'll be feeling no pain."

They followed the crowd through the barn and past several displays of artwork for sale. Dozens of people swarmed the booths, eyeing the paintings, photographs, jewelry and metal work of all shapes and sizes. The designs ranged from drop earrings to towering sculptures.

"She really has a keen business sense," Regina observed. "Display the goods for sale in the most populated area."

Seth threw his arm around her and announced, "I love it when you talk business-speak."

She poked him and Lenny smiled. They were so happy together. *It's because of Sloane.* Regina had told her about Sloane's master plan, and she'd explained that the phone conversation Lenny had overheard was merely a ruse. Sloane didn't think she was a hick. Lenny had left her a few messages to apologize, but Sloane hadn't replied.

Several people waved and called out to Lenny, and one gave her a thumbs-up. Many wore goofy expressions as if they were privy to a secret. She just kept smiling.

What's going on? It's like they've never seen me before.

Even Seth noticed and asked, "Mom, why is everyone being so weird to you?"

"I have no idea."

They exited the barn into an open amphitheater. A few hundred people were sprawled across the raked lawn, which stairstepped down to a small stage. Large burlap bags lined the stage, each imprinted with a name like barley, corn and wheat.

"How about over there?" Seth asked, pointing to a spot a few rows down.

"You two go get settled with Rocket and I'll get us some wine," Lenny said.

"Oh, none for me," Regina said. "I'll be the designated driver."

Lenny patted her arm. "It's okay, honey. I'm only going to have a tiny bit. Besides, I'm used to Dreama's wine."

Regina still looked worried. "It's just that the statistics of designated drivers who imbibe even a little indicate there's a significant increase in the likelihood of an accident."

She imagined Regina's concern had little to do with statistics and much more to do with the death of her parents on a highway. "Well, then I'll just get you two some."

Regina smiled, relieved. "Oh, okay. Are you sure? I'm happy to refrain—"

"No, sweetie. I want you and Seth to have a good time tonight. You'll probably need it to get through the performance."

They wandered into the crowd and she sighed. She wondered how often Sloane endured Regina's constant referral to statistics. Had she been this way since childhood?

She joined the end of the long line and felt a friendly hand on her bicep. A voice whispered in her ear, "Have you recovered from yesterday morning?"

Carlotta held one of Dreama's cast-iron goblets. The Endless Goblet was a marketing ploy to sell the wine. Anyone purchasing a goblet received free refills throughout the performance. From the look on Carlotta's face, Lenny guessed she was already on her second round.

"Hello, Carlotta."

"Hey, baby."

Before she could stop her, Carlotta kissed her and squeezed her ass. She quickly stepped away. "Whoa. Hold on."

"What kind of greeting is that to the woman who made you come? Where are you sitting? I'm hoping you'll invite me to join you." She stepped into her personal space and added, "I want to hold you in my arms, and when the sun goes down, who knows where I'll touch you in the dark?"

"I'm with Seth and Regina."

Carlotta took a gulp and struck a pose with her hand on her hip. "So what? He's not a little boy. It's time he knew his mother has a love life and a girlfriend."

Her volume increased and soon others were staring at them. It suddenly dawned on Lenny that her private affairs were no longer private.

"Have you been talking about us?"

"Honey, everybody is thrilled! The mayor and the leading Pinedale businesswoman becoming an item. This is great news."

Realizing that a dozen people were staring at them, she grabbed Carlotta's hand and led her behind the barn. "First, we are *not* an item. I am not your girlfriend."

"Then what was yesterday? I'm well aware that the great Lenny Barclay doesn't sleep around, so our morning tryst must have some deeper significance."

She slurred the end of her sentence and took another drink. "Here, have some. It'll make you feel better."

She held out the goblet, but Lenny shook her head. Dreama's wine was mind-blowing, and she'd promised Regina she'd be the designated driver, but more importantly, if she started drinking, she'd probably wind up naked in the barn loft with Carlotta between her legs.

"Carlotta, you can't tell people we're together. Yesterday was a moment of weakness. I was upset. You told me Pru had cheated on me, and I wanted to get back at her."

"Get back at her?" she laughed. "Earth to Lenny! She's dead. You can't get revenge on a dead person."

She winced at the rawness of the statement. "That's not what I meant, not really." She searched for the words, but she couldn't explain her actions.

I was mad at Pru, but I was even angrier at Sloane.

"Then what did you mean?" Carlotta pulled her into a tight embrace and said, "We make a great team, and we have excellent chemistry. I know you enjoyed it, Lenny. You're a much better lover than Pru."

Lenny pushed her away and wine splashed onto her western shirt.

"Hey! This is silk!"

"Stop talking about Pru. I don't want to hear you say her name ever again."

"Pru, Pru, Pru. I can say her name anytime I want. She was *my* lover too." Her lips curled into a wicked grin. "Come to think of it, now I've had you both."

Her last sentence was said with such smugness and finality that Lenny couldn't help what she did next. She grabbed the goblet and threw the wine at her. Carlotta stared at the giant red stain seeping into the silk. When she looked up, her white teeth were bared, and she growled like an animal.

She hurled herself at Lenny, and they went down. Lenny was naturally stronger, but she knew Carlotta's rage was fueled by alcohol and love of fashion. Within seconds she was pinned to the ground and Carlotta hovered over her. A crowd had gathered around them, but using their small-town wisdom, they didn't intervene. They knew neither woman would really hurt the other, so they just stood and watched.

"You bitch!" Carlotta screamed.

"Get off me!" she cried, trying to wriggle free.

Carlotta pressed her knees into Lenny's thighs, and she yelped in pain.

"That's gonna leave a mark."

"It won't be the only one," she hissed. "You are mine."

Carlotta tightened her grip on Lenny's wrists and smashed their lips together. Lenny's emotions fell into a whirlpool as she continued to protest.

I don't like Carlotta. We will never be friends, and we'll never have a relationship. If I'm honest with myself, I'll probably never have another relationship, and if I do, it won't be what I had with Pru. Sloane would never want a relationship, but I didn't even give her a chance. She wanted me. I was the one who pushed her away, but she's gone now. So why not enjoy a little fun with Carlotta? She's an excellent lover, and if I stopped fighting her, I'd really be enjoying this kiss. Maybe…

"Ouch!" Carlotta screamed and scrambled off Lenny.

The crowd was laughing hysterically. When Lenny sat up, she saw Rocket close by, his little body in fighting stance.

"Your dog bit me!" she cried.

"Hell, Carlotta, he just nipped you," a man shouted.

"Yeah, it was nothing," someone else agreed.

Seth and Regina emerged from the crowd. Their expressions suggested they had no idea what to make of the scene. "Mom, what is this? I thought you were getting wine."

A voice cried, "It's Carlotta who got the wine!" and everyone laughed.

Dreama appeared wearing a dress made out of cornhusks. "What's going on? The show's about to start." She looked at Lenny and Carlotta on the ground. "You'll have time to profess your lady love for each other during Act Two, but not now, not before the detasseling."

Regina helped Lenny to her feet. "Is that true? Are you and Carlotta together?"

She couldn't hide her embarrassment. She glanced at the dispersing crowd, realizing how ridiculous she looked. "No, not really."

"So Sloane was right. You did hook up with Carlotta. Why am I helping you keep your store if you're just going to give it to her?"

She turned away and Seth followed her, but only after shaking his head in disgust. She looked at Rocket, who almost seemed to be smiling.

She gave him a pat on the head. "Yeah, you're a good boy. Nothing like giving a pain in the ass a pain in the ass."

CHAPTER TWENTY-EIGHT

Regina flew back to Boston on Tuesday, searching for some normalcy in her life. Seth had asked her repeatedly about what was bugging her, but she couldn't explain it. She was irritated with Sloane for lying to her, but she was also angry with Lenny, who, it seemed, had chosen Carlotta over Sloane. More than anything, though, she felt the entire week had been a personal limbo and that she'd accomplished very little as the vice president of Wilderness Campaign. As she scrolled through the seventy new emails in her inbox, her thoughts drifted further away from Colorado nearly as fast as the 747 carrying her.

Oddly missing was any communication with Sloane. There had been no texts or emails, not even regarding the other four potential locations they were currently scouting. No doubt she was still placating the board regarding the Colorado debacle, and indeed the effort could be eating up her life—all because she wanted to make Regina happy.

It wasn't easy to acknowledge how much she owed to Sloane, a woman who wasn't humble, gentle or compassionate. Yet she'd given her everything and asked for nothing in return except her loyalty. The fact that she was sitting on a plane headed home rather than helping her fiancé redesign his mother's shop proved she *was* loyal. She'd left him to help Lenny and Toby, the well-meaning but somewhat unmotivated college student, complete the store. They calculated it would be another two weeks before Pru's could reopen, just in time for the July tourist season.

She wished there was a way to make Pinedale work as a Wilderness Campaign location, and she wished Lenny and Sloane could make the personal connection they both needed. Statistically Pinedale needed the Wilderness Campaign to save its economy. Carlotta could open six more businesses, but she couldn't create enough jobs, not that she cared. She only cared about herself.

Regina tapped on her iPad and pulled up the *complete* file on Pinedale, the one she'd not seen until Sloane's secret was revealed. R and D had a thick file on Carlotta, including her personal bio and financials. She'd inherited everything from her Dollar Mart CEO husband. There were several photos of them together cutting ribbons at store openings and standing arm and arm at various charity events. After he died, she continued to run the company, and while she owned three businesses in Pinedale, she regularly trotted around the United States opening new Dollar Mart stores.

Regina tapped through the photo gallery, doubting she'd learn anything meaningful. The dirt was probably in the financials, but until she was back in her office sitting at her desk, she didn't want to deal with anything that detailed. She quickly scrolled through the last fifteen pictures and was about to give up when something occurred to her. She started back at the beginning of the gallery, paying attention this time to the background of each photo. She smiled when she spotted the pattern. In the background of several Dollar Mart openings was a Happy Burger Joint.

"There has to be a connection," she said, pulling her headphones and a pad of paper from her carry-on. She cued up her classical playlist and began to uncover what Carlotta wanted to hide.

* * *

She went straight from the airport to the office, determined to find Sloane. Perhaps she could convince her to pack a bag quickly and head back to Colorado that night. She flew past Cullin, the assistant she shared with Sloane, and into her office, unceremoniously dropping all of her belongings onto the leather couch before she swung open the connecting door. Surprisingly, Sloane wasn't at her desk. Cullin appeared behind her, holding a message.

"Where's Sloane?"

He handed her the message. "I've already made your travel arrangements."

Go home and do your laundry. I expect you on the morning flight to McMinnville, Oregon. Cullin has all the details.

"What's in Oregon?" she asked.

"Don't know. Sloane called this morning and told me to get this to you ASAP."

"Has she been in the last few days?"

He shook his head. "No, she never came back to Boston."

"What? She left Colorado three days ago."

He shrugged. "I have no idea." He leaned closer and whispered, "I do know that Steve has called five times, and he's pretty upset. He's asking for an unscheduled board meeting."

* * *

She spent the evening doing her laundry and sorting through the stack of mail she and Seth had received in their absence. The dog sitter was happy at the prospect of making more cash, but Regina noticed her pets were mopey when they saw her repacking the suitcases she'd just unpacked.

She tried to call Sloane, unsuccessfully, and when she sent a text, all she got in return was a terse, simple message. *Get here and I'll explain.* She rolled her eyes. Typical Sloane. So she was incredibly surprised when the phone chimed again and Sloane sent a follow-up message. *I love you.* Something was definitely going on.

"Do you know anyone in McMinnville, Oregon?" she asked Lenny on the speakerphone when she called Seth that night.

"No, why?"

"Because Sloane is in McMinnville, and I've been ordered there tomorrow."

"Ordered there?" he laughed. "Wow, that didn't take long. She gives up on Colorado and sets her sights on Oregon."

"I hope that's not it. We can't give up."

"What are you talking about, Regina?" Lenny asked. "The town council voted down Wilderness Campaign. They won't go for a chain."

"What if I told you that's been Carlotta's plan all along?"

"What?" she cried. "How?"

"Didn't you say she just bought the storefront next to the Happy Burger Joint on Harrison?"

"Yes, she's telling everyone she's putting in another restaurant."

"Uh-huh. How big is that space?"

"It's pretty big. We were all surprised, but everyone was okay—"

"Because you thought it would be better to have Carlotta there rather than another person with a chain."

"Uh, yeah. How did you know that?"

"Lenny, she's going to put in a Dollar Mart."

"She can't do that!"

"Actually, she can. And there's more."

When Lenny said nothing, Regina asked, "Are you guys still there?"

Seth finally interjected. "Mom's listening, hon, but she went and got the whiskey. She's pouring herself a shot. So what else have you learned?"

"The parent company of Happy Burger Joint is Dollar Mart. Carlotta's been telling everyone she hates chains, but she's the one who brought in the Happy Burger, hoping no one would ever pick up on the connection. In the fine print it talks about subsidiaries, but the bottom line is that she purchased that property as the Dollar Mart CEO. I guess no one caught that." In the background she heard Lenny shouting profanity, and then Rocket began to howl. "I'm sorry," she added over the din.

"It's not your fault, Regina," Lenny bellowed, "but I'm going to crucify Carlotta."

"Well, hold on. Don't do anything yet. I think Sloane's up to something, and that's how McMinnville's involved."

"Are you sure, honey?" Seth asked suspiciously. "Maybe it's not even related."

"I think it is."

"Well, you need to figure it out quickly. We had some news out here too."

"Oh?"

"Carlotta and her buddies called for an unscheduled town council meeting for this Thursday. Seems they've all conveniently planned vacations for the end of the month. They've put the tax grace period on the agenda."

"That's two days from now. Shit."

"You got that right!" Lenny shouted. It sounded as if she was already inebriated.

"I'm going to text Sloane. She needs to know the time frame."

Lenny continued to shout, but Regina could tell Seth had taken the phone outside. "Reg, I really hope Sloane's not going to let us down. It'll crush Mom."

"Don't worry, babe. We'll take down Carlotta and then fix Lenny's love life."

"I take it you have a plan?"

"Don't I always?"

* * *

Wednesday morning's trip to McMinnville seemed to take forever. She had to fly to Portland and then rent a car for the hour drive south. She realized her destination wasn't an office but a residence, a fact that was confirmed when she pulled up in front of a simple one-story ranch house with yellow siding. Parked in the driveway was Sloane's trademark Range Rover rental so she knew she was in the right place. She just didn't know why.

A woman in her early forties answered the door. When she said she was looking for Sloane McHenry, the woman nodded, clearly expecting her.

"I'm Dawn. They're around back in the shop."

She followed her down the driveway and into the backyard. A light rain began to fall and they quickened their pace toward a building with a single window. A large fluorescent light hung from the ceiling and two people were huddled together.

Dawn opened the door and announced, "Regina's here, Sloane."

The room held all kinds of tools and machinery for different types of repair. In the center was a table with a computer. A young girl who bore a striking resemblance to Dawn was holding up a piece of metal and showing it to someone on the computer. Sloane stood beside her, and when she saw Regina, she came and gave her a hug.

"Hi, I'm glad you're here."

Sloane looked as if she hadn't slept in days. She wore her hiking shorts and a wrinkled T-shirt, which Regina guessed was the last clean item in her suitcase.

"What's going on? Do you know Steve is about ready to blow a gasket?"

She nodded and pulled her to the table. The girl looked up at her curiously. "Allie, I'd like you to meet Regina. Regina, this is Allie. She's our new business partner."

"Hey, don't forget me!" a voice said from the computer.

Regina leaned over and looked at the screen. Dreama was smiling at her. "Hi, Regina. Did you like *The Harvest*?"

CHAPTER TWENTY-NINE

Lenny had been given one simple direction by Regina: just go about your business and don't think about the store. So that was what she was doing, despite the fact that she'd spent three sleepless nights worrying that by the end of the day, she would be a few technicalities away from losing Pru's dream.

She and Seth had made great progress remodeling the shop, but she wondered if it was just a huge waste of time. He constantly assured her that Regina had everything under control. She hoped he was right.

Thursday morning came and she headed out to the mountains with Rocket in the passenger seat. She chuckled when she passed the various mile markers where she'd pulled over just a few short weeks ago, unable to drive any further, afraid that with each step forward she moved one step away from Pru. She realized now that Pru would always be with her, and while she'd very much like to have a word with her regarding her affair with Carlotta, she could let it go.

Lenny, you're not the easiest woman in the world to live with.

They hiked the Blue Lakes Trail, and she turned around at the halfway point. Rocket barked, wanting to continue.

"Sorry, boy. It's a big day. I've got a lot to do before the meeting. If things don't go so well, we'll have a *lot* of time for hiking."

They headed to Kate's Place and then to the shop. She sensed Sloane was nearby, but she didn't see her. Regina had assured her that Sloane was the mastermind behind what was transpiring but that didn't put her mind at ease.

When they arrived, Seth was putting up new railings for the multiple platforms he'd built. Walls had been painted, nouveau lighting fixtures had been installed and signage hung from the ceilings.

"This place doesn't look anything like it used to," she commented. When he looked at her with a pained expression, she said, "That's a good thing. Pru would approve."

They worked through lunch, hoping Regina would call, but she didn't. She'd texted once to say she'd see them at the meeting and to save her a seat. At four Lenny trudged across the park to the library to meet with Maddie. She glanced over her shoulder at the store, hoping Seth's hard work wouldn't be for nothing.

"You look deep in thought."

Sloane sat at a bench, holding a book. She smiled and Lenny felt her knees buckle. It was all she could do not to rush over and plop on her lap. The desire to kiss her was nearly overwhelming. She'd never been so grateful to see anyone in her whole life.

She sat down next to her and noticed the title of the book she held, *The Seven Ps of Business: How to Ensure Your Success.* "Pru had that book."

Sloane turned to the inside front cover and pointed at Pru's name. "I know. This is her copy. I found it at the Schoolhouse Emporium. Apparently you sold it."

She shook her head. She had no idea what had come and gone in the last several months.

"I brought it for you to read. You're going to need it."

"I hope you're right."

"I know I am."

There was smugness behind her smile. She was far too calm, given that Lenny could be just ninety minutes from her life unraveling. While she appreciated Sloane's business savvy, she knew her town and how much they hated chains. They were incredibly loyal to their neighbors—to a fault. She worried their well-meaning small-town values would be their downfall.

"I just don't think you know what you're up against," she said simply. She shifted on the bench. She didn't have much time, but she needed to apologize for jumping to conclusions, and she wanted to tell her about Carlotta. "About the other morning…"

Before she could launch into an explanation, Sloane kissed her. The soft pillow lips lingered, and Lenny responded with another kiss. They held each other, and she whispered, "I wish I'd stayed that morning. I actually undressed while you were on the phone."

Sloane sighed deeply and the next kiss was full of desire. When she pulled away, her frustration was obvious. "We should probably stop," she said, deliberately moving a foot away from Lenny on the bench. "It's probably not appropriate for the town mayor to engage in lascivious PDA in the park. What would people think?"

"There was nothing lascivious about that kiss," she argued.

"No, that part was in my mind." Sloane grinned.

Lenny's phone chirped with a text from Maddie. *Can't meet. Too much work to do. See you at the meeting.* "That's odd. Maddie canceled our meeting. She never cancels our meeting."

"That is odd," Sloane said innocently, returning to the book.

She stared at Sloane, who ignored her. "What have you done?"

* * *

Lenny took her seat and faced the enormous crowd. It seemed nearly every Pinedale citizen was in attendance, and Paul told her they'd run out of chairs. Even the children's chairs from the youth section were in use, and it was comical to see several adults trying to balance on the tiny seats. She imagined the high attendance was Carlotta's doing, making sure their previous vote on Wilderness Campaign wasn't overturned.

It had happened before with other issues. She had learned that small-town politics had a mile of leeway, and no vote was ever final.

Seth, Regina and Sloane sat toward the back, but she could see them clearly. Only Seth looked nervous, wringing his baseball cap between his hands. She remembered how often he'd done that sitting in the dugout when a game was close. Regina leaned over and took his hand, and he smiled at her. They were perfect for each other. Her gaze drifted to Sloane. She looked amused and confident, completely the business professional.

She glanced around the table at the other council members. Donny and Joe sat to her right, each wearing a stoic expression. To her immediate left was Dreama, who seemed to be studying the audience. Carlotta sat next to her, busily scribbling on her copy of the agenda. To Lenny's far left was John Snyder. When their eyes met he winked at her. Having John at the table made her feel better. She pounded the gavel once and called the meeting to order. They ran through the formalities of the pledge and the reading of the minutes quickly.

"Are there any changes to the agenda?" she asked hesitantly, remembering what had happened at the last meeting.

"I have one," Maddie said. "We can remove the discussion about the grace period."

The entire council looked at her. Carlotta asked, "Why?"

"Because it's no longer necessary."

Carlotta glanced at Lenny before she said, "What do you mean it's no longer necessary? Collecting taxes is a cornerstone of government."

Maddie coolly folded her hands in front of her. "They're already paid. No one owes anything."

A murmur rippled through the crowd and Lenny looked at Sloane. She was leaning back in her chair, her arms crossed. She blew Lenny a little kiss.

She couldn't believe it. Her mind reeled as the weight was lifted. Pru's wouldn't go under! She was in such a fog that she was momentarily oblivious to the shouting around her as Carlotta drilled Maddie for details. It was Dreama who grabbed the gavel and pounded it on the table.

"Order! As vice mayor, I demand order!"

"There's no such thing as a *vice* mayor," Carlotta spat.

"Well, there should be," Dreama said.

Carlotta pointed at Maddie. "I want to know how those taxes got paid."

She shrugged dismissively. "It was anonymous. I received a notice in the mail today from Ouray County."

"I want to see that!"

Maddie handed her a copy of the notice and she scanned it, her anger growing with every second.

"Are there any other changes to the agenda?" John prodded. "The NBA Finals start in an hour, and if we can get out of here on time, the first round's on me for anyone who comes and watches at the café."

Several members of the audience applauded, and Lenny banged the gavel once. "We're at the public comment portion of the meeting. Maddie, do we have anyone who would like to speak?"

She waved a thick stack of papers. "A few."

Lenny leaned back in her chair, prepared for the onslaught, but she was unprepared for what happened next. The first speaker was an artist living at DreamaWorks. He wanted a revote in favor of a Wilderness Campaign to bring more tourists through the town. She was even more surprised at the reaction from the crowd. Only *half* of them booed as he sat down, and they were silenced with a single bang from her gavel.

She glanced at Carlotta, whose eyes had narrowed to slits. When the next three speakers, also artists at DreamaWorks, echoed the sentiment of the first speaker, she noticed several audience members nodding their agreement. Something was up.

Much to her pleasure, Carlotta fidgeted and sent a text message. Lenny wasn't surprised when Donny's phone, which was sitting in front of him, started to buzz. With a single punch of a button, he silenced it and continued to stare at the audience. While Donny and Joe were always quiet at meetings, they weren't usually stone-faced statues.

One by one each person at the podium demanded a revote on the Wilderness Campaign. Some talked about the town's livelihood while others spoke of their own hardships. Lenny continually looked at Sloane, who seemed completely captivated by the speakers.

After Olaf Koskinen shared his story in broken English, John looked at his watch and then the crowd. "So, is everyone who signed up to speak asking us to revote on the Wilderness Campaign store?"

"Not me!" Chance Devitt raised his hand. "I'm totally against it, and that's why I'm here. I want to make sure you all stay committed to the small business owners, people like Carlotta who do so much good for the town. We don't need big chains or outsiders, like this lady," he said, pointing at Sloane, "telling us how to run our town. I feel for everyone's pain, I really do, but we need to solve our own problems."

Carlotta beamed from her seat at the table, and Lenny thought she saw her mouthing the words to Chance's speech, as if she'd written it herself. A few clapped, but the audience was clearly divided.

John sighed and turned to Lenny. "Madame Mayor, may I ask for a straw poll?" She nodded and John continued. "Will all of the homeowners who are present and in favor of us considering a Wilderness Campaign store in Pinedale please stand?" Roughly half of the audience rose. "Thank you," he said. "Will those against a Wilderness Campaign please rise?"

When the other half of the audience stood, Carlotta said, "I think it is plain to see that we are divided on this issue. It would not be prudent to move forward."

"Would you at least *study* the issue?"

Everyone turned to Regina, who was standing at her seat, holding the familiar portfolio Lenny had seen the first day Sloane had arrived. "It would seem to me that if half the town already thinks this is a good idea, then perhaps a subcommittee could actually read the proposal and make a recommendation? Wouldn't that be the most fair idea, given that your economic livelihood is at stake?"

"I vote for a subcommittee," Donny said, his tone flat.

"I second it," Joe added.

Carlotta gave them a death stare, but they ignored her and continued to gaze at the audience.

"All in favor?" Lenny asked.

Only Carlotta didn't raise her hand. She turned to face Joe and Donny. Lenny couldn't imagine what Sloane had offered for their support, but it must have been significant.

Regina advanced to the front and handed the report to Maddie. "I do have one question about the issue of signage, which of course, is critical to a company's success."

Obviously looking for anything to break the momentum, Carlotta said, "We have strict ordinances about the size and height of free-standing signs."

"So would this one be too big?"

Regina gestured to her left, and Lenny realized she held the SmartBoard clicker in her hand. People gasped and shouted before Lenny could remember where to look. They'd bought the SmartBoard at Paul's urging. He insisted that in addition to providing necessary technology for the library, it would be a great way for the town council to display information. Unfortunately, Maddie had been less than thrilled so it was never used during their meetings.

Lenny's gaze settled on the middle of the west wall and the two pictures being displayed in split-screen fashion. On the left was a wide shot of the Happy Burger Joint on Harrison and the adjoining property that Carlotta had purchased for her supposed second restaurant. A large sign, similar to a political sign, sat in front of the empty building, but it was too far away to read. Fortunately, or unfortunately for Carlotta, a close-up of the sign was displayed on the right side of the screen. Bright yellow letters against a deep blue background announced, *Great Savings Are Coming Your Way! Dollar Mart Arriving in Your Community Soon!*

Several people had risen from their seats and moved closer to the SmartBoard, as if their proximity could change the message. They pointed and shouted, some unable to believe what they were seeing.

"What the hell is that, Carlotta?" Donny shouted. It was the most animated Lenny had ever seen him.

Carlotta sprang to her feet. "How did that get there?"

Regina shook her head. "I have no idea. I saw it about an hour ago."

Carlotta grabbed her bag and ran out the back exit. Lenny pounded her gavel until everyone sat down again. She looked up in time to see Sloane follow her.

Is she going after Carlotta?

"That bitch lied to us!" C.J. Dooley cried. "I will never, *ever* step foot in Charlie's again." He pointed at John and said, "True Grit's the only place I'm drinkin'."

John gave him a thumbs-up, and others nodded their agreement.

"I think we've had enough for one meeting," Lenny said. She looked at Maddie. "Is there anything else that can't wait until next month?"

"Nope," Maddie said plainly.

"Meeting adjourned," she said, slowly threading her way through the crowd. Most of her neighbors remained in the library, sharing their disbelief and anger over Carlotta's treachery.

"How did you get that sign up?" she asked Regina.

She shook her head and said, "You know, sometimes there are mix-ups in PR departments, and the right hand doesn't know what the left one is doing."

Seth kissed her cheek. "You are truly wicked sometimes, and I love you for it."

"We need to find Sloane," Lenny whispered. "Carlotta's so mad that I don't know what she'll do. I've heard she carries a pistol in her bag."

Ten minutes later they finally exited the library after several neighbors had stopped Lenny and shared their anger. They headed across the park looking for Sloane or her crumpled body on the ground.

"There's a light on at Pru's," Regina said.

They found her standing next to the cash register, pouring four glasses of champagne.

"Thank God," Lenny cried. She threw her arms around Sloane, who pulled her into a tight hug.

"I'm glad to see you too," she whispered.

They kissed until Regina and Seth started coughing. "A little too much PDA, Mom," Seth teased.

"Sorry," she said, blushing. She gazed at Sloane. "Thanks for saving the store."

Sloane caressed her cheek. "My pleasure."

"Did you see Carlotta? I was worried she might hurt you."

Sloane passed out the champagne and explained. "No, that wasn't going to happen. By the time I was done with her, she was in no position to hurt me."

Regina gazed at Sloane over the top of her glass. "Did you do what I think you did?"

"What was that?" Seth asked.

Sloane smiled at Regina with a look of pride. "I caught up with her outside, and yes, she did take a swing at me, but I ducked. Then I handed her an envelope that contained a check for a very large amount of money. At first she was confused, but then she understood."

"Well, I don't understand," Lenny admitted. "What were you paying her for?"

"I bought Schoolhouse Emporium for the new Wilderness Campaign store. I'm certain once your little subcommittee hears *all* of the facts, they'll be convinced it's what Pinedale needs. Regina will take care of that."

A thought occurred to her. "How did you get Donny and Joe to support your subcommittee idea?"

Her eyes sparkled with the joy of the *deal*. "I negotiated with them. Donny's tired. He'd rather be using his own fishing rods than selling them to other people. He's going to move his shop into the Wilderness Campaign, and Joe is going to become a building supervisor."

"Really?" She couldn't believe it. Maybe she didn't know the townspeople as well as she thought.

Sloane raised her glass and the others followed suit. "And here's to Pru's Curious Curios and its impending wealth."

She snorted and the champagne bubbles flew up her nose. "I don't know how you expect *that* to happen. I think we'll do better after this extreme makeover, but Pru always knew collectible shops weren't huge moneymakers."

"This one will be."

Sloane reached into her briefcase and pulled out some eight-by-ten pictures of several beautiful metal locks shaped like various animals or bugs—a butterfly, a beetle and even an elephant.

"What are these?"

"This is your future, if you want it to be. The girl who designed them calls them Backpack NoJack." She chuckled and added, "Definitely a name that will appeal to teenagers. They are a simple security lock for school backpacks so no one can 'jack' your stuff while you're at lunch or on the playground. They're cheap to make and boys and girls are going to love them. She's agreed to let Pru's Curious Curios market them exclusively, and they will be produced here in Pinedale by no other than DreamaWorks."

"You're going to make a fortune," Regina added. "We're going to need more employees just to keep up with the Internet offers."

"It's a complete win-win," she added, sipping her champagne. "Pru's increases its profit margin, and Dreama has another source of income for her studio. I should also add that she's very much in favor of a Wilderness Campaign store coming to Pinedale."

"Imagine that," Lenny said drily.

Regina and Seth set their glasses on the counter. "We're going over to the café to watch basketball. Are you coming?"

Lenny opened her mouth to agree, but Sloane interjected. "No, we have other plans."

Regina and Seth stifled a giggle and headed out. It wasn't until the door was firmly closed that Sloane reached for Lenny. The deep kiss was permission to caress the soft flesh of Sloane's breasts and the wonderful curves of her buttocks. Lenny wanted so much more. She reached for the fly of Sloane's pants.

"Not here," she said, taking her hand and bringing it to her lips. "There will be time for that. Let's just savor this moment."

Lenny feigned surprise. "What? You're going to live in the moment."

"I am."

Physical

(consideration)

The consumer's interactions and experience with the product or service must be positive, enriching and, if possible, life changing.

CHAPTER THIRTY

"Where are we going?"

"You'll see."

They passed the turnoff to Lenny's place and headed toward Telluride.

"Are we going to your summer home?"

Sloane grinned, but she doubted Lenny could see her expression in the darkness. "Nope. Better."

Lenny chuckled and took her hand. Sloane glanced at their entwined fingers resting on the console between them. There was nothing sexual or provocative about it. Lenny wasn't stroking her thumb or making suggestive remarks about what she'd like to do with those fingers. In fact, she was gazing out the passenger window at the bright stars that filled the Colorado sky. She was simply holding her hand to create a connection. Sloane resisted the urge to study the gesture in fear of careening off the road. She so rarely held hands with women, the last time being on a crashing plane when Chris practically broke her fingers.

She'd held hands for foreplay and fear. *This* was not one of those times. In the quiet of the SUV, the connection was relaxing. It was reassuring. It was intimate.

She glanced down again, making sure it was real. This was an important moment, but she wasn't sure she completely understood its significance. When her cell phone buzzed, requiring her to pull her hand away from Lenny's, she wanted to apologize to her, and more importantly, she wanted the caller to go away so she could reclaim the connection. She couldn't recall a time when she more resented an interruption.

"Sloane McHenry."

"I've called five times, Sloane. Why are you avoiding me?"

"I'm not avoiding you, Steve. I'm putting together the deal of the century here. I have to stay focused."

"If your focus has anything to do with commissioning a fourteen-year-old girl and her cutesy backpack locks, then I'd say you're a little *out* of focus."

"And I'd say you're worrying about matters that don't concern you."

She could afford to be disrespectful because she had the backing of the majority of the board. Until that changed she would continue to put him in his place, hoping he'd resign his seat. She had no idea how he'd learned of her arrangement with Allie, but there was clearly some low-level secretary or data entry hack who was feeding him information. God help that person if she learned his or her identity.

"You're out on a limb, Sloane, and I'm not the only one who thinks so. It's very interesting that you have time for little side jaunts to Oregon when Pinedale is still so precarious."

"Nothing precarious at all, Steve-O." She knew he hated it when she called him by his old fraternity name. "I'll have my report to the board by the end of next week. But you know I always appreciate you looking out for the welfare of the company. Gotta go."

She disconnected and tossed the phone in the backseat. "Son of a bitch. I hate that guy." She stabbed a few buttons on the control panel and Van Morrison's "Tupelo Honey" began to play.

She realized Lenny probably had heard most of the conversation and would want to ask her a lot of questions—just like all of the other flings. *They always do, and they get mad whenever the phone rings since I'm supposed to be on vacation.* She'd want to make it better. She'd want to help.

"I don't want to talk about it," she said curtly. "Just in case you were going to ask."

"I wasn't," Lenny said quietly. "I'd rather sing."

Sloane enjoyed listening to her gorgeous voice, and when she nudged her to join the chorus, she did, but her mind still swirled with pieces of the Pinedale deal. She needed to form a game plan and create a timeline. There were so many considerations and variables that could affect the profit margin. She'd conceded a few points already, such as the fishing rod sales, and Steve would inevitably hold that over her head. She'd have to negotiate hard with the builders and come in under budget to make up for the concessions she'd made.

She wasn't even conscious of her drumming until Lenny leaned forward and reclaimed her right hand from the steering wheel.

"Stop multitasking! Just sing," Lenny ordered.

She laughed at Lenny's fake angry tone, shoved the deal from her mind and sang along. She glanced at Lenny's face, a beautiful silhouette against the night. She was still, peaceful.

She finally understood. Lenny didn't need to say anything. The simple touch was whatever Sloane needed it to be. Lenny was happy just being with her. She didn't need to be showered with gifts or dine in fancy restaurants.

She could never be just a fling.

The turnoff appeared in the headlights and they headed toward Priest Lake. Lenny peered through the windshield, most likely wondering where they were going. Sloane bit her lip, unwilling to give away the surprise.

They passed through a residential area and for a few minutes the Range Rover was illuminated by the glow of streetlights.

She caught a glimpse of a smile on Lenny's face that sent a pleasant shiver down her back. They turned onto a private road that cut through a meadow. The narrow bridge wasn't far away. She could see the creek, a dark line that cut a path between the trees. She lowered her window and Lenny followed suit. The smell of fir trees and the sound of the rushing creek flooded their ears.

She slowly drove over the bridge and around several fallen logs. She veered to the left, grateful for the off-road capabilities of the Rover, and followed the tree line into a meadow and their campsite. The headlights illuminated a firepit, a large tent and a mess area with tables and chairs. She looked over at Lenny, who was studying the scene with amazement.

"What's all of this?"

"This," she replied, "is our little retreat from the world, at least for the next forty-eight hours, if you want it to be."

She couldn't tell if Lenny was pleased or annoyed. Her eyes darted around the campsite, and she leaned out the window and studied the surroundings. "Who owns this land?"

"I do." Her jaw dropped and Sloane grinned. "My house is on the other side of that hill. I don't get out here much."

"Why not?" Lenny asked incredulously. "If this were my place I'd be out here all the time. I can't see much of it right now, but I'll bet it's gorgeous at sunrise."

She leaned across the console and stroked her cheek. "It is, and I can't wait to see it with you."

Lenny's kiss was a sign of surrender. She pressed against Sloane, offering her lips, her breasts, all of her. It was tempting to wield her power and take Lenny in the SUV. There was certainly enough room for both of them in the passenger seat, but that wasn't what she wanted. She hadn't come all the way out here to set up a romantic rendezvous only to behave like a sex-starved teenager. Lenny would have to wait, but they could have a little fun in the meantime. She slid her hands down Lenny's front, unbuttoning the simple cotton shirt and discarding it in the backseat. The darkness freed her imagination, and she pictured Lenny's cleavage surrounded by the pink sports bra she'd seen during their make-out session in the cottage.

She buried her face between Lenny's breasts, working the straps, nibbling at the soft flesh until she was naked from the waist up. Temptation washed over her; the control she craved and the power she possessed as Sloane McHenry, CEO of Wilderness Campaign, rising up. Lenny would become another conquest on her list, one of the flings who satisfied her aching libido.

Perhaps Lenny sensed her hunger, or perhaps her own desires surfaced, but she pushed Sloane away with a laugh, maxed the volume on the stereo and fled from the SUV. Sloane watched through the windshield as she casually stepped into the headlight beams and swayed to "Moondance." The white light glowed against her skin, and her breasts jutted forward, the nipples hard from the cold night air. She stroked her belly and slowly peeled away her shorts. She stretched and her body extended beyond the headlight beams, her face in darkness. Sloane studied the sinewy muscles of her arms and her legs, picturing those strong thighs wrapped around her shoulders.

I can't wait much longer. This was supposed to be my surprise, my seduction.

When the song ended, Lenny slowly relaxed her body and walked out of the headlight beams like an actor leaving the stage. Sloane killed the ignition and plunged the campsite into darkness. She grabbed the flashlight from the console and stumbled out of the Rover, her legs weak and her heart pounding. She opened the back and dug through the rucksack that sat upon three coolers she'd loaded up with food, drink and goodies for their outing. She could hear Lenny making noise in the darkness, as if she was moving things in the tent.

No, no. Don't touch anything. I had it arranged perfectly.

She swore quietly until she found the matches. Leaving everything else behind, she trudged to the firepit and struck a match. She'd already set up the campfire earlier in the day so the tinder and kindling caught quickly. A small yellow glow illuminated the campsite—and Lenny, who was sprawled upon an open sleeping bag a few feet from the fire. Her hands were clasped behind her head and she lay in a suggestive pose.

"How did you get that sleeping bag out here? It's pitch black."

"I have great night vision, almost like a superhero." She sat up on one elbow and stared at her. "Take off your clothes and get down here."

She stripped quickly, made somewhat self-conscious by Lenny's stare and remembering the little show she'd given her in front of the headlights. The night air chilled her, intensifying her need and making her keenly aware of the heat between her legs. She eagerly lowered herself to the ground, and Lenny enfolded her in warmth.

They kissed and touched, nuzzled and nibbled. It was delectable. If they sat up, the night chill converged on them, the fledgling fire still gaining strength. They giggled in the cold and quickly dropped back onto the sleeping bag. Their passion grew, emboldened by sheer animal instincts. They were outdoors. They were naked. They were making love.

Soft moans and sighs drifted into the crackling fire, its intensity increasing as each log was consumed. Lenny's wetness glistened in the bright light, and joy radiated from her face, each time Sloane's tongue caressed her center. She arched her back and rocked her hips much like the fire's burning tendrils of red and yellow.

"Yes, Sloane, please," she chanted.

It was time. She buried herself in Lenny's taste and felt the powerful thighs wrap around her shoulders. Darkness surrounded her as Lenny came over and over.

* * *

She awoke first, just before the sunrise. Even though she was on vacation, her routine was established, and if she were in Boston, she'd be heading to the gym right now. She sat up and let the sleeping bag fall away. They'd had quite a workout, first under the stars and then inside the tent. Although Lenny's fireside lovemaking had been spontaneous joy, the romantic scene Sloane had planned, which included some fun play toys and tasty treats, was equally well received.

She watched Lenny sleep and grinned when a light snore escaped her lips. She kissed her cheek and her eyes fluttered open.

"Hmm, what time is it?"

"The sun's coming up soon. Do you want to see it? We'd need to take a walk to the edge of the meadow."

"Do I have to get dressed?"

"Not as far as I'm concerned."

"Great, let's go."

Lenny jumped up suddenly full of energy and pulled her into her arms. Between the kisses Sloane said, "We're going to miss the sunrise. I really want you to see it."

"Okay," Lenny said, grabbing her hiking boots and heading through the tent flap.

"Are you seriously going naked?" she asked, pulling on her shorts and shirt before she emerged.

Lenny stood in front of her with her hands on her hips, clad only in her hiking boots. "I am."

She licked her lips. "I'm learning new things about you all the time, Madame Mayor."

They walked the few hundred feet to the edge of the meadow and spread out a blanket just in time to watch the sky explode into yellow and orange. She encircled Lenny in her arms and buried her nose in her hair. They sat quietly together for almost an hour while the sun made its full appearance, only occasionally breaking the silence for a brief comment about the beauty of the outdoors. It occurred to her the serene scene bore great resemblance to holding hands with Lenny in the car—until she guided Sloane's hands against her breasts, and they found an entirely different purpose for the blanket.

When they returned to the camp, Lenny went back to the tent and emerged wearing clothes. "I'm going to go exploring. Wanna come?"

She had just poured a cup of coffee and was planting herself in a chair. Surprised by Lenny's offer, she said, "No, I just want to sit here and enjoy the birds. Why don't you stay?"

"I feel like walking." Lenny leaned over and kissed her. "But when I get back…"

The statement hung in the air between them. She recognized her own contentment was matched by the look on Lenny's face. She watched Lenny meander through the meadow, periodically bending over to look at a flower or study a plant. Her breath caught thinking about her fine derriere. *And those muscles.*

As she sat in the silence, she couldn't help but compare this tryst with the previous flings. Granted, most of her women were outdoorsy and readily slept under the stars. Most of them hiked, fished or rafted, but none of them would *ever* go off for a walk without her if she didn't want to go. When she said no it was *no.* The fling quickly changed her plans to spend more time with *her.* Yet Lenny's head was moments from disappearing out of sight. She'd left her—alone.

She frowned. Instead of enjoying the next hour listening to the birds, she downed two vikes and consumed a Red Bull. She was frantically throwing together breakfast when Lenny appeared carrying wildflowers. She held them out like a first date.

"For you."

She looked up from the eggs she was scrambling and nodded. "Great."

"What's wrong?"

"Nothing."

"Well, you're scrambling those eggs like they've committed a felony, so something is clearly wrong." She didn't answer and Lenny pressed. "Sloane?"

She dropped the spatula and faced her. "Why did you leave me here?"

She stared at her with a puzzled expression. "Because you said you didn't want to go. Did you *want* to go?"

She shook her head. "No, I didn't want to go, but I didn't want *you* to go either."

"Why not?"

She started to reply and realized it was a terrible answer. Instead she said, "I don't know. I just didn't."

Lenny leaned over and turned off the camp stove. She took her hand and gave her the flowers. "When I left, you looked completely content to sit in your chair and enjoy the morning air. I was glad you didn't want to come."

She shot her a look. "Why not? Are you already tired of me?"

Lenny chuckled, whereas any of her other flings would have readily launched into the fight she was trying to pick. Instead she leaned into the flowers and breathed deeply. "Smell them. When we woke up this morning, I was certain there had to be flowers nearby. I wanted to surprise you. I wanted to give you a gift as a way to thank you for this wonderful trip, but it wouldn't have been a surprise if you'd come with me, now would it?" She shook her head. "We don't have to do everything together, honey."

Her face fell and she busied herself with preparing the breakfast plates. She couldn't help the shocked expression that creased her face.

She called me honey.

"I just don't want you to be upset when I leave in a few days. I want us to get as much out of this time together as we can."

She couldn't look at Lenny, but from the corner of her eye she watched her drop into a chair. When she handed her the plate, she knew the mood had changed, and she'd changed it— deliberately. It was for the best.

They ate in silence until Lenny asked, "Why did you want to put a Wilderness Campaign in Pinedale?"

Between bites she explained, "It's good business. Do you remember when you heard me on the phone refer to the townspeople as hicks? Well, I don't believe that at all. Small towns are the bread and butter of our stores. Who do you think has the most time to hunt, fish and camp? Certainly not the city folk."

"Won't Carlotta find out you paid those taxes? Isn't that public record?"

She shook her head. "That's highly unlikely. The money came from one of my private offshore accounts. She'll give up looking long before she finds the source, if she's even here. She lost a lot of friends last night. I'm sure she'll be moving soon."

"You have offshore accounts?"

She looked embarrassed. "I'm not proud of everything I've done in my life, Lenny. For a long time I wasn't a very nice person, and I took what I could get."

She stopped chewing and started to feel her stomach tighten. *What's happening here? Get control, Sloane!*

"I'm happy to use those funds to help the town," she said coolly. "Just seeing the look on Carlotta's face when Maddie told her the taxes were paid was worth every cent."

"So how was paying *my* taxes good for your business?"

She focused on her eggs. She didn't want to have this conversation.

"Tell me why, Sloane. Why did you do all of this for Pinedale?"

She shrugged off the question, the one question she didn't want to answer. "Because I could. I did it for Regina. Helping you helped her."

"For Regina," she repeated. "I think that's very noble of you." Lenny finally asked, "But is that right? Is it ethical?"

She set down her plate and got up. She conversed better when she stood. This was just supposed to be a few days of getting laid before she headed home. She ran a hand through her curly hair, her exasperation showing. "What's ethical? Everything is about relationships and timing and nepotism. We do things for the people we know."

"Is this really a good deal for you? Does this meet the Seven Ps?"

"It meets *some* of them," she admitted. She threw up her hands. "Can we change the subject?"

When Lenny met her gaze there was a sadness she'd never seen. "No, I don't think we can. You need to take me home."

CHAPTER THIRTY-ONE

The grand reopening of Pru's Curious Curios had coincided with the Fourth of July weekend, which, according to Regina, was perfect timing. She and Seth had worked eighteen-hour days for two weeks straight to finish the shop, create the website and launch the newest featured item, Backpack NoJack locks. Seth had quit his job at the bar, and Regina had somehow magically been freed up to help.

"Doesn't Sloane need you for some other projects?" Lenny had asked several times, but she insisted she had remained in Colorado with Sloane's blessing, not because she was in trouble or had been fired again.

The opening proved to be a huge success, and by the end of the summer season Pru's was doing steady business, and the Backpack NoJack had become an Internet sensation. Young inventor Allie Kennedy was featured in several business journals, always crediting Regina Dewar as the woman who discovered her. Sloane was never mentioned.

Lenny needed to forget Sloane. The morning at the campsite had confirmed her suspicions. She was just another fling or, rather, that was all Sloane would allow her to be. She just couldn't bring herself to have more. Having taken several classes in interpersonal communication, sociology and psychology during her prolific undergraduate career, Lenny understood the human heart.

"What's wrong with her?" Seth had asked one night at dinner. "She loves you." He'd turned to Regina for support, but she remained silent, feeding the end of her pizza crust to Rocket.

She had tried to explain. "Honey, having feelings and having the courage to act on those feelings are two different things."

He'd nodded and since that night they hadn't discussed it. She was doing her best to move on. The store kept her constantly busy, and Toby, her unmotivated college student helper, had become much more motivated when he was promoted to website manager. Regina and Seth had returned to Boston, but he assured her it was temporary. Sloane was toying with the idea of opening regional offices, and if that happened, they would be moving to Colorado permanently.

The entire town was abuzz about the scheduled fall opening of the Pinedale Wilderness Campaign. It was going to be everything Sloane had promised. In a single weekend it would become the number one employer of Pinedale citizens. Donny's fishing rods would find a home, and Joe would be named manager. Several times she'd heard Joe's story of being flown first-class to Boston to meet with Sloane in her "ginormous office" and being treated to a steak lunch at the classiest restaurant he'd ever seen.

It wasn't the only surprise. Sloane kept her promise about the non-competition clause and didn't include a Wilderness Café in the store. Anyone wanting to eat while in town would have to visit local establishments like Kate's Place or the True Grit Bar and Grille.

They wouldn't be visiting Charlie's or La Casita. By the end of summer Carlotta had shuttered the restaurant and bar and put her home at the top of the mountain for sale. Lenny wasn't sorry to see her go, and she was grateful for the peace and quiet on her walks with Rocket.

Her life was full, but each time she passed the growing Wilderness Campaign store that summer, she craned her neck to see if there was a sleek black Range Rover amidst the construction vehicles. There never was, but she really didn't think there would be. Sloane was far too busy and important to oversee the construction. That was Regina's job, which suited Lenny just fine since it meant she and Seth visited regularly.

"The store is opening in two weeks," Regina announced one evening when they were enjoying dinner. "We are ahead of schedule and we'll make hunting season and be in the running for winter sports purchases."

"That's great." Lenny nodded.

"There's one more thing that I think you need to prepare yourself for, Lenny."

She looked at Regina and then Seth, who clearly knew what she was about to say. "What? If it's about Sloane coming for the opening, I'd figured she would. We're adults. I think we can be in the same town."

"Well, it's a little more than that, Mom," he added, his eyes on Regina. "You know, you're the mayor."

"And?" Then she understood. "Oh."

"We always have the mayor cut the ribbon...with Sloane."

"I see. How does Sloane feel about this?"

"I haven't mentioned it to her yet. She's so busy that I doubt it's crossed her mind."

"Don't you think you should tell her, babe?" he asked.

Regina sipped her wine. "Nope. I'm not buying that bag of trouble. She'll figure it out. Probably when the plane coming here is somewhere over Topeka."

* * *

On the day of the Wilderness Campaign opening Lenny decided to start her day with a hike. She knew Sloane had arrived the day before, and it felt odd knowing she was so close. She needed to clear her head, and a trek up to Blaine Basin would do the trick. She'd been there a few times since that adventure with Sloane, always stopping for a few seconds to stare at the tree over the mud bog, the place where Sloane had fallen and shown her true self, the woman Lenny had grown to care about.

Yet, by the time she reached the lower basin, she was frustrated and her head certainly wasn't clear. Thoughts of Sloane, Pru, Seth and her wasted life jumbled together. She dropped amidst the tall meadow grass and stared at the sky, Rocket hovering over her curiously. She lay there for some time, unwilling to address the issues or make a plan. That just wasn't in her genetic makeup. She saw absolutely no reason to get up. The rest of the day promised a public appearance in front of the whole town where she would say a few words she hadn't yet compiled and stand next to the woman she desperately wanted and couldn't have.

Not the way I want to spend the afternoon.

She peered up at Rocket. His head was cocked to the side as if he was listening. "What if I don't go, boy? It's not like they're *not* going to open the store. Joe can do it. No one will care that I'm not there."

She closed her eyes to meditate on her plan.

* * *

"Lenny? Lenny?"

She awoke to crystal blue eyes staring in to hers. *Sloane.*

"Good news, Rocket. She's not dead."

She wasn't sure if this was still part of her dream, but she doubted it since Sloane was clothed. "What are you doing here?" she mumbled through a yawn.

"I thought I'd take a hike before the opening. Apparently, you had the same idea." She glanced at Lenny's prostrate body and said with a raised eyebrow, "Long night?"

She wasn't in the mood for banter. She just wanted to be left alone. She closed her eyes again, and soon Sloane was shaking her. "C'mon, Lenny, you need to get up. The opening is in two hours. If Rocket hadn't charged up to me, you'd have slept through the whole thing."

She opened one eye. "That was the idea. Have Joe cut the ribbon."

"Uh, no," she said, her voice turning shrill. "You're the mayor. You need to be there."

Lenny could tell she was getting angry, but that didn't matter. Just because Sloane could turn off her emotions and go back to business as usual didn't mean Lenny could. She pulled away from her grip and sat up.

"Sloane, I'm not going."

"Of course you're going."

"No, I'm not," she insisted.

She stood up and dusted off her cargo shorts. "That's just fabulous, Lenny. Way to look out for your town! They did a great thing when they elected you."

"Well, hopefully they won't make the same mistake twice."

"I doubt it." She started to walk away but stopped and turned around. "You know what I don't get. You talk all about living in the moment, but what about loyalty, friendship and commitment? Those people are counting on you. Some things are about the long term."

Lenny shot up and confronted her. "You're going to lecture me about the *long* term? The woman who can't sustain a relationship for more than two weeks? You? The queen of the summer fling?"

"I never promised you anything. I never made this more than what it was."

She rolled her eyes. "How trite and convenient. Do you keep that phrase handy for every woman you sleep with?"

Sloane looked away, and Lenny stepped very close to her. She was almost certain that in the quiet of the mountains she heard Sloane's heart racing.

"That's right," she whispered. "You never promised me anything. What do you promise *yourself*, Sloane? What little agreements do you make with yourself late at night when you're all alone? How do you negotiate your happiness? Do you only get a piece at a time, or have you just decided to wait until it's more convenient and go for the whole deal? And when will that be? When do you get to have it all?"

"We're going to be late," she insisted.

It was as if she hadn't heard her. "Why did you pay my taxes? Why did you help me out, and don't say it was because of Regina. She had nothing to do with that debt."

They stared at each other and Lenny said a silent prayer for the truth, but the steel returned to Sloane's eyes. "The opening is in two hours. Your presence is critical to the messaging. A small town gets a shot in the arm from a huge corporation. You *need* to be there. The town *needs* you to be there."

"No, *you* need me to be there. It's *your* message, not mine, not Pinedale's."

"Fine," she said through clenched teeth. "I need you to be there. More importantly, *Regina* needs you to be there. This is her deal and her future."

She was pulling out all the stops and playing every card she had. How much would she risk?

"Follow me," Lenny said.

She trudged across the meadow to the fallen tree precariously sitting over the mud bog. She looked at Sloane with a little grin, but Sloane was already shaking her head.

"Oh, no. We're not doing this again. There will be no wagers."

She hopped on the log and jumped once. "If you can jump three times, I'll come to the opening." She jumped a second time and added, "I'll effusively sing the praises of Wilderness Campaign, and," she said as she jumped a third time, "I'll make sure the world knows how much our little town owes your great big powerful company."

She jumped once more and shouted, "What do you say?"

Sloane looked as if she could commit murder. "What do you get if I fall?"

She paced along the log. "Then I don't go."

Sloane debated what to do. She drummed a tune on the bark

Lenny didn't recognize, all the while shaking her head. Finally, she murmured something about bullshit under her breath and pulled herself onto the log. She faced Lenny, who grinned broadly.

"I can't believe I'm doing this again. You'll probably just jump off like last time."

She shrugged. "You don't know that. I'm older now, wiser and more mature."

She muttered something unintelligible again and checked her stance on the log. She was all business, Lenny saw, and completely focused. She was doing this simply because she saw no other way to control Lenny's behavior. She bounced once and didn't acknowledge Lenny's clever comment of encouragement or her applause. She bounced a second time quickly and nearly fell off. She steadied herself and prepared for the third bounce. She stared straight ahead and wouldn't look at her. Lenny realized then that this was no friendly competition, and even if she won, she'd lose.

Sloane glanced at her, making sure she was still standing close and not at the end of the log where she could jump off and send her into the bog. She took a deep breath and jumped up.

Lenny jumped off—into the bog. Sloane swore as the log moved forward and her feet failed to find purchase. She fell backward into Lenny's waiting arms. Lenny slowly lowered her into the muddy bog until they were standing next to each other, mid-calf deep.

Her cries disappeared as she realized she wasn't covered in mud. Confusion was all over her face. "What? Why did you do that?"

Still holding her, Lenny gazed thoughtfully into her crystal blue eyes. "I wanted to show you that I could catch you. I won't let you fall, Sloane. I'm here for you. That's what I do. That's what I've spent my life doing. I'm there for people, and I could be there for you."

Lenny could see the wheels turning and the internal struggle raging in her mind.

"I don't know," she said. She shook her head. "Do you know

how rarely I don't know something or admit I don't know?"

She started to cry and Lenny kissed her, not waiting for permission, not allowing her to take control.

"Well, I *do* know. Let me take the lead."

Sloane wrapped her arms around Lenny's neck and jumped into her arms. It was enough to make her lose her balance and they tumbled into the mud. When they sat up, they were laughing and flicking mud at each other.

"I thought you said you wouldn't let me fall," Sloane joked.

"Well, you jumped on me!"

"And I'm going to do it again!" she cried, pouncing on top of Lenny. She held her tight and whispered, "I paid the taxes for *you*, Lenny. This deal wasn't just about a store. It started out that way, but then it was about you. The deal may not meet all of the Seven Ps, but you do, at least for me."

Rocket started to bark, and they looked over at him, standing on the shore, wagging his tail and cocking his head in curiosity.

* * *

They hiked double-time back to the parking area, holding hands, singing "Days Like This" and not caring about the open stares from other hikers.

"I'm not moving to Boston," Lenny declared.

"Fine. I can't move here, but I can visit a lot."

They grinned and Lenny added, "I'm not good with Skyping or emailing every day."

Sloane gasped and said, "You think I have time for that? I'm a busy executive who works eighteen-hour days."

"Well, I'm going to be busy too. You've seen to that."

Sloane stopped and pulled her tight. "I'm sure we could negotiate a meaningful compromise." She kissed her quickly. "We've only got an hour."

They reached the parking area and decided to leave the Range Rover until later when they were free of mud. Lenny laid plastic bags over the Jeep's seats and they headed back to town.

As they pulled into the Pinedale Lodge, Lenny's expression turned serious. "So, would this compromise involve seeing other people?"

Sloane paused before she replied. "I don't want to see other women, and I don't want you to see other women either."

She snorted, "It's not like there's a lot to choose from."

Sloane laughed. "Oh, honey, I think you're about to meet a lot more people, the whole town is. When the heart's ready, love finds you."

"Is that what's going on here? Do you love me?"

Suddenly Sloane couldn't look at her and struggled to continue. "I love...I love everything about you, your wit, your compassion for everyone around you and your zeal for life." She looked far away as if an enormous epiphany had occurred. When she faced her, she smiled, but it was nothing like her usual electric PR smile. "Yes. I love you. I love you and I want you to be mine."

"I love you too."

Sloane kissed her and hopped out of the Jeep. Before she ran inside for her shower, she leaned through the open window and asked, "Have you ever wanted to go to Greece?"

EPILOGUE

Rocket loved the chance to sniff around his yard in the early mornings. He followed the scent of a raccoon around the fence until it disappeared under the house. Uh-oh. Lenny probably wasn't going to like *that* at all.

Everything was better now that Lenny was happy again, especially when Sloane was around. That day at Blaine Basin he'd decided Lenny and Sloane needed to be together. They smelled *good* together, so he'd made sure that Sloane found Lenny sleeping.

Now Sloane visited a lot, and she loved giving him attention and dog treats! One time she accidentally called him Cookie, but he didn't mind. She even took him on walks when Lenny was at the store.

A car pulled into the driveway and he ran to the fence. It was Seth and Regina and all of his friends! He gave a quick bark and zipped back inside, ready to greet them at the front door. Five noses pushed past Seth, and the room was filled with yipping, barking and sniffing. He could tell they'd all just had a bath at

Seth and Regina's special dog shop because they didn't smell like each other all rolled together.

Regina came in last and stayed near the door, waiting for Seth to undo all of the leashes so they could go outside and play! Rocket ran to her and barked, but she couldn't lean over and pet him like she usually did. Her belly had grown huge and she smelled *very* unusual.

"Hi, Rocket, sweetie. Where's Lenny? Where's Sloane?" He let out a little bark and she looked up the staircase. "Still in bed, huh?" She rolled her eyes and waddled to the treat pot. "Don't worry, boy, we'll take care of you."

At the sound of the treat pot opening, all of his friends joined him, and Regina gave each one a snack. She cooed at him just like Pru used to do, and he looked around, wondering if she'd returned. His friends dashed outside, and although he was eager to follow, he wanted to look for Pru. He sniffed the furniture and the baseboards, making a circle around the living room.

Seth called to him from the kitchen. "Rocket, what are you doing?"

He sat in the middle of the room and thought about all of the smells—Lenny, Sloane, Regina, Seth, all of his friends...and Pru. He headed outside, happy.

There was still a little of her all around him.

Rocket's Story

The real Rocket is a two-time winner of Maricopa County's Hero Award. He earned his first award in 2006 for his story of survival. Abandoned in a yard for a month, he was near death when he was found by animal control. So many people wanted to adopt him that an essay contest was established to find a new owner. Barb Steele's heartfelt and touching words persuaded the committee that Rocket belonged with her. She launched Rocket's Rangers, a non-profit organization that teaches children about proper pet care, kindness to animals and the importance of spaying and neutering pets. In 2011 Rocket again won the Hero Award for his community service. You can visit Rocket at rocketsrangers.com.

Bella Books, Inc.

Women. Books. Even Better Together.

P.O. Box 10543
Tallahassee, FL 32302

Phone: 800-729-4992
www.bellabooks.com